BY THE SAME AUTHORS

Secrets of Strangers

LOSS OF THE
GOOD AUTHORITY
The Cause of Delinquency

Tom Pitt-Aikens
Alice Thomas Ellis

VIKING

VIKING

Published by the Penguin Group
27 Wrights Lane, London w8 5tz, England
Viking Penguin Inc., 40 West 23rd Street, New York, New York 10010, USA
Penguin Books Australia Ltd, Ringwood, Victoria, Australia
Penguin Books Canada Ltd, 2801 John Street, Markham, Ontario, Canada l3r 1b4
Penguin Books (NZ) Ltd, 182–190 Wairau Road, Auckland 10, New Zealand
Penguin Books Ltd, Registered Offices: Harmondsworth, Middlesex, England

First published 1989

10 9 8 7 6 5 4 3 2 1

Printed in Great Britain by Richard Clay Ltd, Bungay, Suffolk
Filmset in Monophoto Imprint

A CIP catalogue record for this book is available from the British Library

ISBN 0-670-82493-3

To Feltham Borstal

Contents

Prologue

TPA I think of the following excerpts, from letters quoted by Thomas Carlyle, as the literary epitome of the Loss of the Good Authority. The first describes Frederick the Great in August 1785, one year before his death, passing through the village of Hirschberg on his way to the Silesian military reviews.

Concourse of many thousands, from all the Country about, had been waiting for him several hours. Outriders came at last; then he himself, the Unique; and, with the liveliest expression of reverence and love, all eyes were directed on one point. I cannot describe to you my feelings, which of course were those of everybody, to see him the aged King; in his weak hand the hat; in those grand eyes such a fatherly benignity of look over the vast crowd that encircled his Carriage, and rolled tide-like, accompanying it. Looking round when he was past, I saw in various eyes a tear trembling. ('Alas, we shan't have him long.')

His affability, his kindness, to whoever had the honour of speech with this great King, who shall describe it!

The second letter describes him in June 1786:

A man adjusted to his hard circumstances and bearing himself manlike and king-like among men. He knew himself to be dying.

*

ATE I don't myself care for Thomas Carlyle and at first I was hard put to see the relevance of Frederick the Great to a book that I imagined to be all about delinquency. I had preconceived ideas of my own on the subject, and Frederick the Great didn't come into them. The concept of authority has been out of popular favour for some time in the circles in which I move, and I was surprised to see these royalist sentiments quoted with approval. I am not overtly republican because I do not care enough either way. Our Royal family seems harmless and that is all that we expect it to be. Some of its younger members tend to be faintly ludicrous, but not sufficiently as to incite a people to revolution. This very blandness is what keeps the monarch on the throne and indeed power-lessness is at the heart of the constitution. A ruler in an apolitical role may do many things, but ruling is not one of them, so he can't get into much trouble. Authority on the face of it is no longer vested in the monarch but in 'government' – politicians, bureaucrats, civil servants: faceless people who control our destiny, arouse our ire but seem, when it comes down to it, curiously remote and therefore not worth bothering with. A lack of visible, tangible authority can give rise to inertia in the populace, which makes widespread insurrection unlikely but leads to cynicism, depression, division and – some say – crime. The second rank of authority (police, judiciary) assumes an undeserved importance and acts as flak-catcher, as do the tax-man, traffic wardens and other menials. After some thought on these lines I contrived to twist myself into a stance from which I could look afresh at the whole concept of authority, beginning with the odd notion of

genuine respect and reverence for a real leader; TPA
helped here by informing me that Frederick the Great
was regarded by some people almost as a saint.

Introduction

TPA In 1977 I was a British delegate in Norway at the United
Nations European Seminar on 'New Approaches to the
Treatment of Young Offenders'. There I saw clearly that
although the various expert delegates were confident as
to the novelty and validity of their own arguments and
methods, in most cases their approaches were essentially
the same as those adopted by other countries some years
before and now abandoned. Indeed, in many cases the
'new' standpoints being arrived at were the same as
those that other countries were currently discarding as
inadequate.

The delegates who attended that conference represented many nationalities, political persuasions and disciplines. Their causal views of delinquency embraced
political, genetic, socio-economic, moralistic and an-
thropological arguments. Methods of treatment, including medical, social and psychological, ranged from the
most liberal through to the most punitive. It was,
however, the mass failure of self-perception – that is, the
inability or lack of attempt by the delegates to look at
themselves, to see what they themselves were actually
doing at the conference – that most struck me, since this

is, ironically, the very phenomenon that I identify as the
key to the understanding of delinquency. I remember my
free association at that time, gazing at the big blue and
white flag with its 'Organisation Nationale Unie': 'O – N
– U' – 'O – NU' – 'O – New' – 'Nothing new under the
sun'.

*

ATE A lack of self-perception amounts to delinquency? TPA
assumes that I understand and share his ways of thought,
but I need further explanation. I do not doubt him, but I
am not accustomed to his view. I think in terms of mortal
sin – full knowledge and full consent. He sees the failure
to know oneself and one's motives clearly as a dereliction
of duty, delinquency; and he may be right. The sacrament
of confession is intended to compel the penitent to scour
his conscience and his motives; a refusal to do so is
sinful. I learn that the delegates of whom he speaks did
not even abide by the rules they had made for themselves,
but arrived late for their discussions and frequently
wandered from the point. While I see this as a mere
venial sin, almost a technicality, I begin also to see the
ramifications, the consequences in muddle and confusion.
A refusal to see clearly, whether wilful or not, leads to
blankness and despair. In order to understand him, since
I have little respect for civil, lay authority, I have to
translate even further than he does, into terms of
ecclesiastical authority. The laws of the religious life,
which I do respect, leave little room for either self-
conceit or self-deceit.

*

TPA No one is unaware of the growing level of private, public
and world-wide anxiety about increasing crime and civil
disorder, and yet here at the United Nations, the
foremost European experts in the field were being
unwittingly delinquent – at a certain level, they weren't
aware of what they were doing!

My thesis demonstrates that there are many factors that can produce a lack of self-perception in individuals and groups: fear and anxiety, enthusiasm and excitement, over-involvement or alienation; and that this lack constantly manifests itself, not only in the delinquent himself, but even more worryingly in those who are attempting to understand and help.

*

ATE For example, one common human failing is a disinclination to get out of bed in the morning. This can seriously impair the worker's chances of promotion or even of remaining in gainful employment. He will say to himself, 'But I had a heavy night last night. I am tired and deserve my sleep. It is unreasonable to expect me to go to work.' A well brought-up person will refute this argument himself, totter off to work and, it is to be hoped, remember in future to defer his heavy nights until Friday. If, however, his mother was in the habit of lying abed until lunchtime, he will feel justified in staying there. More – should he not, should he take to leaping out of bed at the crack of dawn, he will feel that his actions are an implicit criticism of his mother and her way of life. Precept and example are important. This mother might have exhorted her children to rise betimes but, ignoring her own advice, she would not have been a good authority. By saying, 'Do not do as I do, do as I say,' she would have lost her good authority.

*

TPA The capacity to prevent historical familial pressures and human failing from distorting or limiting self-perception I describe as the good authority, and once one comes to recognize the implications of this concept, approaches to delinquency, which are capable of ever-increasing return in terms of real understanding and consequent benefit, may be created and developed.

In the twenty or more years that I have been developing my understanding of the concept of the good authority, I have become increasingly aware that the many narrow-fronted approaches adopted in the treatment of delinquents – so often old ideas in new guises – can never stop the delinquent process, but merely ensure that the related and underlying crises are not discovered and tackled. In this book I shall attempt progressively to bring out the understanding of authority and the myriad varieties of good authority. Gradually the implications for good of the good authority and the implications for evil of its loss, its absence or its failure to be recovered by mourning are brought home.

CHAPTER ONE

Authority

*Definition of authority – Invisible nature
of authority – Importance of authority –
Common misconceptions about authority*

TPA The subject of delinquency arouses in the onlooker such
a mixture of reactions, ranging from fear and outrage to
bewilderment and even fascination, that it is extremely
difficult to study dispassionately. Most people engaged
in the study of criminal behaviour have attempted to
conform to an apparently objective scientific tradition
and to classify delinquency in precise terms of theft,
violence, sexual crime, drug abuse and so on. This is the
result of a false, archaic and misleading approach, and
fails to take into account deep-laid causes of criminal
activity. It is of no more value to us now than the views
of Dr William Buchan. In 1783, when few broad
pathological concepts existed, he considered diabetes to
be 'a disorder of the kidney and bladder caused by acute
diseases, fluxes, excessive evacuations, great fatigue –
hard drinking, the use of strong medicines – cantharides,
turpentine and such like.'[1] As carbohydrate metabolism
had not then been recognized, now, similarly, it is
essential in a study of crime to understand certain basic,
almost metabolic, principles. The most important is
authority: its beneficial effects and the consequences of
its absence.

Authority may be confused with both *influence* and *authoritarianism*, but I shall here define authority as 'that which within a definite area may allow, disallow or insist upon change, with or without any further references'. Influence, however, may be effected over any area and may have to make reference to someone or something else, while authoritarianism is simply a particular kind of authority that exists at the expense of freedom. The relevance of these definitions will become clear as we go along.

*

ATE Definitions are, by definition, difficult. Dr Johnson, faced with the self-imposed task of defining a net, grew skittish and parodied himself: 'Anything reticulated or decussated with intersections at intervals between the interstices.' The temptation is to refine a concept down to a very skeleton of a technical phrase and leave the public to figure it out for themselves. It had never occurred to me even to attempt to grasp the second law of thermodynamics until somebody explained that it posed the proposition that it is not possible to unscramble eggs. I got that at once. I asked TPA to simplify his definition of authority, but as he had spent some time on rendering it as spare and concise as possible he was naturally reluctant to put the feathers back on it.

*

TPA Quite often one of the neurotic patient's actual symptoms is a profound belief in the efficacy of his therapist who may, in fact, be fairly useless. This gives them both a measure of confidence, justified or not. But in the case of the delinquent, mistakes and omissions will produce effects that cannot be denied – by the patient, the therapist or anyone else. Such things as assaults and burglaries are difficult to overlook. The practitioner in the field of delinquency, working with hundreds of commonplace problems in commonplace settings such as clinics, community homes, custody centres, children's homes and prisons, finds that the usual psychiatric approach – with its attendant jargon: psychopathy, personality disorders, etc. – tends to become irrelevant. Instead, other simpler, more easily understood and communicable ideas present themselves. For instance (since all delinquent acts are in some sense committed in defiance of authority), where does authority lie, how is authority recognized, how can it be usurped, who is liable to usurp it, who might wittingly or unwittingly allow that to happen?

In our society this usurpation has already occurred to the concept of 'elders and betters', which has fallen on lean times. The fact that nowadays so little is said in its favour tends to suggest a poor understanding of the meaning and usefulness of authority. The degradation of the old by moves to earlier retirement can be seen as vandalism, as a disregard of the value of experience and authority. Grandparents are seldom revered and are not encouraged to 'interfere' with the upbringing of their grandchildren.

It might be useful here to compare the systems of royalty, autocracy and democracy as a means of highlighting a quality of 'hiddenness' inherent in the kind of authority that is linked to the genesis of delinquency. The sovereign no longer overtly legislates or leads cavalry charges, but occupies key positions that are beyond the reach of even the most able and ambitious citizen: the sovereign is the head of the armed forces and therefore no one else can be – the matter is beyond debate.* Autocracy and democracy are popularly thought of as politically right and left, and seen as good or bad depending on the political bias of the observer. It is more important to recognize that autocratic authority is

---

* An example of this was Hitler's inability to come to power as long as Hindenberg was alive, although the latter was old and feeble and played very little part in government. It was unthinkable that anyone else could be in power while he was still there.[2]

potentially immediate in its effect, while democratic authority is necessarily slower. Obviously, there are circumstances where a rapid decision is imperative, and others where deliberation, discussion and shared authority are appropriate. This has nothing to do with left or right or good or bad.

There is a danger that one type of authority may be discredited or accredited at the expense of the other. For instance, democracy may be seen as 'damned bureaucracy', while autocratic measures make it appear that 'at last something is being done'. Such autocratic regimes may then become reluctant to relinquish power; eventually too much will be expected of them and they will inevitably be found wanting, abusing or seeming to abuse their position in situations where wider debate is vital. On the other hand, it would be inappropriate to set up a debate between the passengers and crew to discuss what to do about the listing and imminent sinking of the ship they all happen to be on at the time. It is for the captain to order: 'Abandon ship.'

*

ATE Many different disciplines and schools of thought will give varying reasons for the loss of respect for authority, lack of parental/school discipline being probably the most popular, though bearing the attendant implicit question – whence the loss of confidence on the part of parents and teachers that they feel it somehow unseemly to impose their will on the young? The libertarian sixties are also blamed in retrospect for some of the excesses of today, but here again the question poses itself – why, in that decade, did a good proportion of mankind collectively go off its head? The experience of the past has demonstrated that such supposed delights as unlimited sex, unrestricted indulgence in mood-changing drugs and universal love are variously neither well advised nor feasible. It has been said that only a fool learns by experience, and this appears to be depressingly true, the

lessons of 'history' being largely disregarded by succeeding generations. And here again we have the chickens
and the eggs. Whose is the responsibility for the repeated
errors and tragedies? Does it lie in the weak incompetence
of the 'old' or the wilful intransigence of the 'young', and
is it beyond the power of humanity to master? Tyranny
and injustice certainly foster resentment and ultimately
revolution against all forms of authority, Church and
State being linked in the popular view; monarchs,
ministers, land-owners, clergy: the inchoate focus of
mass despair and rebellion. Under Hitler and Stalin, as
they overturned the old order, children were encouraged
to betray their parents in the name of the 'cause', and the
concept of authority became meaningless, morally and
spiritually destitute, a deformed and monstrous rootless
growth. The aforesaid pair who can be regarded as the
ultimate in *authoritarianism* can perhaps be held responsible for, amongst other things, the widespread
distaste for *authority* current today in the West. Anybody
giving a peremptory order, no matter how valid or
necessary, is liable to be called Hitler or told to go back
to Russia. Perhaps a half-recognized, half-acknowledged
guilt – the awareness that powerful old men send out
helpless young ones to fight and die on their behalf – has
brought not only power but, by extension, old age into
disrepute. Not only strength and beauty, but worth and
virtue are seen as residing in the young. The old
increasingly are ignored, abandoned, stacked away in
'Sunset Homes' and disregarded; they are fair game for
muggers and con-men and nobody wants to sit down and
listen to their reminiscences. The young, feeling in need
of advice, will not call upon their grandparents – who
will, in all probability, by reason of blood, social milieu
and proximity, have had similar problems – but will turn
to an 'expert', or read a manual. The writers of manuals
have much to answer for. Truby King, for one in the
thirties was responsible for unnaturally distancing many
a mother from her child; and many an anxious lover has

sprained a muscle or two at the dictates of the experts on sexual intercourse, not to mention worrying himself to death counting orgasms. In an ideal world older blood relations would be the ones to consult in these – not really esoteric – matters. The birds and the beasts, left free of human interference, muddle along quite happily without undue innovation or the need for outside advice. A simple, unchanging power structure and a simple, accepted means of establishing dominance are essential to a species' survival, but unfortunately man, being a complex and devious animal, has invented new rules and devices and distorted answers to fit questions.

*

TPA It can sometimes be difficult to identify the proper site of authority, especially in an institution where strong influence such as tradition or charismatic leadership prevails. For example, in my own field, soon after the coming into force of the England and Wales 1969 Children and Young Persons Act[3] it became evident that in some residential establishments for delinquents the principal, superintendent, headmaster, even the ethos of such places, were felt to be more powerful and of more importance than the frequently young and frequently female social worker whose employing local authority (which she represents or personifies) is the actual legal authority of a child 'in care'. Similarly, probation officers exercising supervision orders are often thought of as having more clout with a fifteen- or sixteen-year-old client than social workers exercising a care order. This is simply not the case. I have heard people who should know better imagine aloud that a probation officer would be 'tougher' than a social worker, or that a child in care should be 'handed over' to the probation service – which would actually be an illegal rejection.

Then, frequently, probation officers who do not understand the implications of their own authority make the mistake of not instituting proceedings that could result in the return to prison of a newly released client who has committed some technical offence, such as not notifying his probation officer of his change of address. Technical offences nearly always precede actual crime, but the probation officer, apart from wrongly imagining that his action would destroy his relationship with his client (who, of course, would not consciously want to go back to prison), feels that his application will anyway be turned down by a higher authority (in England and Wales the Home Office) because the offence was 'only technical'. Unfortunately, this might well happen, but the probation officer must realize that it is *he* who has the authority to *institute* recall proceedings – no one else. His client, at least unconsciously, expects and hopes that his probation officer will do what he thinks best – succeed or fail.

To give one small but clear example of the usurping of 'ordinary' authority by 'charismatic' authority: a chaplain entered a prison wing, and, without thinking to announce his presence to the officer in charge, beckoned to one of two inmates who were peacefully playing snooker, one watching, cue vertical, the other crouched, cue horizontal over the table. The 'vertical' watcher obediently and silently left with the chaplain. Later 'horizontal' made a severe 'unprovoked' attack on 'vertical' when the latter was returned to the wing by the chaplain.

The concept of 'non-consensus' decisions suggests to me that the individual and group unconscious are aware of these definitions of authority and influence. For instance, it happened in a prison wing that a new, young, unassuming assistant governor was the only staff member who thought that a 'perfect' inmate should have his release date postponed following a minor peeping Tom incident during his pre-release parole. After some discussion with me and realizing that even very slight misdemeanours indicate an unreadiness to re-enter society, he decided to go against his staff's opinion that the boy be released as planned. The staff, far from being annoyed, showed signs of relief that he was able to realize and demonstrate his authoritative role so clearly.

Sometimes 'value judgements' are neither here nor there. What is important is the decision: that it should be made, who makes it and whether the maker *is* the proper authority. People are greatly relieved when a decision is made in a difficult matter. The relief stems from the knowledge that the appropriate authority has decided what to do and is strong enough to accept the consequences, even should the decision prove to be the wrong one. The responsibility lies with the authority itself. An organization, institution or family that knows that it has over it an authority that can be trusted, no matter what, may certainly experience anxiety, but the anxiety is more likely to reach only a tolerable and therefore non-damaging level. Life can still proceed in a productive and creative fashion, which would be impossible if there were unspoken doubts as to who holds ultimate responsibility.

Delinquents rightly hate and mistrust the authority that is pathologically determined to be one hundred per cent certain that it is right – as if this could ever be! There are 'authorities' such as courts and borough councils which seem to be primarily concerned for their own public image and reputation. In order to ward off any political blame, they seem to need to festoon themselves with assessments, reports and opinions. In this they resemble over-anxious parents who prefer to leave decisions about their children to 'experts' (or to the children themselves). Even worse, the decision may be made as a result of the pressure of the child's behaviour. It is interesting in this connection to note the derivation of the term delinquent. Chambers Dictionary gives *delinquere*: the dereliction of duty, whether by the individual while in authority over himself, or by an adult over a child. The duty is to do one's best and stand by it, even if one's best will be found not good enough.

Often, in an institution, authority is likely to consist not so much in ordering others about as in protecting the work of the staff over whom the authority is exercised: discussing and politicking at a distance, seeing that the staff do not suffer from interference from above and are able to get on with the job. A traditional, currently highly unfashionable, but still valid view of the respective roles of father and mother clarifies this protecting aspect. Father – the legal head of the household in the United Kingdom – *sees* that the children are looked after; mother *looks* after them. For instance, since the 1969 act the field social worker is now the 'father' figure for his primary client, the care order child. He does not *care* for the child (perhaps then rivalling the residential 'mother' figure staff), but on behalf of his department he ensures that the child is cared for.*

* It is worth mentioning that in England and Wales, before the implementation of the relevant parts of the 1969 act, both father and mother figures were internal to certain institutions known then as Approved Schools. Since the implementation of this act,[4] the father figures of children in care are outside the institution, while the mother figures work, as before, within the institution itself. These Approved Schools are now known as Community Homes With Education on the Premises.

CHAPTER TWO

Change of Site of Authority

Outlines the necessary considerations and implications associated with the transfer of the site of authority (e.g., from parents to a child achieving legal majority) – Factors influencing its successful transfer

TPA I am not concerned here with the changes of site of authority that occur as a consequence of overt revolutionary change, but instead I will concentrate on those with evolutionary changes: the natural, progressive, logical changes of site of authority. A straightforward example would be that which follows the death of a father. The site of legal authority over the family's children would then move from both mother and father to mother alone.

Probably the most important transfer of authority is the change from extra-person to intra-person authority. In the legal sense in the United Kingdom, this begins when a child is sixteen years of age and is completed at eighteen. Curiously, in spite of these legal facts, many referrals of adolescents to helping agencies such as consultants and child-guidance clinics are oddly paradoxical. If the adolescent concerned is over eighteen, then frequently the referring agent (usually the family doctor) will suggest a meeting including the parents. Conversely, if the adolescent is fifteen or under, it will often be suggested that the child would benefit from seeing the specialist on his own! This peculiarity is, I believe, due to a widely prevalent, inbuilt aversion to acknowledging the proper site of authority – before the age of sixteen a person is totally subject to the authority of his parents; after eighteen the responsibility lies in himself.

It is important to note that the changes of site are frequently imperceptible and the *evidence* of such changes is therefore indirect. For example, in an institution for teenage boys there was an uneasy atmosphere and harsh undertones of gossip and criticism amongst the staff. The criticisms levelled at each other by the warring factions were of two varieties. Certain members of staff were criticized for threatening the children with deprivation, such as the loss of pocket-money, etc. (What an awful thing to do!) Others were criticized for not standing up to the children by themselves, but threatening to report the boys to the other house parent. (What an awful thing to do!) What had happened was that with an increase in staff, some houses still had one, while other houses now had two house parents. The critics were simply and unwittingly comparing two standard methods, in everyday use, of confronting children in one-parent and two-parent families respectively. This example enabled the team of workers to understand how, in many one-parent families, mothers on their own find it hard even to form a concept in their minds of abandoning the threat 'I'll tell your father when he comes home,' and resorting instead to threats of halving the children's pocket-money. After the loss of one parent, by death or divorce, the refusal to accept the pain of loss, which is common in situations of unsuccessful or incomplete mourning, may inaugurate a vicious circle of anxiety between the remaining parent and child that can result in the child becoming seemingly omnipotent and ruling the roost. There may be a gap of time between changing from one authority to another, and it is at such times that experienced 'non-executive' but none the less influential people can be extremely useful in preventing tremendous disruption, and even chaos, in families and institutions. It is important for a recently bereft wife who has not yet sufficiently recovered from her grief and shock to have evolved a new way of dealing with her children to be supported by someone who is used to wielding authority and is prepared to do so. Grandparents, uncles and aunts can hold the fort till a parent has recovered and learned a new way of coping with disciplinary problems, or until a new authority takes over. These intermediaries can help a recovering parent (or a new boss) to realize the dangerous implications in a situation that is simply begging for a big foot to be put in it.

Consider the following case. A new superintendent of an institution arrived to take up his post at the same time as three new female members of staff. The new super-intendent was careful to let it be known that he did not consider female members of staff to be 'second-class team members', yet strangely he found himself becoming more and more alienated from the two senior female members of staff who were there already. What he had failed to appreciate was that if, as he insisted, female staff are just as good as male staff, and are so marvellously vital, etc., why was it not acknowledged more fully and openly that the same two extremely efficient women had coped for several years on their own – and had from time to time had to endure the patronizing, almost traditional criticism of the male members of staff for their 'soft, aunty-like ways' with the children? This example under-lines a problem that faces a new authority who wants to do his best and is simply oblivious of extremely important continuity factors. If, in the case above, there had been a continuity figure, such as a respected bursar or matron[1] whom he had thought to consult, the new superintendent could have been made aware of exactly where not to put his big foot.

When statutory orders, such as care orders and super-vision orders, are imposed by a court, it is essential for the professional involved to be acutely conscious of the

exact nature of the order. A probation order or supervision order in the United Kingdom is not only a licence
'to advise, assist and befriend'. The client may be unlike-
able, for a start. He is also liable to get into a sorry plight
about his self-government if the professional himself is
unclear about the precise nature of the order. On the
other hand, if the client knows that a social worker
carrying out a supervision order on him is a professional
who will observe his welfare; using his ears, eyes and
head – and if necessary will direct his feet back again
towards a court – then all concerned are mightily helped
by being clear about their own tasks. I have noticed that
courts sometimes fail to ask a prisoner first, if he
understands and second, wishes to enter into a probation
order contract – the magistrates themselves seeming to
regard the order as a soft option to a custodial sentence,
which is certainly not the case. A prison sentence places
the bulk of authority and responsibility *outside* the
prisoner (in Britain upon the Home Office), providing a
setting that encourages regression. A probation order
demands a considerable degree of self-authority and
responsibility from the client, in addition to the necessity
for him to run his own ordinary life. A probation order
has three compulsory parts, and provision for a fourth
discretionary part.[2] The compulsory parts are related to:
the necessity for the client to live an industrious and
honest life; the notification of change of address or
change of work; the willingness to allow visits by the
probation officer or to attend appointments asked for by
the probation officer. The courts, already having made a
'soft option' misunderstanding, go on to compound this
misunderstanding twice. As well as neglecting to ask the
prisoner whether he understands and accepts the contract
of the probation order, they then add as the fourth,
optional, clause that he submit to psychiatric treatment –
not that he should actively seek it out, thereby unwittingly declaring their failure to have ascertained whether
the prisoner has any self-authority.

Delinquent behaviour is often related to a change of site of authority, but it might be as well to highlight one of the dynamics involved. Unless a father blesses his son when the latter begins to be his own new authority as distinct from being under the old authority of his father or his parents, then the child has in effect 'stolen' himself from his parents. Michelangelo's picture of Jehovah, to me relinquishing his grasp of Adam's hand, conveys an impression of the limitless confidence that should exist between father and son; the significance of this painting partly lies in the importance of this classical handover for all children and all fathers.*

*

* See the story of Jacob gaining Isaac's blessing (Genesis 27). Jacob means 'deceiver, grabber' – also note he was the 'smooth' son, Esau was 'an hairy man'. See also the return of the Prodigal Son, Luke 15.

Imagine the dialogue between Jehovah and the teenage Adam:

Scene: The roof of the Sistine Chapel, Rome.
Time: The Renaissance.
Place: A launching pad in the clouds above Eden (A National Trust garden).

JEHOVAH   Over to you now, son. This is I T. Keep in touch.
ADAM   Thanks a million, Dad, you've done a grand job. Gee, I'm not half rarin' to go.

Jehovah starts counting and lets go of Adam's hand – the latter is a tiny bit 'sissy', because of having neither Mum nor siblings – and Adam is launched into space at the shout of ZERO.

                10 . . . . . . (Ten Commandments)
                  9 . . . . . . (Beethoven's Ninth)
                  8 . . . . . . (Bluebeard's eighth wife)
                  7 . . . . . . (Wonders of the World)
                  6 . . . . . . (Henry VIII's six wives)
                  5 . . . . . . (Fifth Avenue)
                  4 . . . . . . (Horsemen of the Apocalypse)
                  3 . . . . . . (Blind mice)
                  2 . . . . . . (Two's company)
                  1 . . . . . . (Night and day, you are the one)
                        ZERO

ATE   Here we hit, inevitably, upon the question of sex
The father/son transferral of authority is classic and
clear. What is the role of the mother? Traditionally the
poor woman stood wringing her hands or her apron,
depending on her class, and weeping copiously as son
went off to school, college, the colonies, war or a job in
the distant city (I exclude the Roman mother: 'Come
back with your shield or on it,' and the 'little mother' of
the 1914–18 war, who wished she had more sons than the
few she'd lost, so she could lose them all to the glorious
cause) while father abjured him 'to be a man'. Daughters,
being perceived as property, were not offered self-government, but 'given away' to a new authority – a husband,
or, if put into service, an employer. It is only very
recently *sub specie aeternitatis* that the female has been
seen as wholly human, let alone as an independent being
(see the early Fathers, right up to Milton and beyond. It
was debated whether women had souls, and it was
Milton who wrote, 'He for God only, she for God in
him'). Nevertheless, from time immemorial women have
led, if not always a sheltered, always a secret existence
with their own rules and traditions. Even when, as in our
own society, this mode of existence has been partly
forgotten, it appears it has merely gone temporarily
underground to re-emerge whenever the outside conditions seem, if not propitious, at least not too threatening.
One result of this is that women, no matter how little it is
recognized or stated, need the *approval* of their mothers

ADAM (*faintly*)   Dad, are you still there? I'm a mite scared. It's not
half lonely.

JEHOVAH (*loud and clear*)   *Be fruitful and multiply*, son. Try repeating, ever so quickly, *the Leith Police dismisseth us*, and *keep off
apples* for a while.

ADAM (*very, very faintly*)   OKOKOKOKOKOKOKOK, Dad.
The-leith-polith-dismitteth-uth . . . the-leith-polith-dismitteth . . .
the-leith-polith . . . the-leith-the . . .

before they take up their own lives and they need that
approval particularly powerfully when they start to have
children of their own. Even when, as is too often
unfortunately the case – certainly in my own generation –
the daughter actively dislikes her mother and cannot wait
to get away from home, she will feel anxious and bereft
should her mother withhold all signs of approbation from
the newborn. I wonder if daughters need, at any deep
level, the approval of their fathers; as perhaps sons do
not need that of their mothers?

I have always considered the idea of a male holding
any real authority over females profoundly strange, since
he can have simply no conception of the rules that hold
sway in the female psyche and govern her behaviour.
The headmaster of a girls' school seems an unnatural
creature at an unnatural disadvantage. Convents, which
have for centuries enshrined a psychological expertise gained by (essential) long experience and insights,
function, on the whole, easily and fluently with
women in total charge. The convent chaplain is dominant only in spiritual matters, although his influence
may appear to be greater than it is. *All* women have
learned, where necessary, to be adept at soothing the
male ego. It saves trouble. TPA thinks this book
should be called *Sins of the Fathers by ATE and
Mothers by TPA*.

*

TPA In the United Kingdom a child may, with his parents'
consent, live away from home when he is sixteen years
old. That means that the youngest child's brand-new
self-over-self authority may be responsible for leaving
father and mother alone together, as simply husband and
wife, for the first time since the early days of their
marriage. In some cases, if the first child was born very
soon after or even before the marriage, it would be for the
first time ever. There is no doubt that in several of the

cases with which I have been in contact, the parents have
dreaded this eventuality.*

I have frequently found manifestations of the Israel
syndrome in the delinquent population. Some children
seem to have evaded the guilt of being responsible for
leaving their parents alone together by unconsciously
contriving to achieve a custodial sentence at sixteen to
eighteen years of age – so that both delinquent and
parents can blame the authorities and the police for the
separation. The children leave home only to be put in a
'home'. There are more subtle dynamics relevant to
delinquency in regard to the sixteen- to eighteen-years
age group to which I will refer in a later chapter.

The authority that a human being begins to assume
over himself on an unconscious level should be a benign
process. It would be as well to dwell a little more on this
particular vertical change of site of authority (in the
generational sense), which is first and foremost a change
from a double-authority structure, that is of another or
others over an individual person, to a single-authority
structure, that is the individual person having authority
over his own self. The fact that this change of site of
authority, from the double to the single model, is not
sufficiently well understood is underlined by the common
prevalence of a certain supposedly therapeutic strategy.
Delinquent trainees or clients are 'rewarded' by being
given more and more trust, as their course of training or
treatment progresses and is perceived as being effective.
I think, however, that for many people in penal institutions or establishments, being trusted is synonymous
with being neglected, and therefore such a treatment or
approach is fallacious and will engender logical, though

---

* I have elaborated the concept of the Israel syndrome from studies of
families who were in this predicament. How does a new adult child in
a close-knit family structure, such as those found in Jewish homes,
manage to leave home and to stay at home at the same time? The
answer is: he goes to *Israel*.

often unexpected reactions. It is possible that the trainee has simply learned how to work the system, how to please and how to stay out of trouble, without any fundamental change of attitude at all.

The fortunate young child is the one whose parents do not trust him to be left alone, but who anticipate that little fingers will explore electric sockets, who are aware of infant curiosity about window-ledges, matches and pills, and decide to forego their night out. Delinquent children often have parents who have, rejectingly, 'trusted' them, and whom in their turn the delinquents do not trust. (This again brings to mind the derivation of the term delinquency: 'dereliction of duty'.) The unfortunate child is the one who has been left alone by his parents, and who *may* have survived the presence of an electric fire in the room. If he has survived, it is due to good luck and not to good guidance. May heaven help the child whose parents now imagine that since he has survived once, he is safe from other severe hazards inherent in being left alone! Children and the childlike need a parent or caretaker, who is absolutely trustworthy, whom eventually a child or even a prisoner can trust. This is an area where professionals should score over non-professionals such as parents, in that the former earn their living partly by performing distasteful tasks, refraining from natural tendencies such as the wish to physically punish or swear at their charges and having to work efficiently with colleagues whom they may dislike. Parents are not paid and therefore not expected to behave so unnaturally.

In anticipation of the age of majority or date of release, a novel and most efficient notion must be assimilated. 'If I – sadly – hadn't got my trusted parents, and/or jailers, whom could I trust?' The answer is: 'Me!' 'Good' criminals, like some old lags who know and abide by the prison routine completely, including its behavioural mores, are trusted by prison staff, but are actually not trustworthy. The 'trusty' in prison is often the very person whom the people in the world outside do *not* trust, hardly surprisingly since he is always in and out of prison. The same person is seen totally differently in other places at other times by other people. Failure to see both the situations that make up the whole is to be deluded. I would mention here that certain institutions, which pride themselves on cultivating a sense of responsibility in juveniles, frequently, concurrently and more or less covertly seem to denigrate that same self-responsibility in the adult staff by, for instance, senior staff constantly checking on the work of junior staff. I think that this denigration of the adult sense of responsibility is as rejecting as the over-estimation of a juvenile sense of responsibility. Halfway houses are ideally suited to individual ex-prisoners or children who have achieved a level of ability to trust others who are in authority. To reach this stage successfully there must have been a certain sad appreciation of the forthcoming loss of those others. The young people emerging from such institutions no longer have trustworthy staff or parents immediately to hand when wanted. Any institution or any parent who believes with conviction that its inmates or his children really want to be free of outside good authority is likely to be initiating a dangerous chain-reaction. The most important disillusionment, both simple and benign, that a person must go through is to realize the extreme convenience of having an 'own self' that can be trusted – so much more to hand and therefore so much more efficient than a good mother or the best policeman.

The prize of a justifiably trusted self comes from the model of justifiably trusted others. A regime, family or institution based upon trust of those who do not themselves have a concept of self-trust in the first place is mad. A healthy baby trusts himself as being omnipotent, as possessing infinite power, and imagines the world as an extension of himself. On the other hand, a fortunate child eventually learns to trust the outside world only where trust is warranted. A new adult, as time goes on and the trusted people and concepts outside begin to retreat, has to learn to trust the internal images of these people and concepts – 'himself', all over again. A child's trust is built up in imperceptible, unconscious, non-dramatic ways; these ways need to be understood by the concerned professional.

One of the most important of these ways is simply by 'being there'. The concept of 'being there' is not easy for caring staff to appreciate, until they realize that a child in care has had first blood-relations who have themselves 'been there' very little (if at all), or inconsistently. There is no question of a professional replacing a 'not-there' parent, but there is every reason to expect a professional to understand that the working-through of his or her own forthcoming departure, vacation, attendance at a course or absence because of pregnancy is of paramount importance for his or her client.

Frequently, and concurrently with the non-appreciation of the importance of 'being there', both parents and professionals adopt an over-compensatory indulgence towards children. This was underlined by an experiment that I undertook,[3] following up an impression I had gained that certain children's social workers tended to stay with their cases for a shorter period than one might usually expect, after having succeeded in arranging for the children to be admitted to an institution (a very expensive procedure which if unnecessary could certainly be regarded as an indulgence). In studying a series of sixty social workers, each of whom was responsible for a child in care in the institution in question, I discovered that the average time that they remained in post with their particular children was ten months from the child's admission date, whereas I found that sixty social workers selected at random from outside the institution stayed with their cases for an average of eighteen months, that is the over-compensation was perhaps in response to the unconscious awareness that they would soon 'not be there' with their child clients.

A child's development is uneven – sometimes two

steps forward, one step back. A child who is lucky enough to have a parent figure who cares enough to be aware of this staccato development is experiencing someone whose concern for him is genuinely good. It is common for people in institutions, whether families or prisons, to be unable to make up their minds. It is only half the battle – perhaps the lesser half – simply to get clear what plan *is* to be decided upon. More important is to realize that the person in the quandary may be testing for the presence of a special type of caring. Such a person – child or inmate – is unconsciously hoping to experience an authority who does not simply want to know the plan merely in order to keep his own bureaucratic mind at ease, but who is also sufficiently interested and sufficiently caring to have noticed that his dependant has his own varying sets of wishes – even about exactly the same thing.

I remember a young man who nearly had a sex-change operation which was stopped when I realized how much he had vacillated over the years, alternately wanting then not wanting the operation; staff turnovers had tended to obscure this vacillation even further. A successful operation would have left him with a permanent memorial to a lack of this particular type of caring. The wish to bask in this kind of caring often stands for the wish to protract the mourning for an ever-loving, ever-interested parent figure saying to herself and her child: 'Just look what he's doing now!' This is strikingly evident in the mother who indulges her baby lovingly as he goes through his feeding play, in which he alternates between *not* wanting the food and patronizingly accepting his mother's offerings.

A child's realization of the parents' perception of him as metaphorically grey, not black or white, not totally good nor totally bad, is an important building-block towards trust of others. An over-condemning or over-idealizing blindness by parents is perceived as neglect, but the realization that one's parents see one as grey is a confirmation of their interest and their sense of reality. The opportunity to perceive one's parents' realistic perception of one's self provides the model that will enable one to eventually perceive one's self realistically.

The way in which a child or a person in 'child status', whether prisoner or junior staff member, takes delegated responsibility, is a useful pointer to the real solidity of the beginning of their assumption of self-authority. The following somewhat commonplace instance might help to clarify my meaning. One morning a fairly new junior member of staff in a residential institution found that she was unable to carry out a responsible task to which she had been assigned for the first time. She was supposed to plan a rota of staff 'sleeping in' for the following month. Her difficulty was threefold: one member of staff had neglected to make known his annual leave plans; she wanted very much to succeed in her task; and, lastly, the very influential, dominating, 'all-knowing' secretary of long standing had made it clear that she needed the rota for typing that morning. The new member of staff managed to resist the temptation to guess the missing dates, since, if wrong, logistic chaos would have ensued. She didn't give way to her own wish to succeed, nor to the dragon secretary, but waited till her delegating senior returned the next day. This kind of sober giving up of a very strong wish to succeed – to *have* to be right first time – which might result in what looks like failure, is a hallmark of the beginnings of maturity somewhat reminiscent of the resolution of the Oedipus complex, enabling one to give up any notion of marrying one's mother's husband or one's father's wife, but to make do with a 'second-best' of one's own. The staff member gave up the wish to do the job quickly, well and on her own, but instead agreed with herself to do it slowly, well and with help. Unresolved, this conflict can result in an unwitting lifelong chase after an unattainable ideal.

I would like to mention two examples that stress this acquisition of self-authority. The acquisition of the ability to self-help may be particularly vital to people deprived of good parenting, or of any parenting at all, people who may largely have had to bring themselves up.

The first example concerns a patient of mine; the second is about a fictional character, acquiring his self-help ability quite consciously, even delightedly.

A boy inmate in a penal institution complained that he couldn't sleep. During our half-hour interview it turned out that, though only nineteen years old, he had committed very many serious acts of delinquency, and had received eight non-custodial sentences, such as fines, probation and deferred sentences – all in fact significantly reminiscent of the treatment he had received from his over-indulgent parents. When I asked him how these sentences had affected him, he replied: '*I didn't lose much sleep over them.*' We came to the end of the interview happy that at long last he had begun to lose sleep. No sedation was prescribed for this boy, who was probably beginning, after much delay, to take an objective view of himself – that overview which had been kept back, kept unconscious by the indulgent parents and courts who habitually cosseted him and let him off lightly.

The second example I call the Bozo Syndrome, after the character in George Orwell's *Down and Out in Paris and London*.[4] This example demonstrates a common self-educative ploy, which is unconsciously used to cultivate a sense of self-authority. This syndrome has many implications, including the partial answer to the question: why do certain vagrants and others continue to wander, fail to show gratitude for charity and persist in seeming not to learn from direction or advice? Bozo was a pavement artist, or screever, who surprised Orwell in the lodging-house by laughing as he drank his tea. The joke was against himself: he had sold his razor, before shaving. He needed the money in order to make up the necessary amount for his night's lodging, but he would still have received the same price if he had shaved first. One assumes that Bozo would use that grown-up learning about the best order of things to good effect; also that he wouldn't have learned it if the warden of the lodging-house had generously waived the sum outstanding.

Most of life's lessons are of the first, or unconscious, sort, and thus, unfortunately, are usually wasted. I have gained the impression that some people who fritter away benefits are unwittingly, and therefore often repeatedly, attempting self-therapy and creating situations where lessons affecting their own lives *could* be basic and possess wide relevance, but because of the unwittingness are misunderstood and lost – as in the case of the boy who first thought he simply needed sleeping pills. This unwittingness as to the potential of the repeated attempt to self-help should not affect the professional concerned, or much valuable time, concern and money will be squandered. The professional must have *his* wits about him in order to help the unwitting client to know exactly what he is doing, and the reason why he is doing it. Without the witting participation of the professional who does realize the therapeutic potential of apparently self-destructive and nonsensical behaviour, the behaviour remains just that; the patient remains a patient and the professional remains useless.

CHAPTER THREE

'The Good'

The elaboration, with examples, of the meaning of particular types of good authority, that are necessary for the safety and successful development of individuals, families and enterprises

---

TPA Good authority is a huge psychic burden, weighing more or less unconsciously on the shoulders of the bearer, and certainly often perceived only unconsciously by others – except when found wanting. It is taken for granted, not appreciated. Nobody notices authority if it is good. How then does one study a phenomenon that is not consciously visible? It can only be done by perceiving its absence in situations in which it should be present. The relevant situations can be seen in everyday life, and can even be captured, examined and used in specially constructed therapeutic settings.

The unwitting recognition, and the witting non-recognition, of good authority is an interesting and serious problem. If, for instance, we do believe, as is commonly and traditionally held, that qualities of Good are built up through life, why do we commonly indulge in 'ageism', that is, why do we automatically patronize or even reject our elders? Yet we tend to be doubly upset when an old person is beaten up by a mugger. In my view this is due to the unconscious anger felt against an attack on a vast experience of life; but the conscious reaction is still: 'Poor old soul!' – a dodderer, who is not being allowed

even to dodder in peace. The mugger overtly demonstrates society's denial of the meaning of experience.
Experience is felt and only rarely, if ever, defined and,
because of this, often lost. However, it is possible that,
for instance, a great deal of inter-sex, inter-religious,
inter-class and inter-racial vehemence (and for that matter
violence) is in reality a 'debating area' where unconsciously a mass attempt is being made to stress what are
felt to be valuable human resources of experience, which
are as a rule unrecognized. These previously unacknowledged resources, for example sex, religion, class
or race are exemplified by: feminine intuition, masculine
strength, Christian neighbourliness, Jewish hard work,
middle-class solidity, working-class solidarity, Arab hos-
pitality, etc. A general resource of experience might be
expected in mothers who have had trouble-free pregnancies culminating in successful births – happy events.
They are probably less liable to find peace boring –
rather be grateful for it, having enjoyed the benefits of
nine months' 'uneventfulness'.

It is rather sad and wasteful when an experienced
person can only put 'experience' into words by referring
to his 'years in the business' or simply by claiming to *be*
'experienced', forgetting or discounting the real worth of
the knowledge and awareness he has acquired over the
course of time. Another instance of the good of experience
exemplifies just how subtle the non-recognition of a
good can be and shows the experienced person herself
not recognizing her own good: a penal-institution matron
of many years' professional experience was distressed
when told that an inmate's female visitor had written to
the prison authorities saying that the matron had made a
slanderous remark during 'visits', connecting the said
visitor with the inmate's venereal disease. I, being the
institution's psychotherapist at that time (a kind of
boxroom where items were to be put when there was no
specifically ordained quarter for them), became the
receptacle for the matron's distress. 'But was there no

other staff member with you?' I asked. 'Of course there was,' she said disdainfully, as though I had suggested that she couldn't tell soap from butter, and at that moment a pleased yet worried look made her eyes cross slightly. She was pleased because she had been saved from the female visitor's victimization, but at the same time was startled that she had not recognized her own taken-for-granted skill, time-acquired and intuitive, which had made certain that she was never out of earshot of a colleague when talking to the woman in question.

I propose now, as simply as I can, to outline examples and to elaborate some of the features of the goods. Colin Murray Parkes [1] writes of what he calls the lost 'supplies' which, he says, 'we don't know enough about yet'. I think his supplies and my Good are probably the same. I would add that, though I think we do know and even understand about Supplies we are not aware of them when they are present, and awareness only dawns when we feel the pain of their missingness. The Good has to be learned. For one small instance, one must learn that it is possible to feel strongly about something without necessarily taking action. 'I know how you feel, son, we'll work something out together,' is a little, but hugely Good thing to say, since one can imagine on the other hand the infectious terror caused by a Supply-less, not-Good father whose first reaction on hearing of his son's disappointment about something – say at school – is to act on his own strong feelings and to go round to the school and raise hell with the apparent prime movers of his son's unhappiness. Again, a certain kind of ability (akin to cynicism) to foretell the future is a Good or Supply, the absence of which one should dread. It goes largely unrecognized. I call it *Kilroy*. The phrase 'Kilroy was here' never ceases to fascinate. Papers on the subject have appeared in learned journals. It is probably the most common graffiti the world has known. Yet most of us wonder: 'What kind of person writes "Kilroy was here" on walls? (A different kind of person from *me* –

that's for sure.)' In fact, it is so difficult for us to imagine a 'Kilroy-was-here'-writing-person that, if it were not for the actual writing on the wall, we would find it easier to believe that no 'Kilroy'-writing-person existed.

During a discussion, several first-time inmates of a penal institution agreed that on arriving they had had to pinch themselves to realize that they had been incarcerated. But equally frightening in retrospect was the ease with which they had become part of the prison, institutionalized – 'Kilroy-was-here'-writers – people that in their previous world they hadn't believed really existed. The prison officers hadn't seen that under their noses a massive, continuous, sinister psychological event was taking place. New prisoners were being transformed from being surprised and shocked 'that it could happen to me' individuals into becoming Kilroy himself. In this connection, a good-authority father knows and shares the knowledge with his son that 'it *could* happen to you', *really* could happen, whether it means getting killed on the roads, being caught stealing, being imprisoned or even failing to find a job easily.

*

ATE This refusal to accept the evidence of one's eyes or senses is ancient and accords ill with our idea of the 'survival instinct'. Presumably prehistoric man could not afford to be so wilful. Civilization brings welcome distractions, such as alcoholic beverages, to make the things of the night go away – or seem to. Belshazzar must have known or suspected that the Persians were at the gates, yet even as the writing appeared on the walls of his palace he chose to ignore it, doubtless assuring himself that it was an illusion and all would be well in the end.

*

TPA I have already suggested that the distance an authority keeps may be beneficial to those it sees are being looked after. This distance-keeping needs to be understood in order for it to become an appreciated Good, rather than devalued, since such devaluing easily becomes infectious. A father even in this homogenized age may with advantage be generally more physically distant from his children than his perpetually harassed wife. Likewise, a senior member of staff in an institution or organization is much less competent if he fritters away his advantage of distance, becoming no more able than anyone else to see the wood for the trees. A 'testing' staff or an undermining wife, however, would have an easy time making the distance seem like lack of interest, or rejection, even to the actual would-be good authority himself. Distance enables a clearer overview to be taken, both of past, present and future. It is a definite advantage to have a trusted leader who, for instance, knows that a past chance has been lost, and who insists that everyone should realize that there is no turning the clock back. His lack of something like this sort of leadership was sadly recognized by the father of a delinquent boy. Although his problems seemed at first only to be connected with his never-satisfied thief of a son, he began to see that behind this was a hidden matter. He realized that his wife – having herself been one of eleven children, had needed a lot of support to come to terms with being sterilized – even after six children she felt unfulfilled; unconsciously she had still wanted what her own mother had – eleven children. That would have made her a 'proper mother'. Had he understood her nagging sense of insufficiency, he might have been of more support to her.

While in the middle of a crisis,[2] an overwhelmed mother might well appreciate a reminder that difficult times have beginnings, middles and blessed ends. At the time she may have no concept of ends or beginnings – just of awful, never-ending middles. Like other good-authority commodities, the keeping of distance can occur inside individuals and families as well as outside. The usual typically unrecognized quality of this Good, residing in our own common sense or within a professional helper, has to struggle against over-involvement. This can be done by sleeping on it in the case of an individual or just listening in the case of a professional. The wish to be worrying, re-worrying, doing, meddling, fixing, mending, replacing and trying to change oneself or somebody else can often contribute only to an increasing and spreading anxiety.

An important Good is the ability to differentiate between firmness and punitiveness. In the minds of some authorities firmness and punitiveness or violence are often confused. The more an authority is muddled, the more it will be pressed to show its true colours by those over whom it has authority, and it will sooner or later be 'exposed' as punitive or even sadistic. But if there is no confusion then sufficient firmness can be brought to bear in the first place, and this will be perceived as caring, thereby pre-empting the need for the child or prisoner or group to behave more and more badly in order to find out just how far it can go. It should be plain to see how low-profile policing will have a profitable or disastrous result, depending on the level of confusion initially present. The village bobby on his bike would make little impression on a large-scale riot, while bus-loads of police with riot shields would cause outrage if summoned to a disturbance in a school playground, and anyone can perceive the sense of calm when a baby is firmly and lovingly held, and can compare this to the confusion and disturbance evidenced by a panicky bawler in the arms of a scared and scary person.

In the matter of ownership and responsibility, we are likely to feel the unrecognized fact of our authority dawn on us as a tangible reality. An owner, whether a child with a guinea-pig or a householder, can make the connection between care or maintenance with the possession of a healthy pet or a house in good order. But if care or maintenance is lacking, the owner is going to have to face the consequences either of guilt about the dead guinea-pig, or shame at his own laxity in not organizing the repair of the lock on the front door *before* the burglary. A lazy child saying, 'Its hutch doesn't need cleaning, I cleaned it yesterday,' has a problem if his parents collude with this argument, since the guinea-pig will fall victim and, more importantly, the child will be desperately worried, unconsciously knowing that he has parents who cannot take responsibility.

A good authority knows what can wait and what cannot, without having to be rigid. Perhaps it was rigidity that was responsible in part for the 'military delinquency' variously known as cowardice in the face of the enemy, shell-shock, lack of moral fibre, battle neurosis or battle-fatigue. Perhaps the real terror was not only the fear of being blown to bits or being buried alive, but at least in part a fear of being subject to an authority that lacks a certain kind of Good. I suspect that in the First World War there prevailed a post-Victorian lack of ability to know when to stick at it – that is, to stay entrenched – and when to pull out. The balance was perhaps rigidly tilted in the first of these directions. It seems almost as though a kind of ritual suicide was taking place as a perverse and tragic pulling out. It is noticeable in the study of delinquency how commonplace expressions often show hints of their origins. Very often in families having a delinquent member, an authority of the exaggerated, 'big-stick' variety is found, whereas the good of 'sticking at it' has been lacking. The First World War example of the lack of the Good of being able to 'pull out' to advantage probably went hand in hand with another lack of Good – the lack of the ability to face loss and anxiety in public. Troops with commanders beset with these lacks of Good must have been more worried, unconsciously, about their 'crazy' superiors than about their conventional foe.

*

ATE   'The vulgar and licentious soldiery', the raw material of war, must do what it is told without question. Campaigns could not be conducted without implicit obedience in the

ranks. When generals make mistakes, as they unfortunately must do, these mistakes must be concealed or they
imagine morale would be destroyed. Only when many
bones have been bleached by time are old errors and
misjudgements made public for the instruction, if not
edification, of future military commanders. There is a
tacit acceptance of this by the man in the front line. In
war films querulous remarks by the lowest private are
silenced by the sergeant, the middle-man, who may
harbour doubts more acute than anyone else's. He will
not be privy to his commander's thinking, but he will,
being experienced, have some idea of what's in the wind.
He may not like it, but his training will keep him quiet. I
think it's nuts myself, but there you are. A weak person
in a position of authority, having made up his mind, will
not change it, since his fear of losing face may be worse than
his fear of losing the battle, and of all the king's men.

Perhaps this unspoken, unholy conspiracy may be
necessary or at least unavoidable in times of crisis, but it
should play no part in everyday 'ordinary' life.

*

TPA In this connection and in my own field the most
touching piece of work I have ever known concerned a
fifteen-year-old boy in care and his new social worker.
The social worker was able to perceive, at last, the
complete inability of his client's parents 'to stick at it'.
For many years previously his successive professional
predecessors had not seen, or had denied the fact of, the
parents' inconstancy, and had vainly tried to keep the
family together or at least in contact. With a mixture of
anguish and relief, the two of them, professional and
child, faced their disillusionment in the parents with
their selfishness and their habit of passing the buck. A
young adult was born out of this disappointment and out
of his social worker's ability to face reality.

*

ATE   I asked how these parents manifested their inconstancy and learned that they did it in small but ultimately destructive ways. They would agree to get the child to school on time and after a few days would forget this promise and stay in bed. They swore to produce meals on time and shortly neglected to do so. They vowed to give up getting drunk and to be home before ten, and kept that up for less than a week. They said they would regularly see the social worker and never saw him at all. They never kept their word and yet expected the trust of their child.

*

TPA   If it were true that human kind cannot bear too much reality, then there would not be much good in us.[3] Any inability in a person to accept the world as it is – with all its wrongs and shortcomings – denotes a lack of Good. This lack of Good can even be treacherously, self-deceivingly turned upside-down, with the result that the world is claimed not to accept the person; the initial denied reality is superseded by a false or irrelevant reality. This 'reaction formation' can become a consensus that is commonly used by groups of individuals who agree that they have a grievance. Soon such a grievance, that the world does not accept *them*, is seemingly supported by the very numbers involved, all of them laying claim to the same complaint. Certainly some delinquents calling themselves, and often being called, 'homosexual', fall into this category; together denying the rejecting, stupid world for its intolerance, when actually each of *them* separately cannot see the world very well at all. Any group of children, young or older, needs a good reality-testing base in order not to turn into a teeming horde whose aim is to cling together, attached with the glue of their psychologically manufactured unacceptability. They will otherwise truly present an upside-down mirror of the real world which no 'good father' had helped them to accept. Once such a good authority has helped its folk to face a difficult reality, he can then remind them of their future, can dissuade them from destructive anxiety, can encourage the provision of space and time, and a calm atmosphere in which to preserve the power of thinking and the ability to accept innovation.

I hope I am beginning to make it clear that wisdom, not knowledge, is the distillate that is being sought here; a kind of awareness of the danger that over-brilliant tactics can damage overall strategy. The need to realize, for instance, that it is not the points scored within an argument that count so much as the fact that an argument has started and will need ending. Every day smokers and drinkers pull themselves apart trying not to smoke or drink, only to end the argument with themselves by lighting another cigarette or pouring another drink. They could hardly end the argument by holding out – the argument would always feel unfinished. (One unconscious reason for people chain-smoking is to provide themselves with a predicament in which an eventual decision to give up will have more substance than a decision made against a background of intermittent smoking. In the latter case the decision not to smoke again will not feel sufficiently different from all the previous occasions when there was no smoking between cigarettes.)

*

ATE 'There's nothing easier than giving up smoking. I do it every day.'

Mark Twain

There is a considerable difference between stopping and finishing. The moderate drinker is able to crush up the vitamin C tablet, sprinkle it over the remaining wine in the bottle and bung the cork back in after drinking only a glass or two. The immoderate person ('one of us won't live to see the morning') will not be satisfied until the bottle is empty – finished – not merely because he wants to get drunk – he is probably drunk enough already – but because there is, in his eyes, something unsatisfactory about a bottle that is neither full nor empty. The compulsive smoker will not leave a packet with two cigarettes in it, but will stay up ten minutes past his bedtime in order to polish them off. He can then say to himself – right, that's the last cigarette I'm ever smoking – while retaining the chance of enjoying the guilty delight of buying another, brand-new, gloriously full packet the following morning and starting all over again. I know. Eating water biscuits, playing ping-pong and chewing gum are also activities which seem to have no natural, built-in point of conclusion; but that doesn't really matter much. On a more alarming note, TPA says that those with a 'tendency to violence' having felled an adversary will not stop there, but will often go on kicking until the person on the ground is finished off. The ability to stop is clearly a sign of health and maturity, while the compulsion to finish can be destructive. On the other hand I find myself thinking of builders. All the builders I have ever had dealings with evince a notable tendency to keep on stopping and a positively pathological reluctance to finish. Painters often can neither stop nor finish, but go on fiddling with a picture until its original fresh conception is lost; and there are writers who have to have their manuscripts taken from them by force as they neurotically cross out whole sentences, and frenziedly put in otiose adverbs, not trusting themselves to have produced a perfectly adequate book.

*

TPA On a much wider plain, politicians who allow themselves to be drawn into discussions by their opposite numbers in other nations should realize that being a party to discussions implies some outcome to these discussions – maybe not even in their own political lifetimes, but perhaps far in the future. Once the international debate has begun, individual issues assume an (often unwarranted) importance, since the debate is now legitimized. The good political authority is able to resist, in the first place, the temptation to appear reasonable by entering into discussions which with any luck will peter out, and instead refuse at the outset to be led into them. Many people crave for a reinstatement of the practice of hanging felons, and many politicians, whether from personal conviction or out of a lust for votes, claim to feel the same way. As a result, in Britain there has been, and probably always will be, a debate about capital punishment. As long as a matter is legitimate material for discussion, then each such discussion may lead to change. But if the matter remains unmentioned, no discussion takes place and no change is made. A mischief-maker therefore has merely to mention a topic in a particular quarter for discussion to be initiated, and thus to effect eventual change. This particular quarter is unlikely to be the legitimate quarter, and only if the particular quarter has a good authority can trouble be averted.

A new senior executive, recently appointed to a subsidiary branch of a company, was invited to the group's head office to partake in introductory pleasantries which were laced with discussion regarding the hypothetical future, including the amalgamation with or running down of the subsidiary company. The new executive realized that if he were to report back to his own local subsidiary branch management, then discussion would be set in progress and the change would be only a matter of time. During his visit he suggested that the correct procedure might be for the chairman at head office to contact the branch management formally, via its own chairman, suggesting a venue and an agenda. No such letter was ever sent, and the only obvious change five years later was that the new executive was now the chairman of the entire group. He was a good authority in the sense that he was very aware of his own defined areas of authority; he was not authorized to act as the luncheon's messenger-boy. If he had not been so aware, he might well have been the unwitting, unconsciously brain-less vehicle of an asset-stripping manoeuvre that could have resulted in the loss of many jobs. This example shows how a good authority is able to counter a piece of conventionally accepted behaviour that is, in fact, a particular brand of delinquency, that is, the use of, or attempted abuse of, an individual to manipulate a group. Political agitators commonly use the opposite ploy; they will use a group, a local community, for instance, which has no good authority, in order that the reverberations of a neighbourhood disorder may reach the executive ears of an important public authority. The subsequent pub-licity then has the effect of putting an unacceptable and extreme minority view in a position where it has much more exposure, coverage and leverage than it is entitled to. I use the expression 'no good authority' not in any moral, but in the following, precise, sense: there may well be authority figures present in a given situation, but each one of them should be aware of the limits of his authority, and should in consequence be able to take action quite legitimately at the earliest justifiable moment. He should not be intimidated by the fear of seeming to be unreasonable, or by appearing to flout the current dogma – perhaps that of keeping a low profile or not seeming bossy. An authority is entitled, if necessary, to act in opposition to the majority (the anti-consensus decision). Unconsciously, at least, that is the action expected of it, especially by that very same majority who in the first instance chose what they hoped would *be* a good authority. It was they who were responsible for the 'may' and the 'with or without reference' of the stark legalistic definitions I provided earlier in this book. In my opinion, an authority capable of letting a baby, or a mob, regress to such an extent that any fool (let alone the good authority) can see what action is necessary, will incur the double wrath of such neglected 'children'. Looking good is not at all the same as being good. It is fine when the two do coincide, but one of the purposes of authority is to save us from wishful thinking. The ability to be good and yet be prepared to look bad at the same time is an invaluable asset. Even some of General Washington's supporters during the American War of Independence might have thought that the redcoats looked conspicuously splendid, but the lack of camouflage was not good for British prospects.

Let me give an example of this business of being good and not just looking good. A fourteen-year-old boy arrived with his father and social worker to meet the principal of his new children's home. The ceremony went well, not least because father seemed very responsible and concerned. It was a long time before the nice father was acknowledged as the self-same person who now failed to answer brief requests and notes from the house staff and from the social worker about small but important day-to-day matters. This illustrates the absence of a particular Good in a parent. It was heartening subsequently to notice the qualities of other parents who went unremarked in their sober constancy. The very mundaneness of certain assets is part of the curious medium of camouflage and surprise, which can account for a great deal of the excitement that is necessary when working in the field of delinquency, that is, the excitement of understanding, rather than the vicarious satisfaction obtained from the delinquent's outrageous behaviour. The present-day economic revolution, which has enabled adolescents frequently to possess more uncommitted spending power than adults, has probably done a great deal towards putting necessary, everyday things into the background and, conversely, pushed exciting, sensational and immediate issues into the foreground of news and current affairs. This increased influence of young people sees to it that their common and emphatic wish to be involved in the outcome or solution of issues is accommodated more and more. There is a tremendous danger that enthusiastic but less mature participation may swamp, almost by intimidation, the apparently stodgy, slow and frustrating methods and procedures of problem solving, which may have taken years if not generations to evolve.

Earlier I mentioned briefly the discovery of hints of the origins of certain expressions of speech, like 'sticking at it'. Others include 'taking a wrong turning', 'bent', 'going straight', 'going off the tracks', etc. These highlight one of the most mundane tasks that parents need to honour – keeping one another and their family in touch. This keeping in touch is very vulnerable. For instance, a hard-working father at the end of *his* day, and his hard-working wife at the end of *her* day may neglect, out of conscious concern for their own or the other's tiredness, to keep each other up to date. Wives who work days, and husbands who work nights and, in consequence, pass each other by, are not rare. Should something unexpected happen that requires a quick response or decision, judgement is made very difficult and the likelihood of it being incorrect is increased, since the process of catching-up with details, now disclosed for the first time, perhaps in an atmosphere of anger and blame, is most inimical, and implies the likelihood of a wrong turning for a family – a 'going crooked'. The common consensus between husbands and wives who habitually keep *out* of touch may be: 'I leave that sort of thing to my wife', or a somewhat incredulous: 'My husband's got his work to do!' in answer to the query from a professional as to the reason why the father had failed to keep an appointment.

Keeping in touch, though usually taken for granted, is of the utmost importance when establishing a good authority. For example, as I said previously, a young child does not always develop its various skills in a straightforward, progressive manner. Only parents who keep in touch are likely to understand the staccato nature of their child's development. They might even manage to relate this rhythm to family events. Parents who have been mutually satisfied and fascinated by the changes they have observed are in a position of the greatest advantage when it is a question of knowing what is a normal reaction for their child. Its changes of temper, its progression or regression, resemble a dance that is to be followed, never learned, the rules of which are not to be imposed from outside. Children in residential institutions often demonstrate this phenomenon, not so much by their differing performances at different times, but rather by the feelings that they evoke in various members of staff. For instance, to certain staff they might seem to be very mature, yet to other members of staff the opposite. This gives a clue to some of the complexities that, unfortunately, their parents may not have seen. Tasks frequently take longer than had been anticipated. A family or working-group that does keep in touch is able to appreciate the amount of effort and time involved in dealing with the bureaucratic niceties, the unexpected hitches and inevitable distractions that make what had originally seemed a quick and simple task slower and less simple. In a group of people who are in touch with each other, understanding and sympathy are gradually established between the parties concerned, rather than impatience, resentment and disappointment. It is a common fact of life in this connection that people *do* change their minds. A single person living alone who decides, for once, to clean his teeth before washing his face, thus reversing his usual custom last thing at night, will not, I hope, give himself too much of a problem. But in a group that might be discussing various and complex matters, either formally, or informally, a significant feature will be this self-same changing of minds – the very substance of debate. A good authority, responsible for maintaining a situation where the people concerned can and do keep in touch with one another, say, from one meeting to the next, will have seen fit to establish some mechanism to observe and record the making up and changing of minds, since these changes tend to be as complete as is the obliteration of their memory. It is not conducive to further constructive debate if the participants are allowed to believe quite sincerely and state that they did not say what they did say.

*

ATE I've made up my mind, now please don't confuse me with the facts.

Obviously minds might not need changing as frequently as socks or underwear, but there are few things so depressing as utter intransigence – often wrongly described as inhuman. It uniquely typifies our species or, rather, the male of the species. An eminent British Law Lord offered an example of this quality when he made the startling observation before millions of TV viewers that it was preferable for a few innocent people to remain in prison than for the judicial system to be brought into disrepute. The wrong-headedness of this remark *boggles* the mind, and I am surprised that the entire country did not rise up in protest. Most of us are innocent of any crime, after all, and clearly not secure from retribution on that account. I digress. TPA says that the whole business of 'changing of minds' is not sufficiently recognized or discussed; that mind-changing is seen either as weakness or an admission that you were wrong in the first place, when, in fact, it may be that during a meeting facts previously unknown to you are brought to light, and these put a different complexion on the matter. We speak here of *discussion*, not of argument. Reasonable beings, taking all the known circumstances into account, may turn around in the course of discussions but I don't believe I have ever known anyone, starting from an entrenched standpoint, to be swayed from his position in the course of an *argument*. Most people dig themselves in more deeply, close their eyes and start shouting. It is my impression that men suffer mostly from this disability, this inflexibility. While the constant changing of minds can lead to confusion and chaos, blind stubbornness is a terrifying manifestation. Women, for whatever reason, are more open to appeal and less devoted to routine, rules and shibboleths, and perhaps it is a fear of seeming feminine that makes men disinclined to appear to waver. It is most unfortunate.

*

TPA   Again in this context I heard from a social worker about a father who bought three books for his three children, but gave them all to the eldest, the books being too advanced for the two younger children. The eldest boy was supposed to make up his mind as to which of the books he wanted for himself. Some weeks later the eldest boy had not only forgotten his task of choosing one, but had come to regard all three books as his own. The torn dust-covers now spoiled them as future presents for the younger children. The social worker was able to help the family to appreciate that kindness on an authority's part was not enough. The understanding of the business of mind-changing and making-minds-up was a necessary Good. I call this pseudo-benign behaviour hypocritical rejection.[4]

Perhaps certain social policies are experienced as rejections of this hypocritical sort, giving rise to increased angry demands from the so-called beneficiaries. Certain public and political attitudes towards religious and racial minorities often appear to fall into this category. In the United Kingdom recent wider-scale provisions of camp sites for gypsies seems to have met with increased demands from gypsies. Such a problem might be partly solved if the inherent, but disguised, rejection by the authorities were to be openly acknowledged, since as long as it remains disguised it prevents the openly 'indulged' injured parties from belonging either within *or* without society. It is as though the recipients of the overt benefits were bound to remain a troublesome group whose built-in vexatiousness could not be dissipated by the authorities, no matter what the extent of the benefits conferred. It is this phenomenon which results in the quite justified comment – the more you give them, the more they want.

An authority that is able to combine an appreciation of the importance of keeping in touch, together with an awareness of the value of keeping a certain distance, is able to discern what is a muddle and what only seems to be a muddle. Muddles were the dangerous order of the day in one family where the father had no employment save as a 'mother's help' to his wife, so deeply was he immersed in his family affairs. Invariably very serious and important irrelevances like unpaid bills constantly prohibited the key issue of the father's over-involvement from being faced and discussed. The social worker, representing the legal authority of one of the children, was however able to envisage far worse inevitable dangers should she fail to cut through the overt irrelevant anxieties to the less obvious, though far more worrying things that really mattered. Her professional self-distancing made it clear to her that the overt problems were, in fact, loose, easy tangles, designed to keep at bay the opportunity of real sorting-out. It was interesting to read the old case notes about this family and to see how several previous generations of professional case workers had obviously been dying to sort out something or someone, but how the work had come to nothing because they had been sidetracked by a huge carriageway of problems, when the real route to a solution was a tiny footpath.

This perception of reality, plus the ability to confront omnipotence, is a constant theme which the good authority takes upon itself, and which is expected of it. Since we all suffer, more or less, from feelings of omnipotence and omniscience (thinking we can do more than we can, or 'that we will be O K on the night', or that we know what's going on when in fact we don't), the perception as well as the confrontation are hard things to accomplish. The authority, time and time again, will find itself considered impractical by others – and quite likely will be tempted into agreement with this judgement. If omnipotence is taken to be an unconscious and un-thought-out notion that the universe, spatially and temporally, is an extension of oneself, then a person declaring, 'It will all work out in the end,' needs a painful reminder that this is not necessarily so. A true perception, even if it involves pain, can be felt positively, even as real and secure-making. If the true perception is ignored when the opportunity offers, only nostalgic regret is left at the wasted opportunity. When a group of young prisoners was asked why they thought they had been locked up, each had a reasonable-sounding but omniscient answer: as a punishment, for treatment, for training. The staff carefully considered what the real, understandable reason could be in each case, and they felt that the common criterion upon which the law had acted in these particular cases was the wish to reject. When the boys in turn were told why the staff thought they had actually been sent to Borstal, all the boys' composure was visibly upset, and two of them, somewhat surprisingly, wept. It transpired that they were upset because they believed that once they had been rejected they were rejected for all time. There was no idea in their minds of the reality of being given a second chance, or of being cared for afterwards by the same quarter from which the rejection had come. I am sure that some absconders from penal establishments run away in order to test their own concept of rejection, to find out if it is possible to be welcomed back on recapture.

The imperceptible creep-up of squalor or 'going-to-the-bad' [5] is a reality-defying phenomenon experienced by every professional with an entrée to his clients' homes. The mistake commonly made is to jump to the conclusion that a family or a household cannot perform certain simple domestic tasks demanding physical or mental effort. The more useful view is to realize that a blurring or deadening of reality is occurring, and that

this can be very dangerous. Its roots need to be understood. The authority with distance and experience is
then less likely to fall into the error of repeatedly making
heroic efforts to organize clean-ups, and will be more
likely to read the signs correctly.

A remarkable example of this creep-up phenomenon
occurred in an institution that kept a place open for
seven months for a certain boy who was 'never there'.
Police visits to the home of the boy's parents in the hope
of grabbing him often revealed a warm bed and an open
window, even after midnight. During the seven months
the residential staff, who had closest contact with the
resident children, waited for the boy to be admitted, and
by degrees they reached a stage when they found it
difficult to believe that a boy of that name actually
existed. His father would arrive punctually on the dot for
his appointment at the social services department's
reception area, but would immediately leave – before the
boy's social worker, on learning of his arrival from the
reception clerk, had had time to reach him. A younger
brother of the 'phantom' was described as adding to the
constant stench of animal and human excrement in the
home, by making some of the former 'disappear' by
rubbing it into the carpet with his foot. These are only a
few instances, out of many relating to this family, that
have a common feature: *the denial of reality*. Certainly
there was no boy for the residential staff to look after
directly; certainly the social worker was not there physically at reception when the father arrived at the department; and certainly, although the mess from the many
dogs could not actually be seen, the stench, which was
said to be unbelievable, provided evidence which was
convincing enough.

On this occasion, as the psychoanalyst member of the
team, I was able to enhance the Good of the social
worker, who was the authority in the case. Paradoxically,
my contact with this elusive boy was not quantitatively
very different from that of my contact with the children

already ensconced in the institution, with whom the other staff were in more direct touch. Therefore the boy's existence was no less in doubt to me than that of any other boy at that institution, and I thus had fewer reasons to feel like closing the case. The repeated defeats and discouragements had been experienced by the social worker, not by me. The team gradually began to be aware of the incipient creeping growth of what may be termed an anti-authority family. We could see quite clearly how this particular reality-changing family was pervading the psyches of the professionals with the same malaise, together with a growing feeling of hopelessness and the wish to reject.* However, I as the 'distant' psychoanalyst, much less affected, was able to predict the inevitable newspaper-worthy disaster or scandal that must occur in the end. It would bring into disrepute the entire social services department, already overworked and understaffed, as well as providing a legitimate grievance for a family of unco-operative will-o'-the-wisps. Therefore the very effective minimum that the social worker could now do with confidence, which was probably life-saving as well as reputation-saving, was simply to be on the lookout for 'unrealities' where these concerned the child for whom his department was legally responsible. He would know that he was doing an extremely good job, one that was probably appreciated only by his supporting team. It would be understood that in this case there would be no dramatic staunching of blood or turning of inadequate personalities into lord mayors, or even into particularly good mothers.

This last example, where the outcome was far less spectacular than had been hoped for initially (There are no medals when an unknown tragedy is averted!), leads on to the subject of the wished-for ideal – that magic which is just around the corner but is always denied to one. For some individuals the search for that ideal or

---

* The 'pervading of professional psyches' will be alluded to many times throughout this book.

fantasy is unceasing. (Perhaps this is what an interest in pornography actually is.) The search is unceasing for two reasons. Once obtainable, the fantasy is no longer a fantasy and one has to move on to something new. Second is the fact that the person needs real help for real needs, but this is denied from his consciousness by the magical powers of omnipotence and omniscience; that is, the person suffers from wishful thinking, imagining that he knows what's what and that he can cope on his own.

*

ATE This denial of reality can be frightening and maddening in equal degrees to those who come up against it. It is bad enough in friends and relations who may sail gaily along on a clear disaster course, insisting that everything will be all right in the end, but it is bitterly frustrating to see the same phenomenon in the people in power over us. Many of our leaders have so far removed themselves that they no longer have any conception – if they ever had – of what life is like for millions of citizens. I was once in a children's hospital ward (peeling paint, torn lino) helping to look after my daughter and watching TV when a minister came on to announce that there was no shortage of nurses, and that the government had put more money into the country's Health Service than any government previously. The sister in charge, knee-deep in reality, carrying one baby while bottle feeding another in its cot, almost had to have treatment for apoplexy. With increasing disaffection, violent crime and wide public access to sophisticated weapons of destruction, our leaders must distance themselves even further in the interests of their personal safety. How unlike Frederick the Great.

Then there are judges. Judges I have found, unlike policemen, seldom mingle much in low society and so have very little cognizance of the classes they mostly sit in judgement upon.

*

Judge, sentencing an alcoholic Irish labourer: I am going
to let you off with a fine providing you promise never to
drink again. And by that I mean not even one teeny-
weeny little dry sherry before dinner.

John Mortimer

*

TPA The father of a delinquent child who was causing much
anxiety to the grown-ups was himself grotesquely in-
fantile, in fact, a 'baby adult', and saw fit angrily to
address the good authority in myself as follows: 'You're
the expert, and I want you to do it *this* way.' The help of
understanding, which was what he needed, was swept
aside by his 'omniscience' – his fantasy that *he* knew
best. I hope that this example portrays the common
dilemma of opposing needs; the need to deny the
importance of the Good and its nurture, *and, at the same
time*, the wish to acquire those same denied Goods.

I am deliberately underlining a babylike belief that the
Almighty and his heavenly host are intimately in league
with all the baby's whims and longings, or are in fact
part of the baby's own life apparatus. Heaven forbid that
it should be otherwise for a real baby, and that the baby
should have to worry about the factual reality: that his
well-being depends and rests on the good nature, sense of
duty, love or moral obligation of other ordinary mortals.

It is interesting to notice how reputations are made
slowly, their owners' real, enviable and praiseworthy
assets and attributes gradually having accrued to make a
worthy whole. On the other hand, reputations can
disappear and be lost overnight. This is probably because
the real, usually denied, assets, if acknowledged by an
observer, compel an uncomfortable truth to be accepted
– that the observer has a long way to go before he or she
could acquire a fraction of such qualities. It is these sorts
of truths that show themselves in debates about freedom
of the press or open and closed government – do we
really want to know the tremendous problems and

corresponding skills required of many public figures or do we prefer to luxuriate in denigrating able people, who sometimes make mistakes, because that makes us feel more adequate?

*

ATE I am no freer of *Schadenfreude* than anyone else, but do not 'luxuriate in denigrating able people' – even when they make mistakes. What does give me a certain melancholy satisfaction is the sight of eminent people, whose motives and ability I have always found suspect, making a public spectacle of themselves. Mass adulation can be potentially as unhealthy and dangerous a phenomenon as mob violence, and it is salutary, if not edifying, for the populace to realize that an idol may not just have feet of clay, but be solid kaolin up to the collar stud. Admiration and loyalty are, no doubt, excellent responses in the appropriate circumstances, but the rich and powerful are not, merely by virtue of their wealth and status, deserving of approbation. It seems to be true that we do need heroes – not simply because of a human capacity for worship, but because they can give us a better conceit of ourselves as a species – but we are poor at identifying them. The system of canonization, with its scrupulous and minute investigation and assessment of the candidate's life and qualities, offers a safer source of role models, of people who should be appreciated and emulated – but unfortunately the fashion at present is not for sanctity.

*

TPA It can be helpful and salutary to be able to locate specifically and describe precisely some examples of Good in leaders of institutions, organizations and families. Each Good once located and clearly understood can enable those of lesser ability to gain some insight about the good qualities they lack, but which they could hope to possess if not prevented by discontented envy and an uncomfortable sense of inadequacy. For example, a husband took his wife to their doctor to have a very small lump in her breast examined. She was at first too terrified to go but then agreed, and the lump was removed. She was not told whether or not it was malignant. If however she had not been led by her husband to the doctor at what was possibly a very early stage in the life of a cancer, it is hardly likely that anyone would have blamed him subsequently for having given way to his frightened wife, then reluctant to see the doctor and now dying of advanced cancer. He would not have been called a bad husband. As it was, some members of the family accused him of frightening and bullying his wife. They would have preferred to imagine that nothing could possibly be wrong and if no one mentioned it the lump would go away. But the husband with his first decisive action showed that he possessed enviably good leadership – he could tolerate anxiety, combat wishful thinking, when necessary dominate his wife and know that little things sometimes spread and grow into big ones.

Another example concerns the new principal of a residential establishment where educational facilities were provided on the premises. The principal was faced with a very unprofessional but well-meaning staff, who tried to insist that integration and interchangeability should prevail between residential-care staff and teachers. The principal pointed out that syllabuses and timetables were an educational *sine qua non*, and he led the staff to realize the problem of the relative predictability of teachers versus care staff and the implications, such as: the teachers could not be relied upon to muck in in an emergency if they were expected to be teaching geography at 2.23 on a Monday afternoon, whereas the residential staff, with nothing planned, perhaps *should* have nothing planned in order that they could be free to cope with an emergency. It is sure that very many covert disputes, which would have shown themselves subsequently in the erratic behaviour of the inmates, were stemmed by this action of a Good principal.

The third instance deals with an assistant governor in a penal institution who indirectly heard of a boy *talking* of making love to his probation officer. The story was true, and the boy had been talking in that way, but the assistant governor was aware of how rumours develop and was also able to recognize wishful thinking when it came to his notice. He decided to do no further investigation, and the issue faded away. In short, he was a Good assistant governor.

Children don't need trusting very much; they need to be known better than they know themselves, by someone whom *they* trust. The type of parent who knows his sons and daughters better than they know themselves is well aware that it is hard to stop an action or habit once it has been started, that successful little lies, 'only borrowings' and sexual games can escalate and get out of control. A common feature of institutions and organizations is their constant system-changing and introduction of new rules. Rules are made in part to be broken, and only if a system is known well (that is, by a good authority) will it be worthwhile for a boy or girl in trouble to break a rule in order to draw attention to it, or to themselves, or both. In a system where the system itself and the individuals in it are not well understood, where there is no good authority who makes it his business to ensure that people should know the rules, then the negative cost of rule-breaking will be high. In the cry-for-help phenomenon, if the cry is too loud it can be self-defeating. Then again, too much rearranging, an over-indulgence in the changing of systems, traditions and rules can make it more difficult to recognize slightly unusual behaviour or mild misbehaviour which might well be a muted cry for help.*

*

* In AD 66 Gaius Petronius wrote: '. . . We trained hard – but it seemed that every time we were beginning to form up in teams, we

ATE That is rather beautiful and seems to be working well. It must be old. We'd better change it.

Simplicity is a principal element of freedom – in the spiritual and psychological sense – and a rigid structure is an element of simplicity. When firm rules govern every aspect of mundane, daily activity, as they do in the monastic tradition, then the mind and spirit are left untrammelled. Unbridled licence is the opposite of freedom; leading to darkness, confusion and despair. Contrary to popular, Protestant belief, in a well-organized convent there is a sense of light-heartedness and of easy fluent 'mirth'. Conventual rules were laid down centuries ago, tried and proved over the ages by people who needs must live together in harmony without constant discussion, and left unaltered until the ill-conceived 'reforms' of Vatican II. These needless reforms are a good example of the mischievous human urge to meddle and to rearrange, no matter how satisfactory the existing state of affairs. The wish to seem modern and up-to-date can lead to vandalism on a scale undreamed of by the lout with the aerosol spray. Politicians and property developers, from a variety of motives, have destroyed much of the national heritage and frequently got themselves knighted for their pains – which is doubly exasperating for the helpless citizen, expected to either show gratitude for his new shopping precinct or at worst to exhibit his 'stupid, conventional' objections. An old firm that has run smoothly for years may be taken over by new management which will start by altering all the rules and procedures in order to be visibly doing something. A new head of department will make changes so as to be seen to be earning his keep. It is really preferable that most rules, tested by time, should be sometimes

---

would be reorganized. I was to learn later in life that we tend to meet any new situation by reorganizing, and a wonderful method it can be for creating the illusion of progress whilst producing confusion, inefficiency and demoralization . . .'

broken, rather than altered. With constant alteration the structure is slackened until it ceases to exist and its purpose is lost. This makes those who have relied on it disheartened, insecure and indefinably anxious.

*

TPA A good-authority warden in a hostel for ex-Borstal boys was able to manage a group of very well meaning and enthusiastic university-student volunteer helpers who frequently wanted to change the way things were, 'for the better'. He did not overemphasize the fact that they were there on a temporary basis and that therefore their present enthusiasm might make future life difficult for the professionals they would inevitably leave behind; this would have been felt as patronizing and rejecting. Neither did he over-indulge their enthusiasm, which might have been even worse. Instead he made sure that each student had at least one task which was both important and mundane whilst permitting them to continue with their new ideas: group counselling and a drama group. As a result they realized that the abandonment or introduction of any tradition,* system or rule would require an unexpectedly immense amount of thought and consideration to avert unexpectedly immense difficulties in ordinary areas of life. A characteristic example of the absence or partial absence of this good authority is found in a symbiotic (overly interdependent) mother–child relationship, where there is no effective or actual father to help the mother realize that young birds must or should fly.

*

ATE Letting birds fly. Mothers of large families perhaps have less difficulty in permitting their children to fly the coop, may even beg them to do so. Painful perhaps, but not

* Tradition: *trans*, over, *dare*, to give. Never do away with a traditional system unless the new one can become traditional, that is, capable of being handed on.

usually seen as impossibly difficult. Yet for a single mother it may be just that; all her life and all her expectations of fulfilment may have become rooted in her child, and she may be unable to conceive of a separate existence. Nor, in all likelihood, is anyone going to talk to her about it, since few people would see it as their business to do so, and anyway she and her child might be seen merely as a beautiful example of mutual devotion.

*

TPA The last Good I will mention is concerned with the destructive chain-reaction of anxiety that can occur in any group. If a prevailing anxiety is felt to be unmentionable amongst those in authority, then to those under the authority the problem must be perceived at some level of consciousness as *too much for the authority itself*. Over-anxious or anxiety-denying authority is in my view the chief cause of untenable behaviour in a group; this behaviour is likely to persist until the complete destruction of that organization in that form has come about or until the authorities face the anxiety squarely.

*

ATE Sometimes, at the prospect of trouble, not to say mass insurrection, the authorities will 'decide' in order, they announce, not to inflame the situation further, to keep a low profile; to 'trust' the potential troublemakers to police themselves. Over-crossing those fingers that are not already in their ears or over their eyes, they wait for the volatile occasion to pass. It's a nice idea, but it seldom seems to work. The authority landed with the responsibility for preventing or, at least, containing such trouble has an unenviable task since, whatever he does or does not do, he will be criticized. He just has to resign himself to being massively unpopular in one quarter or another, and accept that universal love and approval are not among the perks of political power. The aggrieved expression on the face of a politician who feels himself to have been misunderstood or under-appreciated is of particular interest to the student of human behaviour.

*

TPA The idea of losing face is only a fantasy, and an authority that cannot face anxiety because of its *over*anxiety about having to save its face is unconsciously perceived as the extreme of tyranny.

CHAPTER FOUR

The Losing of the Good Authority

Describes the subtle yet potentially devastating ways in which the good authority can be lost by those whose interests most require it

TPA Probably the most common first crime a child feels he has committed in his life is losing something or someone. *Crime* because the pain of loss can be quickly and magically expunged by the pain of the punishment the loss secondarily engenders. It must be remembered in this context that a baby, we assume, has a strong sense of causality; it probably sees the world as an extension of itself, and therefore anything that happens in the world to which it relates must seem to have occurred because of the baby itself. If the event is 'bad', like warm mother removing herself, then the cold the baby experiences *is* the result of his having somehow made that bit of himself (which we adults call mother) disappear and be lost from his primitive self. Very quickly, the feeling of cold (the prototype of punishment) takes over from the feeling of loss of part of one's self.

But who in their right senses would nurture the sad wound of a lost good when that lost good can be transformed into a bad, and that bad in turn extended into a forthright, 'Good riddance'? What perverse expertise can be acquired as a result of the repeated deprivation of good? Why, a capacity for the most vehement contempt for and derision of what is now felt to be bad. Children who have repeatedly been deprived of good things – like a real mother, father or home – become less and less able to understand the reality – the meaning of a good mother or a good home; these become objects which they do not and cannot possess, and in the child's mind they therefore become bad objects – which of course he can convince himself he does not want.

In a residential institution where it was usual for children to be punished by the loss of their weekend home leave, I noticed that children who had seemed very enthusiastic about their forthcoming weekends would – should that 'privilege' be taken away as a punishment – almost immediately convincingly appear not to care at all. Such a child's 'Who cares?' seemed to be a précis of: 'I'm delighted not to have to endure that ghastly, taken-away-from-me, not-there-anymore weekend; after all, who would want such a thing?' A weekend at home is a comparatively concrete thing, and if that can be jettisoned so casually and with such apparent relief, what is likely to be the fate of the much more abstruse concept of good authority? If its loss is considered at all, it will be as an airy-fairy-will-o'-the-wisp, just a vague idea that perhaps something or other isn't quite the way it should be. This is all very well, but we need to do better, to try to improve on these vague ideas that 'something isn't quite the way it should be'.

It is necessary in this case to make an attempt to be precise, to try to find shared understandings, objective evidence of the loss of good authority. The losing of good authority may well be marked by perceptible changes or even deteriorating patterns of behaviour of groups and of individuals – say in a classroom, work force or military unit. The changes may unfortunately only produce an interest and response in the relevant authority of what seems to me a *dead* or uncreative kind: people will declare that these events are to be expected with this sort of client group every so often, or how lucky they have been to have been spared for so long or perhaps there is an increase in the incidence of this kind of offence or offender which should be verified statistically and more special provision made for these difficulties or difficult individuals. To take an ordinary, everyday example: if a little girl suddenly becomes secretive or fat there is very little to be gained by saying, 'Her Great-Aunt Matilda was shy or fat too,' or, 'Her Great-Aunt Matilda wasn't shy or fat, though.' It sounds pertinent, but it doesn't really tell us anything. The good authority, now lost, which imperceptibly had been originally responsible for determining and monitoring the groups' or individuals' patterns of life and behaviour needs to be understood retrospectively if the latter's future is to make any sense.

The losing of authority can be compared to an illusionist's nightmare. He could be performing the most ingenious sleight-of-hand in front of an audience that is unable to see either the sleight-of-hand *or* the cards, or even the hands of the illusionist. Of course, it may be that no good authority existed in the first place, as I believe is the case in certain psychotic or out-of-control predicaments, whether of individuals or mobs. The question as to whether such an authority ever existed may never be raised, since it may not be possible to determine what was the first place in the first place. Certainly, an unfortunately timed absence of authority, with inadequate continuity figures as stopgaps, can bring subsequent havoc. As an instance, a single mother, who had had three children by three different fathers, demonstrated constantly the losing of a particular kind of good authority. She was rigorously, almost mathematically, fair in the treatment of all her children; if the world had been equally fair in its treatment, those children might have been able to cope more adequately. The particular good authority that she was constantly losing was the knowledge that the future would bring unfairness to her young; her own guilt and her three sons' unfaced and unresolved Oedipal complexes were responsible for her continuing to do her best, her peculiar, particularly damaging best. It was only at long, long last, and with benefit, that a Borstal officer confronted one of her sons – with his young, mountainous and dangerous resentment – whilst the boy was facing *non*-punitive unfairness. (Second helpings at lunch ran out before his turn.) 'You'll just have to lump it, that's the way it is sometimes.'

I have mentioned the usefulness of a continuity figure, even a non-executive one like an uncle or a matron who, if influential, can tide over a family or institution during a period when it is experiencing the loss of executive personnel. Without such a bridge, the losing gathers momentum until it reaches the point when the new executive will be in need of chain-mail and defensive weapons on arrival. In this connection I would mention again the 1969 Children and Young Persons Act (United Kingdom) – important legislation that had an impressive pedigree, but in my view was severely damaged by the loss of several important continuity bridges about the time of its coming into operation. A group under the chairmanship of Lord Longford (appointed by Prime Minister Harold Wilson on behalf of the Labour Party) and composed of people with special knowledge and experience in the field of penal and social policy, had made a study of the problems involved. Their report, 'Crime, a Challenge to Us All',[1] was published in 1964 and served to stimulate informed discussion. Then in August 1965 a paper entitled *The Child, the Family and the Young Offender*[2] was presented to Parliament for internal and external discussion prior to legislation. The underlying philosophy was set out in April 1968 in the White Paper called *Children in Trouble*.[3]

Derek Holtby-Morrell, an under-secretary at the Home Office, was probably one of the most important influences in bringing about a situation that altered the site of extra-parental statutory authority for children in the United Kingdom, but he died less than two months after the royal assent had been given to the act in October 1969. He had been helped in the preparation by Joan Cooper, principal social worker in the Department of Health and Social Security. The act is difficult to keep in mind as a working model in any case, but Holtby-Morrell's absence at the time that the new statute was being interpreted was, I think, the most important intrusive, interrupting and therefore destructive of several influences. The other lost bridges of continuity included: the Seebohm Report,[4] which brought about the reorganization of the social services in 1969: the Maud Report,[5] which concerned the reorganization of local government; certain relevant 'Responsibilities for Children' being moved from the Home Office to the Department of Health and Social Security, as well as to the local authority departments of social services; and the loss of the socialist government (whose ideas as to the pace, if not the nature of the changes, differed from those of the incoming Tories of 1970).

To this day more sway, even to an executive degree, is often allowed to juveniles in care and to charismatic superintendents and/or medical superintendents than is owned, and therefore effectively carried, by local authority representatives of legal authority in the case of these children in care, that is the social worker. I have known instances where children of thirteen have been given the last word as to whether they will accept educational or residential placements – sometimes even being invited to enter into contracts. This is bizarre in the context of the 1969 act, fundamentally brilliant legislation, but legislation that does need (fortunately for some and unfortunately for others) to be *actually understood* before it is used. In this respect it is unlike magic, or the charismatic power of unknown experts, or the unthinking observance of the sanctity of a child's so-called 'needs', which require only simple blind belief. It actually requires the using of brains, knowledge, experience and professionalism.

The way the 1969 act considers authority is like a long, complicated but logical calculation, whereas the situation before 1969 was like a simple-seeming, single-figure answer. The Act has given rise to the need for trained professionals in a field where previously gifted and instinctive individuals had been in positions of tremendous influence. Suddenly the latter had remaining to them only the authority to reject the children they had been caring for, and even that authority was liable to be taken away from them. A great deal of the background to the act and its implications are perhaps somewhat difficult to understand or even distasteful to those whose positions were usurped.

Difficulty and distaste suggest a particular aspect of the losing of authority that I have dubbed the taboo topic. The taboo is liable to make clarification and deep understanding of the meaning of change (at least to the degree necessary to prevent a prolonged losing of authority and therefore chaos) almost impossible. There is also the coincidental danger of a colossal degree of empirical over-anxious reaction. The most common taboo topic confronting people working with families with a delinquent member occurs when a divorced mother, who has custody of the children, marries a new, 'good dad'. The taboo surrounds the fact that it was the *marital* relationship, which actually had in it lots of goods as well as bads on both – not just one – side, that had become untenable, and that the situation is in danger of repeating itself in the new marriage. The way the unspoken, repeated difficulty presents itself is often in the state of the stepfather/children relationships. In many such cases, brothers and sisters take sides, falsely and inter-personally, dividing their loyalties to the separated parents, rather than each achieving a state of mind that is a more realistic intra-personal 'torn' loyalty. The latter may be more disturbing in the sense of feeling torn apart, but is nevertheless the more desirable situation of the two.

A fascinating taboo topic is apparent in the genesis of paranoiac dictators, whether of the trans-global Adolf Hitler or the 'little Hitler' departmental variety. Since a paranoiac is unable to tolerate feeling bad (for example, anxious), this state – which arises if he is faced with another who is good – produces in him in consequence a feeling of 'relative badness'. Professional helpers may recognize a paranoiac person when their best work is seen as bad by the client or senior, and when mistakes or omissions are treated with surprising, patronizing affability. How then does a paranoiac manage to succeed in a world made up of other people, if the others becoming good makes the paranoiac feel bad? The secret is that *the others have to become part of the paranoiac*. Gradually the others sell their souls, unconsciously, until they are in the paranoiac's pocket. 'We' has now become 'I', 'I' has now become 'we'.

Psychoanalytic theory sometimes relates paranoia to homosexuality.[6] This association is also highlighted by everyday crudenesses that contain obsequious overtones (arse-licking, sucking-up, etc.). The (perhaps theoretical!) anal orgasm, said to be yearned for unconsciously by the paranoiac,[7] is commonly brought about symbolically in a devastating form, for instance, in the total collapse of self-esteem and of the esteem of others. In 1943 the psychoanalyst Walter C. Langer predicted, from material gathered for and by the American Office for Strategic Services, that in the event of military reversal, Hitler would be most likely to seek suicide by taking Germany down with him. 'Not one single German wheat-sheaf is to feed the enemy; not one German hand is to offer him help. He is to find nothing but death, annihilation and hatred . . .'[8] This *Götterdämmerung* – or twilight of the gods – that Hitler here describes represents the anal orgasm; and, as we know, Hitler committed suicide whilst Russian guns pounded Germany's 'rear end' as they approached the infamous bunker with its cyanide and cans of petrol.

*

ATE Some members of the psychoanalytic establishment have said it cannot be done – the analysing of historical characters; after all, if it can be done at a distance it makes the shrink's couch seem a little superfluous. For the more venturesome and the less constrained however it makes, at least, a jolly parlour game. For some it can constitute a life's work. There is, for instance, one man who has published a theory illustrating that Joan of Arc was a man, and another who claims to have convincing psychological evidence that Jesus was a woman. As these historical figures are not available for questioning or examination, speculation can run rife. Was Napoleon poisoned by the proximity of arsenical wallpaper? Who killed Mozart, or didn't anybody? Was George III clinically insane? Did Lizzie Borden or didn't she? What happened to the crew of the *Mary Celeste*? And indeed was it Richard III or Henry Tudor (who alone stood to gain by it) who wrought the deaths of the little princes? With no forensic evidence available we have to rely on contemporary accounts to make present-day assessments. Despite the misgivings, it is perhaps simpler to make psychological interpretations than follow the Sherlock Holmes type of detective investigation. It would be difficult now to ascertain from documentary evidence whether George III had porphyria or not, but people do reveal themselves in their writings, and other people have sometimes written, verbatim, what they have said, and we all feel qualified to some degree to judge our fellows by their utterances, do we not?

TPA observes that these psychological judgements of eminent public figures *can* perhaps only be safely done at some historical or geographical distance. Both the libel laws and a certain sense of national self-esteem preclude us from publishing the opinion that some of our leaders are raving. We must leave this insight for our grand-children to establish; and while the rest of the world had few reservations, it would have been an unwary Ugandan who voiced doubts about the mental stability of Idi Amin.

I suppose that in the words 'rear end' is the implication that Germany was in retreat – a doleful, undignified position in any terms, giving rise in the defeated to feelings of rage, despair, black murderousness which, thwarted, leaves the runner with an even blacker suicidal impulse. No possibility of sweet revenge, of return or renewal – just dark death, with a great bang; the destruction of light, hope, fellowship, growth. The end of possibility and the future, since those who run away run always into ultimate disaster, and rather than concede this they would prefer to shatter all around them and let the dust settle on the ruins.

*

TPA Until the cataclysm, however, the taboo and therefore the non-understanding of what is happening continues to exist; good authority continues to be eroded, and megalo-maniacal authoritarianism engulfs nearly everything and everyone. The would-be clarifier in such a vortex is a naive, doomed creature, since even his close friends are possibly at one with, or part of, the paranoiac epicentre and would either be too sucked in or too frightened to listen and to risk facing true comprehension as to what had happened to their integrity of self. Only if a professional worker with a case like this is aware that the paranoiac himself unconsciously realizes his own precari-ousness, can he manage to move constructively and abandon the particularly upsetting failures and anxieties that constantly dog work with paranoiacs. On a simpler plane, the worker's authoritative status may be eroded if he is not conscious of his own anxiety and anger. Often, simple recognition and understanding on the worker's part is all that is necessary to help the paranoiac to be more sane.

The unconscious taboo topic can sometimes relate to a

feared future event, such as the third and probably final coronary of a father. It is not the future coronary that provides the taboo in its entirety; there has to be another sinister element, and this element is best illustrated by examples. A wife wanted to divorce her husband, but did not relish the prospect of losing the large family house, which she was using profitably as a children's day nursery. At every therapeutic session arranged for the family, she and her delinquent son wore, alternately, a large silver ring depicting a skull and crossbones. In each case it was worn on the wedding-ring finger. I had to point this out to them, and before realizing its significance for themselves they claimed that they'd just put it on – 'without really thinking about it'. The piratical taboo was the wife's denied wish for her husband, who had angina, to die so that she could gain entire possession of the property.

A widow said that she felt she had killed her husband because he had suddenly discovered her naked when she was in a late state of pregnancy. The husband had fainted, and had died ten months later of cancer, 'never having recovered his health', as she put it – as though she'd somehow caused the cancer, which he no doubt had already had, and which probably contributed to the fainting attack. This unconscious taboo showed itself by her taking only impotent men as her 'lovers'; her guilt was too great for her to risk killing another 'good man'. This family first came to me because the son had mugged an old lady. It is, I think, probable that he was acting out his mother's projected guilt and need of punishment for her 'murder' of her 'old man'.

Hypocritical rejection is another authority-damaging phenomenon. Some 'improvement' or 'special help' schemes designed to assist minority groups may, as I said previously, be experienced by the latter as *worse than rejection*, since the overt, seemingly benevolent, helping element may tend to render ridiculous the very idea of direct resentment on the recipients' part, and so foster

the hidden, festering, rankling variety of resentful indignation. These hypocrisies that can undermine authority are
closely related to the confusion between firmness and
punitiveness which is common in immature or inexperi-
enced authorities. These authorities may well be confused
about the merits and demerits of autocratic and democratic authority. Not realizing that one is quick and
the other slow, in their confusion they may tend instead
towards a contemporary – say 'liberal' – mode of thought.
Group decisions are, as I have half implied, sometimes
very popular, but 'group' can be another word for 'mob',
which can easily make disastrously wrong decisions. An
individual who gains initial popularity by transferring his
decision-making responsibility to a group can find himself
being trampled to death (either figuratively or actually)
by a mob at a later date.

These inadequacies can act as the straws that break the
back of a weakened authority. A warden in a hostel for
ex-prisoners had never been allowed either to waive
arrears of rent or to evict residents who had failed to pay.
The purse-strings were held by the influential and
ingratiating secretary to the board of managers. The
residents at the hostel knew where the real power lay,
and when the warden attempted to introduce democratic
measures as a palliative to discontent amongst the residents, he (or what authority remained) was metaphorically eaten alive. His instructions were ignored, he
was actually spat upon and the residents did precisely as
they pleased.

It has been known for wives who have no sons, but
who have their own mother and/or several daughters at
home, to completely erode, by sheer weight of personality
and by weight of numbers, an already doubtful paternal
authority in a household.

I have already mentioned that a prerequisite prior to
taking one's own authority, according to biblical tradition,
is the blessing given by the father, and if that blessing is
not given the sceptre, the emblem of authority, is

unconsciously regarded as having been *stolen* by the son. For a boy to reach the age of sixteen, seventeen or eighteen whilst his father is dying is a dreadful combination of events. I have gained the impression that in such a case, the guilt of patricide is thrown in with theft – for bad measure. (In the United Kingdom, a father and mother's legal authority begins to 'die' when the son or daughter is sixteen; 'death' is complete at eighteen.) These correlations occur when the young person's unconscious seems to have become confused between identifications with the parent and the parent's actual physical death on the one hand *and* with the passing of external-person authority-structures (others over self) to internal-person authority-structures (self over self) on the other hand, that is, on the achievement of the young person's majority.

Many family taboo topics are concerned with unconsciously anticipated deaths. A researcher can find eerie age-correlations between fathers today, sons of today, grandfathers then and fathers then. In one case a fifteen-year-old delinquent's forty-eight-year-old father had a stomach ulcer. The grandfather had died of what the father referred to as 'ulcers' aged forty-nine, when the father was sixteen. In fact, times without number I've noticed that children will come into care at the same age as the parent had been when their own mother or father died or left.

*

ATE When we were writing an earlier book, *Secrets of Strangers*, I grew uneasy about these correlations of death. In the family we were dealing with, there was almost a 'tradition', a mute, resigned acceptance, that the men of the family died before they were fifty; as though their psyches possessed a clock, timed to alarum, and when it went off they would go without warning, either by sudden illness, accident or just the loss of the necessity to go on living. It was as though past familial spasms had left invisible but imperative imprints, which as long as they were left unrecognized, would mean the return of more horrifying apparitions. At various salient psychological moments other family members, if not going to the length of dying, would get themselves into trouble. There seemed to be a nasty, Greek inevitability about the whole business; a sense of hopelessness and powerlessness. I was relieved when (perhaps due to being highlighted in therapy?) several ominous dates and anniversaries passed without incident.

*

TPA If the taboo aspects make the losing of authority a secret, hardly perceptible process, the *pace* of the losing provides commendable competition in the 'imperceptibility stakes'. Pace of change (slow or quick) coupled with taboo is the very essence of a secret conspiracy that can undermine the good authority. A father who has been in a sanatorium for most months of the year, leaving his dependants, perforce, to run things in their own way and do as they like, may be joined, physically, by the family *en masse* at his funeral; but his good authority, because of his long absences, will have slowly dripped, dripped away – the last drip being as unseen as the middle drip. Will the family be aware of what needs replacing?

If one cares to look through the case notes of children from broken homes, the word 'home' is often mentioned, actually glibly, but as though it were rock-solid: he can go 'home' for the weekend, 'home' for Christmas, 'home' for good, 'home' if he's good, 'home' if he's not good, etc. If one is attempting to identify with the child, however, through the months and years, noticing the names of several successive professionals flitting past as one skims through the case history one deduces all the different 'homes' that he has had in his short life – home (with mother implied), home (with father implied), home nice, home awful, but *home anyway*. You – the skimmer – are an observer of the changing story – an observer of

time passing; thus you have an advantage over the
current case worker, who is stuck in the present; you are
a privileged and truly sympathetic observer who is more
in tune with the unconscious of the child who has been
mentally battered with this flighty concept of 'home' as
he tries or gives up trying to know with which parent
or whichever place he may settle, now or next time.

In this kind of case-history search it is interesting to
note the switch of favour with each new wave of present
professional workers – the favour switching backwards
and forwards from one to the other of the separated
parents, with the apparent simultaneous falling-off-the-
edge-of-the-earth of the other ex-spouse. Contrast this
with a 'normal' family, where the indirect functions of
the parents' authority will include their children's
friends, their school and possibly also their interests,
simply because children live in their parents' house,
which is likely to relate either geographically or econom-
ically to the school and the children's friends. A shifting
home means shifting education and friends, as well as the
losing of the unconscious connections these have with
authority of the invisible or Good type. The pace of the
changes of home may be imperceptible on the conscious
level, and may be clouded furthermore by empiricism
and common sense, for example if the father has moved
to a better job.

The sudden death of an authority figure can contribute
pace of change at the opposite extreme from the man
who had been in the sanatorium for so long. Sedation
and home-grown mechanisms of denial, like 'going away
for a break' after a death, make mourning even more
difficult, so that the bereaved lose not only the loved one,
but also the concept of the authority that has gone. The
family members arrive at a double standard, with an
authority figure physically dead but, unthinkably, with
his authority presumed by the family to be intact. At
times cultural pressures can be so overwhelming that
good authority can be lost without trace. An instance is

given in the case of a mother whose son was on the point of being admitted to an institution. The mother thought he'd go straight in because '*they* had said so'. True, a *recommendation* had been made, but luckily she was still the child's legal authority, although she seemed to have been stunned into complete psychic dependency on entering a professional system. She was amazed, angry, then thrilled when she had been helped to understand that the *decision* regarding admission was hers. She decided against the residential placement for her son, but elected to use the offer of a safety-net placement in times of crisis. The background security afforded by this arrangement supported rather than destroyed her parental authority. It allowed her anxieties regarding possible future crises to assume a lower, reasonable status, and case-work proper was now able to make more headway.

*

ATE Many professionals in many different spheres seem to have an inadequate, if not a disordered view of the extent and precise nature of their authority. The masculine urge to dominate, if given rein in one legitimate sphere, tends to spill over into other areas, and pomposity is the result. It is self-defeating, since one loses respect for one's bank manager when he is seen throwing his weight about in a restaurant. Many doctors seem to imagine that they are in charge, that they own not only your body but your ailments; the patient being merely a canvas on which they can demonstrate their expertise. Male gynaecologists can be particularly annoying in this respect. Too often patients blinded by science and all the appurtenances of power will submit unquestioningly to whatever form of treatment is proposed. Many practitioners of the law, many ministers of the crown frequently exhibit an air of ineffable self-satisfaction arising from the fact that they are accustomed to being obeyed, and this damages their image in the eyes of the man in the street who sees, not a competent and reliable barrister or MP, but a self-important clown. Fathers of families can make a similar mistake and alienate their children (not to mention their wives). There are times when leadership should consist in being part of the group and pulling your weight (rather than just chucking it around). Figureheads are wooden and of little practical use. In a storm they could be the first thing to be slung overboard.

Because there is something universally attractive and appealing in the sight of a leader leading calmly and well, when an inadequate person, an impostor, is seen to be attempting to do it he brings odium upon himself. Into the tumbrel with him.

*

TPA   It seems sad to think that education and 'progress' might be destructive factors. However, whether or not the feminist movement, together with Dr Spock's very popular first book[9] and certain fashionable moralities are contributing directly to an undermining of authority, I am fairly sure that they tend sometimes to make it more difficult to support the sites of authority. Medical influence in many instances may also be a very powerful factor in the direct undermining of good authority, since doctors have been trained to treat individuals' difficulties and illnesses, and by so doing are liable to generate a cycle of medical omnipotence and/or over-dependency on the part of their patients. For instance, the parents of a child who had been diagnosed as autistic were very much inclined to admit their child for treatment (whatever they thought that meant) at the hands of experts (whoever they imagined these were). It was with tremendous difficulty that this relinquishing and over-dependent situation was avoided, and the child was admitted primarily in order to give the remainder of the family a rest. The offer was made simply and un-omnipotently, subject to the condition that it was acceptable to the head of the household.

Group pressure can be very unnerving for some new

authority figures. I mentioned earlier that group decisions are in vogue at present, and frequently a new
stepfather, fearful of being branded as a tyrant, has
started off in his new role by suffering mental torture,
feeling that he has to act ultra-democratically in spite of
seeing his new family going, apparently unresentfully,
down the drain. An observing professional is sometimes
in a good position to anticipate the disasters that will be
incurred through ingratiating acquiescence to group
decisions. The client population – the family – on the
other hand, is in danger of achieving a retrospective view
only. That is, they may be consciously happy with the
new fairness and democracy – being treated like adults in
the short term – but later they might suffer the results of
the loss of a quick-thinking, sure-footed autocrat.

'Magic' institutions such as hospitals, and professionals
such as lawyers and doctors, tend to detract from
ordinary resources, including ordinary authority. This
occurred at first in the case of a deaf boy who had been
in a penal establishment, and on whom a great deal of
time and concern had been lavished with a view to his
being accommodated in a special training institution
with a staff of specialists. Both the boy's eldest sister and
his probation officer were reluctant to make their presence felt in the face of such white-man's magic. Only
late in the day did they feel able to explain that they had
already made considerable provision for the boy's release
from the penal establishment, and that this would have
been wasted and would have gone unnoticed if the grand
scheme had proceeded. The boy went to live with his
sister, whose home was in the same district as the
headquarters of his probation officer, and within four
months similar training plans had been made by himself
for himself nearer home.

The ownership of property is a useful nuisance that
makes losing one's authority more difficult. Losing
abstract property is only too easy. A professional worker
needs to know who his primary client is. The wish to

work in a family context (which mode of work is at present in vogue) can lead to a social worker becoming completely unstuck should he at any time forget that the child in care is his prime concern, his department's legal 'property'. It may be, of course, that very little is being seen of the child, and that all the work is being done via the mother.

An example might show the dangers of forgetting this principle of ownership. A social worker, who had felt it profitable to work closely mainly with the unmarried mother of a child who was under the supervision of his local authority, was suddenly told by the mother, in strict confidence, of her intention to desert the home. (I call this not uncommon situation the 'confidentiality trap'.) The social worker has to back-pedal and make it clear that the child would, in that case, have to go into care. The mother, who was herself a deprived person, suddenly felt deserted and angry with the social worker, who had failed clearly to explain to her exactly what authority he had, namely, to use his powers of observation and understanding to see that the child (his legal priority) was safe, and, if he thought the child was not, to take the case back to court.

The mother should have been left in no doubt from the start that the social worker was a fully licensed spy, spying for the benefit of her child, and not, except in a bonus sense, a support for her. Paradoxically, I think that the mother would have been more open earlier on had she known that her child was safe in the social worker's professional concern, and that his job was first and foremost to protect the child. Supervision – the authority simply to observe and if necessary to report to a court – is one of those frequently recurring examples of good authority that tends to be overshadowed by the wish to do more. The huge burden is, in part, to be invisible, or nearly so, until a crisis. Even then, part of the burden may be that the work is hardly noticed, even by the professional himself, unless he is able to consider and appreciate that the hard, unspectacular work he has been doing was the work he should have been doing. This kind of case, on the other hand, if not handled properly, can find itself being dissected by the outraged press, having culminated in neglect, baby battering and death.

The Oedipal complex is seen to be an archetypal, unconscious arena where rivalries about authority and sexual property occur. It is not just the unconscious fear of being a sexual rival that can be cited as smashing away at authority, even one's own authority. The bed-wetter demonstrates even to himself that he has no control over his wayward bladder – what chance has he therefore against his father, whose genital apparatus must be kept in the boy's mind as the only genital apparatus worthy of being 'Mum's property'? Oedipal rivalry is no joke, but when there is a chance of winning – say if there is an unacknowledged marital problem – then the child must be careful indeed not to covet the father's place for fear of winning it. Imagine if the parents' secret goal were indeed a divorce (which in my jaundiced experience it often is), how many such bed-wetting sons unconsciously eventually do 'marry their mother', only to find when their own first child comes along that what they have got, in fact, is a *wife* (who is their *child's* mother)? After a while the man may want to leave, and his authority often suffers in these cases. Redundancy at work, for instance, or unemployment because of ill-health may be the trigger that can show up what had existed previously, but had been hidden. Authority in the father and his companionship for the wife can easily be seen now to have been replaced by the rest of the family's presence and needs. This way of losing authority can be acted-out and hopefully diagnosed long before the father's illness, or the possible liquidation of his firm, becomes of serious concern.

A parallel dangerous situation on the professional front often arises and shows itself as follows. When social workers, both field and residential, are seriously thinking of leaving their positions, even though no one knows, symptoms are likely to appear in the children who make up the social worker's case load. This supports (certainly to my mind) an idea that the children and professionals have at least an unconscious awareness that authority is surreptitiously slipping away. Residential workers who have to wear two hats, that is, to be both colleagues and parent-figures, may lose their authority demonstrably and dramatically (the 'false' or superficial losing of authority) if their institution should lose its facility for keeping in touch say it should fail to acknowledge the likelihood or not of the field social worker leaving a case. Senior staff and/or monitoring staff, for example, are among those who must be constantly on guard in this respect. The false losing of authority may be exhibited by out-of-control behaviour on the part of the children or of the adults themselves, and can be confused with the real thing unless a deeper view is taken.

Two young West Indian half-brothers were found by their mother and her co-habitee to be very difficult to look after. I realized first that the boys both had a different father, and secondly that the mother was losing weight quite rapidly. One father (the co-habitee) was indeed losing his authority over *his own son*, as was the mother. He could not honestly say, however, that the situation was the same in regard to the other boy, who was the son of another man. The other man, who had long since deserted the mother, was of course not complaining about losing *his* authority – at least not within sensitive earshot. The question that emerged as relevant to the *real* loss of authority, was, who was going to look after the son of the absent man, after the mother had died of what proved to be cancer?

Another example of this false or apparent losing of authority disguising a real loss of authority was given in Chapter Two, in the case of the young prisoner who complained of not being able to sleep. When he was interviewed it came to light that he had committed many crimes: stealing cars, wilful damage, grievous bodily harm and so on. In each case he had been given what would be considered light sentences, and almost laughingly said of one of his previous sentences: 'I didn't lose any sleep over it.' Now, however, he certainly was. Right up to that moment his criminal actions had not been accepted by him. He was constantly losing his own authority over his body, his thoughts and his emotions, and his present sleeplessness was, in part, caused by his anxiety about having to understand that previous mad behaviour, not, as he had thought, his loss of control or authority in the sense of not managing to get himself to sleep.

CHAPTER FIVE

The Chance of Re-Finding the Good Authority

The authority figure who lacks 'good authority' – paradoxical role of the delinquent, who unconsciously mobilizes those resources needed if the inadequate authority figure is to be redeemed

TPA Broken homes and inadequate mothering have been causally linked to delinquency and psychopathy.[1] There may be some justification for this, but the deprivations have always seemed to me to be too near the consciousness of the delinquent or psychopath to be determinants of repeated misbehaviour that often seems to be beyond the perpetrator's control or understanding. My theoretical framework suggests that the parent who had lost his own external good authority (parent(s) of the parent) in his own childhood will be the parent who is likely to lose *his* good authority over *his* child. The delinquent's parent, in my clinical experience, has certainly always been found to have lost the authority of his own parent. The sins of the fathers (the lacks or the withouts) have been visited on the children unto, at least, the third generation.*

* 'For I the Lord thy God am a jealous God, visiting the iniquity of the fathers upon the children unto the third and fourth generation of them that hate me.' Exodus 20:5, Deuteronomy 5:9. (It is a nice coincidence that our English word 'sin' seems to be linked to the biblical wilderness. 'Sin was a wilderness south of the Holy Land in Arabia; Petraea, lying between Elim and Sinaia'. William Nicholson, *The Bible Explainer*.)

It seems that there may be what is called a repetition compulsion[2] set off at the time when the two-person authority structure comes to be reconstituted in the next generation. For example:

Child B of parent A loses his good authority in A.
When Child B becomes a parent, and has a child C, then parent B will lose his good authority over child C.

Parent B was, unconsciously, entitled to say and to work through as a child:

'I have lost or have never had my good authority in my father or parents,' and years later, in regard to his delinquent child C, he is, once again, unconsciously entitled to say, 'I have lost my good authority over my own child, and my child has lost his good authority normally residing in me, his parent.'

It is also worth looking at Shakespeare's King John.

QUEEN ELINOR	Thou monstrous slanderer of heaven and earth!
CONSTANCE	Thou monstrous injurer of heaven and earth!
	Call not me slanderer! Thou and thine usurp
	The dominations, royalties, and rights
	Of this oppressed boy. This is thy eldest son's son,
	Unfortunate in nothing but in thee.
	Thy sins are visited in this poor child;
	The canon of the law is laid on him,
	Being but the second generation
	Removed from thy sin-conceiving womb.
KING JOHN	Bedlam, have done.
CONSTANCE	I have but this to say:
	That he is not only plagued for her sin,
	But God hath made her sin and her the plague
	On this removed issue, plagued for her
	And with her plague; her sin his injury,
	Her injury the beadle to her sin,
	All punished in the person of this child,
	And all for her. A plague upon her!

(*II.i.173–90*)

In a study[3] of the parents of sixty children who were in the care of local authorities because those parents had lost their legal authority over their offspring, I found that in all cases history was repeating itself, and that when they were minors themselves, these same parents had significantly lost their own normal external legal authority in one way or another, usually through death, divorce or desertion by their parents. My research was undertaken around the issue of legal authority, since that single, important type of good authority would be relatively easy to substantiate. It validated the growing confidence I had in my clinical impression of a repeated compulsion in the delinquent's parent, unconsciously hoping if possible to recapture in the present a sense of mourning for the specific losses of good authority that had occurred in his own childhood.

One can often feel this happening in therapeutic situations. Many uncanny episodes come to light concerning names, events and people's ages from the previous parent/child relationship, almost as reincarnations in the present-day parallel. For example, in the case I mentioned earlier, where a father suffering from ulcers was on the point of going into hospital the father was forty-eight, his son fifteen. Thirty-three years previously, the grandfather had died at the age of forty-nine of what were said to be ulcers. The father was then a boy of sixteen.

In another case, a boy who was taken into care at the age of eight, on the death of his father, had a maternal grandfather who had died when the boy's mother was a child of eight. It made me wonder at the time – did the mother unconsciously become the grandmother and marry the doomed 'father'? Is the boy unconsciously his own mother?

My earliest suspicion of the truth of the 'loss of authority' phenomenon extending through three generations was confirmed for me in a remarkable way. During a family therapy session, I asked a delinquent boy's

father if his own father had died when he himself was
young. He said no. I recovered from this setback and
asked instead, 'Did your father lose his authority over
you in any way?' The boy's father responded astonish-
ingly, by producing, like a rabbit from a hat, a 1930s
newspaper cutting which had extraordinary relevance.[4]
The social worker earlier in the session had complained
that his youthful client was doing quite well except for
staying out late, hanging around street corners with
undesirable *mates* and stealing-by-finding – namely, one
cigarette-*lighter*. The correlation with the father (Arthur)
was that in the early 1930s Arthur had been 'discovered'
at the age of fifteen by Albert *Parker*, a producer for Fox
Films at Walton-on-Thames, and had starred in the film
After Dark. Arthur had then moved from his parents'
home in a poor district of Vauxhall to become the ward
of an American Army Intelligence captain and his wife,
living amongst 'society people' in Berkeley Square. He
was never to see his boyhood comrades again, since all
except one were killed at the evacuation of Dunkirk in
1940. Arthur described wistfully how he and his Vauxhall
mates used to play tricks on the lamp-*lighter* by blowing
out the gas streetlamp as soon as the man had rounded
the corner, and calling him back repeatedly to relight the
lamp. Two days after the session, I learned that the boy's
best friend in 1973–5 was called *Parker*.

*

ATE These coincidences are not only the sort of thing I find it
easy to believe – since I have that sort of mind – but the
sort of thing I like, since patterns, even sad ones, are
preferable to disorder. As I was disposed to be uncritical
of this theory (that the parent of the child will inevitably
be found to have lost his own external authority), I was
gratified to learn that it had been borne out by research.
There has seemed to be a tendency in the world of
psychoanalysis for people to say, 'it is so because I say it
is so'; and this can irritate the layman. Freud's claim that

psychoanalysis partakes of the nature of 'science' has been pooh-poohed by adherents of other disciplines, so a few statistics do not, in this case, come amiss. One interesting twist in the pattern apparently came to light by chance during the research. Children from a middle- or upper-class background who misbehaved had a year and a half longer before they were apprehended than children who were lower in the class scale – otherwise they were no more protected.

*

TPA The important concept to be grasped is not the make-up of the delinquent *per se*, but the loss of authority and the type of authority. In this particular instance, the special loss of authority was related to the traumatic search for old comrades who had been lost when Arthur had left *his* father's home for that of the 'society people' in Berkeley Square, that is, the result of the allowing 'change of domicile in a minor'. This loss of good authority by Arthur as a boy was sudden, and happened under the aura (a positive version of taboo) of good fortune. It was never brought painfully and consciously to the mourning workbench of Arthur's mind, but was left instead to slumber until its reincarnation in his son. Arthur was becoming ill, losing weight and maintaining that he was not long for this world, that his delinquent son would be the death of him; he could do nothing with him; he had given up. 'If I say "do this", he does *that*; "do that", he does *this*; "don't", he *does*; "do", he *doesn't*; "up", he'd go *down*; "down", he'd go *up*; "right", he'd go *left*; "left", he'd go *right*. There's nothing I can do.'

Lily Pincus in her book, *Death and the Family, The Importance of Mourning*,[5] hints at how she herself only managed to appreciate the hidden and precise meanings of the loss of her husband when she later broke her ankle, and therefore lost its use. Likewise, I think that an important function of outright misbehaviour is to enable the authority figure to be conscious of his authority. It is impossible to miss noticing a child who is being frankly disobedient: he is stating, 'You, Parent, have lost your authority over me'; but it is very easy, on the other hand, to overlook the fact that a subtle and invisible loss of good authority is occurring or has actually occurred. The frank misbehaviour (producing a conscious sense of loss of authority in the parent) should be perceived as a *cry for help* by the child on behalf of his parent. Once this overt loss of authority, manifesting itself in the occurrence of delinquent acts, has been perceived, there is then the possibility of getting into contact with and understanding the loss of the particular valuable good authority.*

---

* I think it might be useful to list here just a few of any number of what I call lost good-authority themes – the hard currency, or perhaps the bad debts of delinquency – that are psychically transmitted, in the fashion I have already referred to, from one generation to the next. Some general and specific examples might include:

The lost ability to know when to stick at it and when to cut your losses.

The lost ability to choose between two wrongs, rather than to waste precious time.

The loss of the valuing of thoughts, memory, contracts, words.

Not knowing the value of just keeping in contact.

Not to be able to tell a whole from a part or a part from a whole.

Not to realize that someone who is not crying any more may have stopped being depressed, but is now in despair.

Not to know that resignation is to anger as despair is to depression.

Not to know that just because something obviously needs to be done, there is no guarantee that it will be done (since everyone might imagine that someone else is bound to do it).

Not to be able to realize that little things can grow.

Not to know that a system cannot be used unless one possesses the original, apparently insignificant, key to that system.

Not to know that a group decision is fallible, even if it is comfortable and fashionable.

Not to know that democracy is slower than autocracy, and autocracy faster than democracy.

Not to know that the more successful a cheat or liar becomes, the more often he will cheat or lie and therefore the more liable, by the law of averages, he is to be caught or found out eventually.

In certain family situations, some kind of event or change in the pattern of events is present on the time-horizon, and this possibly threatening event will require a good authority of a particular kind if catastrophe is not to supervene. Imagine a community living beside a river that might one day burst its banks. It would clearly be as well for the local people to keep in mind the advisability of knowing something of the manufacture and function of sandbags. It is quite extraordinary (but very necessary) to realize that some people find it impossible to conceptualize metaphorical sandbags. They are unaware of the necessity to save, to take out life insurance, to arrange for temporary help in a domestic crisis, etc. 'Second nature' is unnatural to the parent who has missed the opportunity of experiencing good authority in his own parents because of the latter's inadequacy, which might be the result of temporary or permanent absence or even death.

The following are some examples of such catastrophes on the time horizon and the relevant or particular good authority necessary to forestall them. Although the need for planning for an enterprise would seem obvious, I have been closely associated with cases in which the

---

Not to recognize those for whom cold, grim satisfaction is to be had from repeatedly losing out and for whom therefore conciliation is wasted.

Not to know that a person or even a country that makes difficulties for others is in difficulties itself.

Not to know that the survival instinct is only interested in its own survival – not the survival of the person who thinks he owns it.

Not to know that a soldier in wartime is living from one day to the next. His family, however, whom he sees on leave, is liable to talk about the war as a whole – when it will be over, etc. – thereby unwittingly demoralizing him by psychically multiplying his chances of being killed. This can be contrasted with the builders of the Great Wall of China, who built the wall in sections, in order to preserve the morale of the many generations of workers.

There are a million such themes – many much more subtle, of course, than those I have listed.

ability to plan was like an amputated limb, or a limb that had never budded, had been lost as a concept, or was never present at all. One particular family's idea about emigrating was 'just to go' at the last moment, and its members became very angry when thwarted by the social services. The latter had been taken unawares, and had been somewhat reticent about cooperating with the family's wish to leave immediately, since two of the children were in care at the time.

Division of labour and responsibility in a family seems a sensible strategy, but a large, extended family suddenly being cut down in numbers (due to the following combination of factors: the death of an aunt; the marriage of two siblings; one sibling's entrance to the army; the father's illness and hospitalization; geographic moves by other relatives) meant in one case that the network method of managing had been made suddenly less effective. The mother had come from a very large, warm-hearted family, where the father was away for long periods of her childhood, and where everyone was used to mucking in. She had no concept of people sharing responsibilities in a defined way – only of people helping each other out, and there being always dozens of reserves; the idea of carrying a specific responsibility was foreign to her and her kin. The social worker had to wade in and dole out specific tasks to each member of the family, and eventually they became more role conscious.

Some tasks can only be carried out by oneself, on one's own. For instance, preparation for a serious surgical operation required a particular seventeen-stone mother to reduce her weight, but she became even heavier, and the operation less likely to be performed. The woman's inability to slim, even on pain of death, gave partial evidence of her inability even to think of doing anything by herself, let alone to *do* anything quite on her own, and without being over-anxious. To her, slimming would only have been possible if she had been imprisoned and forcibly starved.

The delinquent child makes the would-be good parent experience emotions of helplessness, a feeling of loss of authority in the overt, unpleasant, unacceptable, can't-do-*anything*-with-this-bad-child sense. Paradoxically, as long as the parents experience this sense of loss of their authority, there remains a chance of recapturing the relevant Good which they perhaps lost on the death of their own parental authority, or never received from the latter. We know that all that usually happens in this state of affairs is that the child, quite understandably, is seen as 'The Problem', for whom, or about whom, something *must be done*. The present-day parents' craving for the good authority that they lost, or never found, in their own parent takes the form of a wish for the present-day child to be good, and no one is aware of the unconscious parental craving for sandbags as a precautionary measure against impending disaster due to their lack of planning ability, organizing ability or ability to go it alone. Siblings will go to the wall one after the other, thus providing their parents with the repeated craving for the *next* child to be good. The craving, felt at a deeper level, is really always to have their long-lost good authority returned to them, or even to experience it for the first time.

Treatments directed primarily at the persisting delinquent – punishment, individual psychotherapy, behavioural techniques or drug therapies – might well bring about objective improvement, but in my view will in a delinquent family be accompanied by a loss of authority by a parent over yet another sibling or over his own physical or mental state. It is sad, but no one is likely to be aware that little brother's taking to stealing or mother's falling ill is connected with the delinquent's 'improvement'. The 'ex-delinquent's' helpers or custodians might not even know about the new family catastrophes.

I have taken a special interest in what may occur after the youngest child in a delinquent family has attained its majority, that is, has turned eighteen. The parent of an eighteen-year-old is no longer entitled to bemoan the loss of and hope for the return of his authority over his own child, since that authority is no longer an entitlement of that parent, but the entitlement of his child. The apparent need of parents to experience the reality of their own loss of authority, and their unconscious hope of finding or refinding a particular kind of authority, if thwarted by the coming-of-age of their youngest child, may perhaps take other forms. There are innumerable loss-of-control syndromes known to medicine, typified for instance by cancer, which I am prepared to believe take over the provision of the opportunity to bemoan one's loss of authority.[6] For example, 'I have lost authority over my white blood cells (leukaemia), my weight (obesity), my drinking (alcoholism), etc.'

*

ATE This is a tentative approach to a great problem. The individual tackling the possible causes of cancer seems like an ant crawling over a dead elephant. It has often been suggested that cancer might be 'stress-related', and as often – at this suggestion that the victim might somehow have brought his disease upon himself by his inability to treat with more insouciance the vicissitudes of life – the *bien pensants* have risen with expressions of wrath, inquiring whether suffering from cancer is not sufficiently malevolent a fate without *blaming* the patient for inviting a possible premature death. This is doubtless well-meant, intended as it is to protect the person's susceptibilities from further harm, but it is not conducive to open-minded research or frank discussion. Of all the ills to which human flesh is heir, cancer seems to be the most terrifying; regarded with almost superstitious fear, spoken of, if at all, in whispers, and by many people never referred to by name. The bolder amongst us sometimes speak brazenly of the 'Big C', yet this type of nomenclature is only a whistling in the dark, like calling a murderous enemy a cabbage. The guardians of the public's tender feelings do not protest when promiscuity is put forward as a possible cause of venereal disease, but with cancer it is assumed that no moral opprobrium should attach to such common failings as a refusal to face reality.

A responsible, a committed tentativeness is, however, a different matter. The evil have made fortunes by claiming to have discovered a miracle cure for the most frightening of scourges. It is correct to be reticent about a new and not thoroughly researched theory while investigations continue. A proper understanding of the relationships between mind and body is still entirely remote. Nevertheless in a significant number of cases the professionals in T P A's family meetings have been gloomily able to forecast the incidence of cancer in a family member. What is not known, of course, is how often they have been able to avert the threat.

I have been present at some of these meetings, and it is an eerie and disquieting experience to watch a person – often wearing a small, deprecating smile at being the sudden centre of attention – being gently and obliquely warned that he may be next in line for havoc. Sometimes they simply talk past the point, others surprisingly admit to having had intuitive fears on their own account. It has been chilling on the occasions when the predictions have materialized.

*

TPA Certainly I have found that the parents of young prisoners (most of whom are over eighteen) are very commonly ill, that is, have bodies and/or minds that are outside their own control to a greater or lesser extent. It is only fair to say that this has been perceived mainly as a clinical impression as yet, though in my small pilot study of the parents of sixty Borstal boys this was even more pronounced in the parents of boys who were the last born – there were fifteen such boys, and seventeen of the possible thirty corresponding parents were either seriously ill or dead. It might even be that such conditions have a symbolic meaning – that is, that the pathology of the conditions relate in some way to the type of lost good-authority theme inherent in the individual.*

Another specific example. An illiterate husband-father was further distanced from outside contact by his busybody wife who always spoke for the family, completely leaving her husband out. The social worker noticed that, curiously, the father looked relieved on hearing that his son had committed a most horrible act of violence. We gradually came to realize that in this family there had to be a gross degree of seriousness before an issue could break through the communication blackout that engulfed the father. His asthma, I felt, was his way of expressing his 'damned if he'd let anything out once he'd got it in' attitude. Asthma is a condition in which the air is trapped within the lungs, and air is a word used in loaded communication-talk: 'on the air', 'clear the air', 'give it an airing', 'have some fresh air on the subject', etc. The boy's misdeed – seriously assaulting an old woman – may have been lifesaving for his asthmatic father. It may have enabled a message to get through to this communication-starved man, thus preventing him from dying, rather than not deigning to let out what he had managed to get in. Did the shocking news shock him into breathing more easily? It is also possible that the old woman was an unconscious stand-in for the mother who was bludgeoning her husband's capacity to be worthwhile in the family context.

I suspect that, always supposing proper mourning occurs at the time of the first generation's loss of good authority (for instance in societies where mourning is more institutionalized, or at any rate seen as very important), the carry-over effect I have described will be less inevitable and therefore less in evidence.

---

* I have known several cases of spinal-disc problems in parents who appear to fail to understand the importance of the linking and continuity of relationships through time.

CHAPTER SIX

Results of the Loss of the Good Authority

A consideration of the absence of particular types of good authority, and the corresponding results of their absence – application of this to various settings: familial, institutional and commercial

---

TPA The general aftermath of a loss of good authority and the especial denied nature of this loss, which I believe to be decisive in producing delinquency, merit some elaboration and discussion. The loss of an authority might mean a consequent loss of structures. A child's friends are, as I have said, likely to be geographically close to his home, which belongs to his parents. Should the child lose his father and/or mother (an authority), he may lose his home (a structure) and in consequence his friends (a substructure). Friends in this case are therefore a function or resultant of authority. If the loss was in the dim and distant past there might not be any structures remaining in living memory – whole traditions would be forgotten, dead. These structures made up of time and space, known and trusted people and things are all gone or just not there. It is easy enough to understand the change from being allowed the tremendous licence of one's own *legal* authority, to being put in a prison cell where sustenance and companionship are strictly rationed. The feeling that is commonly reported there, of course, is a desire for freedom. I will however in this chapter be dwelling on the abstract, less obvious but more common results of the loss of *good* authority.

How can children and underlings resolve a dispute if the father figure has died before having had the chance, actually or metaphorically, to bang their little heads together? A story describing a particular family's progress after the father's death might well tell of the huge feudings between the siblings but not mention the missing authority, the paternal banger-of-heads, who had with his death taken away the exciting possibility for his children of being friends again, after having been at daggers drawn only moments before. Father, who could not prevent rows beginning but was always on hand to bring them to an end, had gone.

The members of a West Indian family were found to be severally and severely depressed. This at first was thought to be caused only by the recent death of the father, who had been murdered by a person or persons unknown. Gradually a facet or characteristic of sudden unexpected death as a phenomenon became very clear: a sudden violent and unprepared-for death, such as death by accident or murder, can leave a family in chaos. The authority remaining after this murder was filial and cliquish; traditionally subservient to the dead man while he lived, the remaining members of the family were now hopelessly worsening the rifts between them, and were heaping new scores on the would-be-reconciled old scores. There was no one to cut short the feuding by banging the feuders' heads together – father had died in the middle of a family row and the row seemed destined to run on and on, either till Resurrection Day or the depressed exhaustion of the squabblers. It would have done so, if they hadn't been helped in therapeutic sessions to rediscover at least the concept of dead father's head-banging function.

Business meetings, whether commercial, clinical or administrative, evolve a tempo and atmosphere which can be as forceful though covert an influence as some of the meeting's authorized structures, as, say, the order of the items on the agenda. The structure, if damaged by loss of its authority, may give rise to problems that take on a *displaced* form. For example, during the regular staff meeting at a residential institution for children, little progress was being made in deciding on rules to govern a games room, until it was appreciated that the two members of staff who were being most mutually antagonistic about the issue had fallen victim to a temporary loss of the ultra-strict two o'clock start of such meetings – part of the regular authorized structure – while the usual chairman was away on leave. I was acting as chairman in his place, and had arrived at two. One housemother had also arrived at two, but soon after settling in an armchair was called away for a few minutes. During her absence a male member of staff had arrived, and had sat in that comfortable chair. When the housemother returned to the meeting only hard, straight-backed chairs were left. Her comment to a fellow female member of staff, 'I'll just sit here then,' was not understood by the majority of those present, who themselves had been late arriving. The significance of the angrily spoken 'then' was exposed eventually. It was understood that *she* had been on time but no one had known that, and having been called away she was then forced to sit in an uncomfortable chair. Almost magically the atmosphere in the room changed and the displaced dispute about sanctions regarding the games room disappeared; but if I, as the acting chairman, had also been late, then resolution at best would have had to be reached either by vote or by hierarchical edict.

A most serious and common result of the loss of good authority is a sense of omnipotence: the belief in one's ability to perform miracles with very little effort, as in the following case of a child whose father had died and whose mother found herself incapable of changing from a two-person (she and her husband) to a one-person (herself alone) authority style. Consequently, the anxiety-producing nine-year-old son took over as the decision-making mechanism in the family. The mother didn't change her threat from, 'I'll tell your father,' to 'I'll stop your pocket money,' and instead everything was done to keep the boy quiet. He virtually terrorized his mother into doing what he wanted or thought he wanted. Since she always capitulated, he was gradually coming to believe that he could do and have anything – he thought he was becoming omnipotent. The household's loss of father, and the full meaning and implication of this loss, were being denied. Omnipotence gained by causing anxiety in others is only rivalled by what I term the 'power of the pathetic', the means by which we are disabled from saying no to someone, not because we should or shouldn't but because of how guilty they make us feel if we do.

Commonly, the reaction to a loss of authority in a multi-person context does not show itself in discussion of thoughts and feelings by all the people affected – rather, the response is metamorphosed or condensed into an issue involving a single person – usually his unacceptable behaviour (so-called acting-out). This single person is of course directly or indirectly associated with the group who has lost their authority. The anxiety to which the group as a whole was originally entitled due to its loss of authority is now focused on and fuelled by that one person's acting-out. This unconsciously condensed and misdirected, falsely convenient anxiety reinforces the feeling that control or authority is lost and needs to be re-established, but unfortunately, of course, only in relation to that one person who is preoccupying people's minds because of his misbehaviour – the scapegoat. What is really needed is the regaining of the original authority in relation to the multi-person or total situation. This was well dramatized in a family where a stepfather with several new stepchildren felt panic-stricken and wanted me, the psychiatrist, to *do something* about one single stepson – a 'liar'. The stepfather, newly married to the boy's mother, had no concept of patience and sticking at it in the sense of gradually getting to know intimately his new, large, ready-made family. The result was entanglement with health services, social services and legal bureaucracy for himself and for all of them. There was also the possibility that his stepson, the scapegoat 'centrepiece' of the drama, would go to a detention centre. The lying epitomized the difficulty of knowing what was what, and made it clear that if one was ever to find out, one would indeed have to be patient – patient not just with the lying child, but rather with the whole new and different interpersonal structure that now existed and needed to be understood in the family. As it was, the whole family had been lying to itself that it knew its own self.

*

ATE Imagine winter. The pond has frozen overnight. No one has yet tested its strength. The village children clamour to be allowed to go and slide about on it. They make a terrible nuisance of themselves. The village elders briefly discuss the whys and wherefores, the nature and their own past experience of freezing – it varies from one to another – and the advisability of permitting the children, the future of the community, to slither around on dodgy ice. They agree that there *may* be some risk involved, but argue that the ice *may* be solid as a rock. They do not wish to appear to be curtailing the natural freedoms of the community members, and the children are raising a racket – so the elders give their permission and hope for the best.

No one has any real idea of the effect of the portrayal of violence, night after night, on the young, the impressionable or indeed on the rest of us who would describe ourselves, if questioned, as mature and stable. It has not been *proved* that it causes harm, say those who have entirely ceased to rely on common sense and have turned instead to the false gods of 'scientific' proof. In thrall to this pantheon, this ersatz 'authority', they are blind and deaf to the obvious.

What do the young and vulnerable 'think' of an

authority who will allow TV violence when there is even the remotest possibility that the young and vulnerable might go through the ice? I'd go through the ice for the hell of it.

*

TPA I said previously that it is a function of a good authority to produce a good atmosphere in a household or work-place, an atmosphere which is, of course, conducive to good thinking and planning. The loss of this facility is akin to the losing of patience already mentioned. Several requests for institutionalization of a number of adoles-cents were thought by the team dealing with such referrals to be due to the temporary loss of a good working atmosphere at the referring department of social services. This we felt had led to short-sighted tactics (institutionalizing) rather than well thought out or wise strategy for the long term. This opting for the less worthy choice was, moreover, probably felt by the clients or designated patients as a rejection that would tend to bolster anti-authority traits in these youngsters.

In my experience, in all anti-authority situations the authority has at least to some degree 'asked for it', usually, as already described, by allowing a sense of omnipotence to develop in its charges, but also in other ways, which sometimes smack of a semi-conscious abuse of the trust placed in an authority (to be a good trustworthy authority). For example, a harmful anti-authority situation resulted when two institutions came to an agreement whereby one, an adolescent unit, would give another, a children's home, a three-month respite from an impossibly violent youth. After five days the adolescent unit found it could not cope with him, and this led to special procedures that resulted in the boy being locked up in a third institution, a closed unit. After much discussion the fact emerged that if the original agreement had gone to its full term of three months the children's home would have been in a serious staff situation, bordering on mutiny, since the staff found themselves quite unable to cope with the boy but no one wanted to admit it. It was agreed that a hypocritical hope had been unconsciously entertained that the adolescent unit *would fail in its commitment*, thereby unfettering the children's home from *its* commitment – 'hypocritical rejection'. It was subsequently realized that the boy's parents, who were separated, were both alternately and constantly catapulting away *their* own authority over their children in just this fashion, both in turn having contrived their children's rejection by the other parent. The situation was parallel to that which had been recreated at the two institutions in question.

The infamously vicious killers of prostitutes probably catch the public imagination in the way they do because their actions graphically epitomize this secret, false method of rejection, which is used, in day-to-day life, when one person hypocritically rejects another. The whore with her come on is disguising her wish for her client to be finished and go (the come-and-go syndrome), and such outrageous cheating is surely deserving of death. A common everyday example is the adolescents (whether seventeen or fifty-five) who endeavour to get themselves rejected by their lovers in order not to have to do the dirty deed themselves.

The common preference for omnipotence over help-lessness is similar to the slightly rarer preference for grievance over grieving. Authoritative handling is vital if such a switch is to be prevented. A legitimate grievance is to the spirit as cancer is to the body. Feuds are a well known, almost classic repeated mode of reliving a loss of opportunity to grieve: grieving having been supplanted by a grievance with its accompanying wish for vengeance; vengeance once realized probably leading to yet another lost chance for the adversary to grieve – *ad infinitum*. Grieving if not traditionally important (a temporal structure supported by authority) may be supplanted by traditions of vendetta.

Up to this point I have referred to the fairly simple results of the straightforward loss of good authority. After such a loss the future, of course, brings with it conscious balancing acts and unwitting compromises, because of the anxieties (especially denied anxieties) or dreads about a possible loss of structure. For example, if people unconsciously anticipate threats to the structure of their organization because authority is likely to be lost, there occurs a very basic sense of lost control, and the subsequent reaction to that sense of lost control often re-achieves a new, but unfortunate, equilibrium.

In a residential institution for adolescent boys it was invariably found that should it happen that the position of the local-authority social workers, the key residential social workers and the parental situation be simultaneously in unforeseen jeopardy (say the key residential worker becomes pregnant, the field social worker suddenly gains promotion and one of the parents becomes ill), the child concerned would automatically become impossible to manage. The untenability of the child would bring about an emergency wherein the child would be relegated to utter dependency on 'controlling', ever-ready, relatively unthinking – what I call 'lower level' – procedures, whether this meant pleas for his transfer to another institution or an automatic appointment with some specialist such as a psychiatrist. The Good in the authority (either having gone missing, or, as in these early cases in the history of that institution, never existing) was resurrected by the realization and making use of the knowledge of the 'tripartite untenability syndrome'. Nowadays the position is that all members of staff can, very quickly, if they wish, seek a case conference in order to discuss a predicted tripartite loss, thereby in all cases preventing untenable situations from arising.

At present in that institution the case conference is a highly structured, highly valued tool and is therefore well understood both in its format and its purpose. The danger for the near future is that as time goes by the formality of the case conference will be eroded as staff become more and more sophisticated as individual practitioners – they will be able to foresee untenable situations miles ahead and be able to forestall disaster in their own way: unobtrusive discussions with parents in their own home, chats with a child whilst at a swimming pool, timely and tactful phone calls with a relevant member of staff at the social services department. This phase of 'loose structure', though more efficient and at least as effective as the formal 'highly structured' case conference procedure, poses significant dangers, since eventually when there has been considerable staff turnover – as there will be – not only will the structure of the formal case conferences of old be forgotten, but their purpose will have been lost from the minds of the staff, since the work will not be as recognizable in its scattered individualistic 'loose structure' form. Gradually the tripartite untenability syndromes may reappear, once again producing the 'very old', lower level control procedures, usually readymade systems focusing on questions such as, 'Where is the proper place for him to be?' or, 'Who should see him?' perhaps resulting in transfer to a psychiatric unit for the individual child, or even in the decision that he may as well go home.

An example of the way the old case conferences could be lost, in the dim and distant past, is exemplified by 'triage meetings' in a hospital family unit. Most staff members imagined triage meetings to be so called because of the presence at those meetings of three groups – doctors, nurses and patients. It was only at a staff training seminar that the term was found to have derived from war-time casualty clearing originating in the Old French 'trier', to cull. The expression had been brought to the hospital after the Second World War by its medical director, a colonel in the Royal Army Medical Corps. (The particular hospital had been instituted in the first place to cater for the 'civilian equivalent of shell-shock victims' of the First World War.)* These sources illustrate how, not only is a new 'improved' structure bound to supersede an old good structure, but also how it seems that the *meaning* of the old should be stored safely, not forgotten, to be brought out, looked at and dusted now and again by the good authority. Changing patterns of life can throw up or make necessary an authority that can enable a new, adaptive structure to be created, while the old, good, authorized structure should be taken down, oiled and put away, but frequently inspected and tested, often by legend and fable, and never despised. Anachronism is a word tainted with denigration. 'Its time may well come again!' should be engraved, perhaps on stainless steel, alongside its museum case.

*

ATE While 'antique' means money, 'old' merely means worthless. As fast as new machines are invented, old ones are thrown away, old skills discarded as unnecessary. Bank staff seem to be incapable of functioning at all when their computers break down, never having bothered much with mental arithmetic and having no abacuses to hand. The woman who has also retained her old gas stove realizes the wisdom of this as her microwave oven melts before her eyes, and the woman with a luncheon party pending thanks heaven – as her food processor whirrs to a stop – for a mother who taught her to make mayonnaise by hand. These obvious truths are too often ignored by those dazzled with 'progress'. (What'll we do when the fossil fuels run out and nuclear power really is recognized as too dangerous and no one can remember how to rub two boy scouts together?)

*

* It was learned moreover, that another meaning of triage had to do with the grading of coffee beans. The sorting left a final residue of husks and broken beans, from which a cheap form of coffee – 'triage' coffee – could be made.

TPA History, tradition, present predicament and fashion determine what structure is good for now – there is not one static rule for good and all. We know, for instance, that boys learn at school that they should not tell tales. When they leave for business and positions of professional trust, in certain situations tale-telling may be necessary and must come easily and with dignity (not 'out of school').

The next case demonstrates the need for a good authority that can support a new good structure of independent mindedness, whilst an old good structure of loyalty is seen in relative perspective, rather than as under threat from the new. An ex-Guards officer and his wife, both from military families, were distressed by the behaviour of their adopted son, a miscreant scapegrace of seventeen, who did nothing right as far as they were concerned. The concept of a boy doing his own thing was as missing in the family as any idea the parents might have had of criticizing their own parents for sending them to boarding schools at the ages of six and seven. Loyalty for them was completely dominant, and their own parents *had* to have been right. It is possible that the father's regiment might have done him a service if they had incorporated the words 'but moderation in all things' after any mention of the term loyalty.

In Chapter Two I mentioned Bozo the vagrant, who eventually learned that it would have been more sensible for him to shave before selling his razor. An 'expert Bozo' is a person who, being self-taught, is extremely self-sufficient. I encountered such an expert Bozo who was brought to a surgical unit having collapsed after vomiting blood (a massive haemetemesis), but who left hospital too soon after surgery and died. It was felt by the staff that their highly skilled nursing was experienced as an attack by the expert Bozo; I felt that perhaps he had feared, in an unconscious way, that the nurses might steal his self-sufficiency. Only on understanding this did the nurses realize the nature of his complaints about all his property being stolen from him when his clothes had been taken to the hospital laundry – an act performed for kind and sensible reasons. This hospital Bozo with his idealized self-sufficiency had come crashing tragically into the nurses' own idealized notion of patients' dependency. His property *was* his self-sufficiency.

The flexibility I'm implying – being able to be soft, hard, loyal, disloyal, to keep quiet and to be frank at the right time and place – could almost be regarded as a gift. Probably the right word is *grace*, implying change from one Good to another Good, giving up the former position with due respect, entering the next with due respect and therefore always able to return to the first with few mistakes or even no mistakes at all. How often are such terms as 'falling from grace', 'disgrace', 'there but for the grace of God go I', used in connection with work in the field of delinquency? The psychopath who, it is said,[1] does *not* learn even from repeated experience may be in part a demonstration of the need for more than a simple, complete change to a new attitude. Perhaps he ironically personifies, with his intense sense of expediency, the necessity for holding on to all the options, old and new, in order to be able to go back to the old if it again becomes expedient to do so, or move on to the new if it suits him. He is the reflection – the 'projection' – of the unconscious disapproval that most of us feel towards the changing of our own attitudes, from old to new and back again.

I am really talking here about creative deviancy, which is unarguably worth keeping. Art, for instance, would cease to be art, and would become arid and static if people were not prepared to experiment with new concepts and techniques. Art comes from the gracious ability to produce unique artefacts and place them within an authorized structure, while being aware of the prevailing influences. I might cite two examples of how a full awareness by individuals themselves or with the help of others can bring rewarding developments out of stasis. The awareness enables something helpful and new to develop, or the resurrection of something good and old to have an impact. I remember a speaker at a seminar on delinquency,[2] who was aware that an atmosphere of doldrums had beset the seminar; he also felt safe in the knowledge that he had engendered in the other seminar members a respect for his own professional qualities. Thus, on the fifth day of this rather august-seeming conference, he felt able actually to *sing* the first part of his address from the dais. If he had done this on the first day he would have been regarded as mad; on the fifth day, however, his performance was heartily welcomed. At the same conference a woman speaker was noticeably frustrated by feeling unable to mention very exciting, new and helpful child-care concepts based on her own work in her home country, since, it turned out, she had been imagining that these concepts would be outside the conference's authorized frame of reference. The members of the seminar as a whole were able to bring her up to date with the revised frame of reference, which she had not heard about beforehand because of a brief illness that had caused her to miss the early days of the seminar. As a result, she had been anxious in case her deviancy would be considered out of order, that is to say, delinquent. The other members' awareness of her earlier absence and consequent *un*awareness enabled her to speak about those same helpful items – much to the benefit of all present – which she would otherwise not have mentioned.

Structure, as I said previously, can be seen as the usual item for debate – the football that is most commonly kicked about as being good, bad, lacking, not good enough, needing improvement, scrapping or too good. It may gain respect, recognition or loathing. It is an authority, however, which has brought about that structure and it is that authority which is, in my view, given far less of an airing than it should be given. It is sad to think that authority is so commonly hidden, covertly based, as it often is, in patronage, political bedchambers and corridors of power.

A father who is not seen as someone who ensures that secret quarrels within the whole family are worked through productively may be displaced by the extra-familial power of professionals 'secretly' or 'magically' deciding how best to deal with one 'delinquent' or 'sick' family member. The professionals often reinforce the artificially neat 'sick-member structure' with the main issue now being seen as simply what to do about the sick member. At the same time the professionals unwittingly conspire with the family to decay its normal, messy, complex structure, subduing the variety of its several personalities, dulling their conflicting hopes, prejudices, alliances and rifts. A good, recognized and respected authority can construct a safe holding structure, which enables toleration of what would otherwise be overwhelming anxiety about things going wrong *between* people. The loss of this type of good authority results in things going wrong (or seeming to go wrong) actually *with* people.

In one family where this kind of situation prevailed, I noted that when the family were at peace with one another the elder daughter suffered relapses of her chronic medical condition, Hodgkin's disease. I, as the psychiatrist, was seen as trying to cause friction in the family, both parents were then twice divorced, and are now thrice divorced. This syndrome of an apparent preference for things being wrong *with* somebody in the family, rather than things going wrong *between them*, became known by the therapeutic team with which I was involved as 'generating badness'. Interestingly, in that family therapeutic situation the three-year-old 'passenger', who nobody thought would have much, if anything, to contribute, was seen to rummage in his mother's handbag and, to everyone's surprise, proudly stick a piece of elastoplast on his chin – thereby claiming *his* ailment.

How does a young adult leave home unless he is emotionally permitted to do so by good authorized structure? Through apparent stupidity? A marriage of convenience? Pregnancy? Prison? I have frequently found that Borstal boys have repressed, but very sound, reasons for leaving home, and I often find them to be the very boys who had the 'sticking-est' sticky-sweetest relationships with their families. These negative solutions, which nonetheless allow for leaving home with no feelings of guilt, comprise the Israel syndrome I mentioned previously. What is instead required is a good recognized authority that can provide a structure that allows leaving in a developing way, maybe with sadness, maybe with guilt, but authorized, open, right.

New stepfathers, typically, seem to have an initial reticence or even difficulty in combating minor infringements of standards in cleanliness and manners, preferring to wait until intervention is undeniably justified; but if the deterioration is gradual, they may still be waiting for sufficient justification to act when the smell, symbolic or real, has become overwhelming to a fresh nose. The fresh nose is generally unconsciously called in by a member acting as envoy for the family, which needs to wake up to the fact that things are changing, or could change, since the old family's chaos is now dangerous. On the other hand, some families will ask for help consciously and directly if actual long-standing trouble has outgrown a paradoxical usefulness.

In the case of Clare, a fifteen-year-old girl who was taken by her mother to their GP in a clearly psychotic state, it was learned that the child had been socially cut off to an extreme degree for many years, and had shared her parents' bed at her mother's instigation. Only when Clare's father suddenly died did her male-fearing, 'daughter-in-the-bed shielded' mother see her little girl as alien. The girl was now redundant as a marital barrier. Clare had delusions of persecution, was whining, self-conversational and lost in her own mental space. In the old structure – the previous state of affairs – it would not have suited the frigid mother to have taken her child to a doctor, who might well have disapproved of the sleeping arrangements. It was a great pity that Clare's very frequent absences from school, and in class her loneness, apparent preoccupation, as well as her tendency to talk to herself, had not been taken seriously by the fresh noses, unconsciously going collusively stale, amongst her teachers. Clare is now a chronic patient in an adult mental hospital and engenders periodic pious outrage in politicians, who side with Clare's mother in her 'righteous' indignation at the lack of resources for mentally sick young people.

This kind of unconscious hypocrisy is in my view responsible in part for explosive and unmanageable anger in certain people whose unspoken resentment has festered for years. The resentment's chronicity is encouraged by other features as well, such as the resenters' own denial of anxiety, their fear of rejection (which may have a once rejected, always rejected connotation), their low self-estimation and their denial of the defects of quality that they share with their ordinary imperfect fellow-creatures. I feel that professionals are often hypocritically abused (as in Clare's case) by relatives and by the public who are prone to a cynical abdication of common sense in times of stress. Parents in general will quite often allow their children to be treated or even institutionalized without question, without interest, without using their brains at all. If people (children in particular) are treated because those who should be responsible for them delegate that responsibility to others – to 'experts', since it would be 'the best thing for them' – a very dangerous situation immediately arises. After all, who says it is the best thing – who could know for sure? It is better to arrive at a reason for giving some sort of help that may indeed make the parents feel guilty, but which will none the less make sense to everybody concerned.

In a residential institution for adolescents I discovered that frequent abscondings of a particular nature were associated with an unclear reason for admission. The 'particular' nature was the tendency for the youngster to abscond to a non-statutory, non-related third party, typically an adult sometimes known as an uncle or aunt – but actually neither – and often known to the social services department for harbouring children. It seemed that if the children were admitted compulsorily, against the conscious wish of one or both parents, they became very torn emotionally when faced with a staff who were found to be likeable and fair in their dealings. This divided loyalty – to stay, do well and imply defective parenthood, or to flee and imply professional inadequacy on the part of well-liked staff – calls for unconscious compromise – illegal dead centre – and entails the illicit running away not to the parents but to a middle-ground 'uncle' or 'aunt'. (For some reason the 'uncles' and 'aunts' seem to choose to live mostly on housing estates.) The assumption in these cases that the parents are illegally harbouring their children is usually wrong.*

The above is a common result of the loss of Good; that loss of Good being the failure to establish and state clear reasons for the child's admission. Explanations that the admission is for 'treatment', or, 'it's for the best', just won't do. This loss is seen too often in clinical practice. *Legal* dead centre can be established if the reasons for and the purpose of the treatment and/or admission are clearly understood and stated by the current authority. It must be understood by the non-professionals concerned, and supported by other professionals in the case. For

---

* In practice, this split between the professional and non-professionals often mirrors denied parental splitting.

instance: 'John is to be admitted to the adolescent unit because his social worker says so.' 'Why?' 'He doesn't know precisely yet, but he feels uneasy about leaving a child, for whom he represents legal authority, at home with his parents.' The why and wherefore burden is taken on by the proper quarter, together with the directed anger, resentment and threat, but the child himself is spared and can sit tight, leaving the battle *outside* himself, and get on with whatever good opportunities arise.

Symptoms of delinquency are always over-determined – always have a multiplicity of causal roots – but, having mentioned absconding, in this connection I should point out that it occurs frequently as a result of the tri-partite untenability syndrome, and that when these episodes occur and are being discussed, people do often say, 'I wonder what he's doing?' 'I wonder if he's all right?' and, 'Is he committing more offences?' The realization comes about, in parallel with the regular discovery of the tripartite loss of good authority, that everyone is now depending upon whatever small amount of good authority the child is carrying around in his own person – that is, his own quotient of indelible authority. Sometimes it is possible to see the irrationality of anger at such a youngster, on the run with no legitimate funds and no sanctioned accommodation. If he has absconded and commits further misdeeds, he has done no worse in fending for his own needs, baby-fashion, than did the three groups of adults who had failed to arrange for takeover care in anticipation of their own official 'absconding' from the authority stance.

Offences committed while on the run are not always straightforward attempts at self-preservation. A deeper meaning is frequently found to consist in the attempt to resurrect the good authority (unconsciously perceived as dead) in the form of the reliable law – a man in blue – 'a fair cop'. The relief at capture after some doomed to fail criminal escapade brings a look to an adolescent's face that all policemen know. Not only does the offence bring authority back from the dead, but at one and the same time the relief of punishment and retribution for having unconsciously killed the good authority is experienced.

It is hard to calculate just how good is the Good demanded by the unconscious, but to get some idea, imagine a heroin addict who succeeds, once again, in persuading a referring agent to undertake, once again, the difficult task of persuading a choosy hospital to admit him, once again. Undoubtedly the addict will fail yet again, amidst all sorts of trouble, again, at the hospital; and the referrer's name will be mud, again. All this indicates the immensity of the demands and the immensity of the Good demanded; as the mother who would do and risk anything, absolutely anything, for her child. If the good authority is so colossal in unconscious terms, the void in its absence must yawn to be filled. This is demonstrated in the following situation.

The recently appointed principal of a formerly authoritarian institution for delinquents found that vandalism was becoming rife amongst them. This was eventually understood as being a projection from the staff who had, unwittingly and mindlessly, abandoned and abused the professionalism (good authority) that was expected of them under the new regime. They were continuing with an unspoken dependency on the boss ('He should have said something if he wanted us to do it'), together with a mindless non-realization of their own adulthood and responsibilities. One facet of the children's vandalism without doubt showed festering anti-authority revenge against a staff-society that was responding to its own anxiety with blocked understanding. When the dynamics of the situation were understood, the vandalism simply stopped, and the staff actually managed to realize, and to bear in mind, that when asked by the principal for their opinion in regard to geographic bounds for the boys, he *actually did want their considered opinions*. He wanted them to use their minds and not to nobble the boss by leaving him to decide the boundaries on his own. It was the parasitic mindlessness of the staff that would have subsequently enabled them haughtily to portray him as having been too lax or too severe in whatever decision about the boundaries he finally had chosen. During the early or non-understood part of the episode the apparent problem seemed simple – which children deserved to be kept, and which should be rejected from the institution? There were 'bad children against good children', that is, bad, anxiety-producing children and good, caring-for-staff children. Some members of staff left quite soon after the 'understood' phase, probably because of the threat they felt from the new, increased responsibility for thought and decision now clearly expected of them.

The 'thinking' quality in good authority is tremendously taken for granted. If thinking ahead, with all its implications and complications, is lacking in the correct quarter, then the results of this theme will be evidenced in the disturbing episodes of the moment. The theme will be projected hither and thither in the family and its associates, as in the case of two brothers who were scornful of the idea that it was necessary to prepare emotionally and thoughtfully for their transfer from one children's home to another. The boys had a mother who had married without considering her own future, *and* an accident-prone elder brother who was nearly killed by a motor-car through not thinking to look as he crossed the road. These facts, when it was realized that they had a common theme, were helpful in bringing to light the point that the superintendent at the first children's home, who was supposed to have been 'solid as a rock', might well leave (and in the event did leave) quite soon. He left an institution that had never thought that it might lose its permanent superintendent and was barely prepared for the uncertainties and bureaucratic mayhem which lay ahead, or for its task of coping with the acceptance and admissions of yet more adolescent children – an extremely anxiety-producing situation for those staff who remained.

*

ATE Projections. What *are* these projections? – people ask with varying degrees of curiosity and scorn, depending on their cast of mind, as though expecting that one could draw a picture for them and that, if one cannot, then they are not there. The professional sceptic has grown rather less cocksure of late since his colleague in the pragmatic, scientific field, the physicist, has come up with some remarkable observations on the nature of matter. Several saints have had the power of being in two places at the same time (known in the trade as bi-location), but now it seems that particles can do it too. Things are more peculiar than it has been fashionable to admit since the Age of Reason took us all off on its tangent. Faced with something inexplicable, people may now cautiously hazard a suggestion that it may be due to telepathy – a concept previously dismissed by the learned, flung together with apparitions, portents and marvels into the rubbish bin, but now retrieved, still with due reservation, as the least blatantly offensive of the disreputable conglomeration. Ever since Adam, his sons have believed that naming confers power. Once it is accepted sufficiently to be given a name, then a concept belongs to humanity and largely ceases either to disconcert or alarm.

Which gets us no further with comprehending the nature of projections. Some things can only be described by delineating what lies outside them. A hole wouldn't be a hole after all if it wasn't a hole *in* something. Would it? TPA says it's probably what some schizophrenics go on about when they complain of being got at by X-rays, waves and electricity – he wonders whether Reich ever caught any alive in his Orgone Box.

*

TPA A child needs to stop idealizing its parents to become an adult, but this needs to be a benign, not a malignant process. It must be acceptable that father is not omnipotent, that the woman next door makes better biscuits than mother, that a friend's father is better at fishing, or the adolescent himself is better at football. However for a youngster to know, unconsciously, that his own parents cannot think ahead produces at best nothing worthwhile in the make-up of the child.

CHAPTER SEVEN

The Delinquent: The Personification or Anthropomorphism of the Loss of the Good Authority

Robin Gasmeter, Frank Disobedience and Peeping Tom – Concept of the delinquent, as in varying degrees not a person at all, but a living container for certain loss-of-authority themes – How this can happen all or some of the time – How the delinquent embodies and caricatures the very features of the loss of the good authority

TPA Delinquency can be seen as the individual personification of themes related to the repeated loss of, and repeated mourning for, the good authority. The delinquent is the one who yells at us to 'watch this space!' – the space that contains the symbols of mourning. I think of delinquency as unconscious satirical characterization being given full play. What could be regarded as a classic example of this phenomenon is embodied in the syndrome of the Right Bastard. An illegitimate person mourning for his parents is entitled to feel hatred if his parents irresponsibly desert him, but he is also entitled to feel love towards those missing parents, since it was probably that same irresponsibility to which he owes his creation. This only unconsciously ambivalent predicament I refer to as the

Baton sinister (Bar-sinister). Indicating illegitimacy – the marshal's baton laid diagonally from left to right over the family coat of arms. (Sinister from Latin '*Sinistrum*' meaning left. Baton from low Latin, '*basto*', meaning stick)

Left (abandoned) Bastard, or Baton Sinister. It is the next generation, however, that gives us the consciously appreciated Right Bastard. (The ambivalence of the parents towards the grandparents is passed down to the child, and is then projected outwards to the observer who now experiences the ambivalence.) As a rule there is no way of changing such characters, who are fascinating, almost to a hypnotic degree, in the intense mixture of feelings they evoke. They are beloved or hated central characters, whether in history or literature.

The delinquent can make himself the embodiment of a multi-personal difficulty by accurately compressing a précis of the others involved into his own person with the glue of anxiety. The anxiety certainly gains attention, but also engenders in the minds of observers the inability to think. Often we are faced with a silent, frustrating youth who will not satisfy our need to know about the problem. On a conscious level it might be to do with committing an offence, but on the unconscious level it is to do with the fact of the delinquent 'knowing' – 'being in the know'

– in other words, having all the familial thematic unconscious information packed tight inside him. It is best to think of the silence as modesty – 'It is easy to be modest if you are in funds'* – and the delinquent is, unconsciously, replete.

Broadly speaking, delinquency produces a sense of urgency and anxiety in the present, and it is that production which is frequently found to represent the long-term unconscious mourning for all the vicissitudes resulting from the sudden loss of authority during the childhood of the delinquent's parent. It is this taboo loss that needs identification and urgent working through. The unknown (lost) Good is needed *now*, for the well-being of the family, and the delinquent himself provides the coded opportunity to acquire it, but if he were simply to answer straightforward questions with straightforward answers we would be led away from any chance of understanding the significance of what the delinquency really portrayed.

A very worrying theoretical notion arising from the above is that from time to time, or constantly, the delinquent seems to become inhuman, a moving bag of skin, with important symbolic messages rattling about inside. This may be why people describe some criminals as brutes or animals; it may also lend some solid justification to the demands made by the protagonists of corporal and capital punishment. Certainly, the pain-experiencing skin is the same, and the body can be hurt or killed whether its owner is human or a delinquent rattling bucket. Is this indeed then a rationale for corporal or capital punishment? Does it imply that physical punishment is effective whether the individual is human or not? Whereas rehabilitation or reason is not possible with a thing.

* Said by the Prince de Ligne to Frederick the Great at Potsdam in 1780, about the admired military genius of Prince Eugen of Austria. Thomas Carlyle, *Frederick the Great*, Vol. 10, Chapter 8.

ATE The ordinary human view of 'justice' is both simple and hit-or-miss. A person apprehended flinging a brick through a plate-glass window has committed a crime and must take the consequences. The law has no time for the psychological subtleties behind his action. It seems fair to punish him, yet this 'superficial' fairness bears no relation to the complex web of emotional and psychological reactions that lies below the surface of all human behaviour. Only when a positively dreadful and outrageous crime has been committed (although some magistrates grudgingly accept that some shoplifting, compulsive thieving, may be dignified by the term kleptomania and be a form of mental aberration) do the courts turn helplessly to psychologists of one sort or another. Both courts and public seek reassurance that the perpetrator is mad, a creature from another world with nothing in common with the rest of mankind – the species that goes home to its wife, has its tea and takes its boots off to watch the telly. It is supposed that the effort to ascertain whether or not the criminal is in his right mind is in the interests of justice, but – as it applies in so few cases, when logic would indicate that here we have a question of degree, and if one form of anti-social activity is evidence of 'insanity' then the concept must extend over the whole spectrum – it seems clear (to me at least) that the desire to label the mass-murderer as crazy is merely a sanitizing move, unconsciously intended to clear the rest of us from the imputations of original sin. (The courts would reject as blatantly unjust the idea that, in the sense of retribution, the sins of the fathers should be visited upon the children, while failing to understand that the 'children', the criminals, are helplessly governed by old, unacknowledged guilts and sorrows.)

*

TPA Should the child container be shifted, say, to an institution, the rattling bricks and oddments tend to be taken over and taken in, almost magically, by another sibling at home.* It may turn out that when Peter is doing well under *his* individual 'treatment' or 'training', the campaign's cudgels are already being taken up by his younger brother Paul. Perhaps this unwitting game of pass the parcel is what we really mean by the term 'dehumanizing' – each succeeding child accepting his containing role in turn.

It is not only conscience or remorse that is found to be absent from time to time, or constantly, in the delinquent, but less obvious human commodities or senses as well; a sense of time,[1] for instance. What would one expect from a mother and son, who hadn't seen each other for two and a half years, suddenly meeting? Surely something on these lines: 'How nice to see you again,' or, 'I wondered how long before you'd show up, you old so-and-so,' or, followed by mutual tears, 'God, Mother, I've missed you!' Surely not what actually took place: the apparently rational – but unnatural (at least to me, the observer) – continuation of a mundane conversation between a boy, an institution staff-member and the boy's mother who had arrived suddenly, in the middle of the conversation. Boy and mother addressed each other as though they had been in each other's company all the time, and at no time did they acknowledge the gap in their acquaintance, either to each other or to anyone else. That the ability to register the passage of time seems non-existent may appear inconceivable enough, but on closer inspection it was found that even more of these everyday commodities or psychic abilities were absent in that boy and his mother. No memory, no being able to 'stop oneself', no apparent correlation between act and consequence, no

* Christian in *The Pilgrim's Progress* was 'glad and lightsome' when relieved of his burden, but subsequently Christiana and her children felt impelled to start on *the same journey* that he had undertaken. John Bunyan, *The Pilgrim's Progress, from this World to that which is to come.*

use made of experience, no evidence of ability to use advice, no loyalty, no shame, no sense of honour, no sense of humour, no sense of purpose, no sense of failure nor of degradation, no ambition, no sense of caring, no common sense existed at all. All these deficiencies can be seen to come into force in these cases from time to time *or* constantly, making the person inhuman from time to time or constantly.

The sexual act provides us with an evocative and extreme paradigm. It has no intellectual quotient. It may indeed be regarded as a brainless form of recreation. Imagine, however, *being* the sexual act itself; not Tom nor Dick nor Harriet, but actual intercourse. So, if *I am* sexual intercourse, I would writhe, make no sense to others nor to myself, become ecstatic, swear; I'd not stop even if I should or could, I'd whisper to me and me would whimper back.

I am sure, having heard about and read a number of individual and family case histories, that the infamous Gille de la Tourette syndrome (a condition that entails a triad: tics, the shouting of obscenities and juvenile onset) occurs in those unfortunate persons who were never intended to exist in their own right. In other words, their actual futures were never considered by their parents after the sexual act responsible for their existence. It is likely that they were 'mistakes', undreamed of pregnancies, or that the parents intended them to be 'mementoes' or 'souvenirs'. (One sufferer whom I met was the son of a Second World War bomber pilot whose wife wanted 'something to remember her husband by'.)

In my own encounters with a few such cases the primary theme has always been the perpetual lack of all thought for the future of the individual – repeating the original lack of consideration in the parents for any future life of their offspring. The sexual portrayal in the individual patients was almost overt – not only in their bodily movements but even in their own vague belief that if they truly wanted to, they could stop their tics: a latter-day pre-orgasmic misapprehension wickedly lampooning the parents on their way to a one-night stand's 'mistake'. When I pursued with these patients the theme of their identification with their future-denying parents, individuation or self-realization was achieved to the accompaniment of the most frightening exhibitions of liquid hatred I have ever seen.

There also seems to me to be a connection between both the offences with which these people had been involved and an increase of their symptoms on the one hand, with genuine but denied reasons for being anxious about the future on the other. Of course, not all 'mistakes' exhibit Gille de la Tourette syndrome. I have stressed that set of deviations as a means of emphasizing the basic principle of personification of themes. Swings of mood in a patient, for instance from mania to depression, can also be understood as a 'one-man show', the living personification of themes – this time of tenses: 'Now you see me sad. Look! I'm sad, sad. D'you agree? *Now*, I'm happy, happy! D'you see I'm happy? Same *me*. Sad then, happy *now*, sad next . . . and it doesn't make any sense either, does it?'

The following example should help to make the portrayal of tenses as a theme clearer. A few years ago the very experienced staff of an institution for adolescents were preparing their unit for the reception of a disturbed thirteen-year-old boy, Robin. They considered their unit a very good one, and were satisfied in a professional way with their work in preparing for Robin's admission. Now, at Robin's home that same day, the boy and his parents were distraught at the idea of him being sent away to 'that place'. The mother and son shed tears, the father was 'brave', the social worker and GP were staunchly supportive. At one and the same time, therefore, the subjective views of the forthcoming admission to the institution were at variance in those two geo-graphic quarters. Once admitted, Robin spent from Mondays to Fridays at the institution, appearing to find everything very much to his liking, but he was reported as 'positively hating the place' when he was at home for weekends; he cried on Sunday afternoons when leaving his home, yet seemed delighted to be back at the institution a little later in the day. Robin's fluctuating moods were his ambassadorial insignia, invit-ing the staff to realize that *their* now-good unit was at that precise moment the going-to-be awful place in the minds of the boy's family. The staff are still as proud of their unit as ever, but they no longer imagine that new clients will automatically hold any particular fan-tasy view of it. When eventually a residential social worker met Robin's family and said, 'I am sure you were worried what we were going to be like here,' a barrier was beginning to break down.

The implicit parodying by an individual of an under-lying wider situation carries not only the clues to the necessary but missing Good there, but also lampoons the idea that magic or omnipotent methods of dealing either with him *or* with the underlying portrayed situ-ation will suffice; the unfortunate and recurrent states of the delinquent himself are the overt messages for the family or group who might not otherwise discover and retrieve the Good in time. Some examples follow of the delinquent's caricatured loss of Good (against the background of the family's or group's missing Good), together with some indication of the mechanism whereby the Good was lost, or was never available in the first place.

One fourteen-year-old boy was frequently involved in serious offences, consistently finding himself going along with the crowd – not actually carrying out criminal acts, but somehow always being with others who did. His mother was an unmarried woman who had an untrustworthy co-habitee; she perpetually entered into debates and arguments with people and bodies – such as neighbours and social services – or worried away at issues such as bills and debts, which were very important in themselves, but quite irrelevant at the time. Therefore the key issues about which it was imperative to decide, such as whether or not to leave her co-habitee, were never debated. She, it transpired, when she was eight years old, had had to look after her younger siblings after her father's death and her mother's desertion, and had never learned to get down to things, instead always becoming sidetracked by the grand, but less personally relevant issues. Her son (the portrayal) was more obviously getting drawn into fringe involvement with criminal acts that were actually none of his damned business, thus caricaturing his mother who, when small, had not had the maturity to know what to stick at but had been sidetracked by the apparent priority presented by her pressurizing younger siblings. The danger that she was slipping into was that of getting more and more sucked into a relationship with the totally unsuitable and un-savoury co-habitee because she did not have the Good that would allow her to get down to working out for herself whether or not she should stay with this often dangerously violent man. Rather she would always be taken over by some seemingly pressing topic that appar-ently deserved her attention more.

A thirteen-year-old boy had been making very serious attacks on helpless old people whilst he was with a gang. The other boys had only to suggest, in a joking kind of way, that an old person should be 'done over' for the boy in question to race off and attack his victim in an orgiastic manner – so much so that one member of the gang said, about one typical attack, 'He just went mad – for no reason. He's a nutter.' The missing Good this time was found again in his mother, who had a very similar history and life to the unmarried mother of the previous example. It was her inability to choose a wrong or the lesser of two evils – for instance, whether to marry the owner of the comfortable home where she was living or to leave that house – and the man whom everyone described as the 'wrong man for her' – and become a depressed recluse. She again had lost both parents when she was very young, and had been left to look after her younger siblings. She managed this without difficulty when it was easy for her to see what was right and what was wrong, but when it was necessary for her to choose the lesser of two evils her thought-processes became paralysed; her pseudo-parental authority did not extend as far as that. The attacks made by her son highlighted the relief she would have experienced if *she* had possessed the necessary choice-mechanism – the choice-mechanism that would have permitted the doing of a wrong. This case is very important in a general sense, in that I think it goes some way towards giving the lie to simple explanations and reasons for some senseless crimes. The more *wrong* the crime and the more vulnerable the victim, the more relief is experienced by the criminal when he is given even the flimsiest licence by his gang peers to perpetrate the wrong. Some people might imagine that this sort of crime is an example of the game of 'chicken', where gang members goad one another into committing offences as a kind of virility test. It is not.

A third example is a case of rape: a twenty-year-old rapist epitomized, by his crime, his father, who was soon to lose his last child. All the other children had grown up and left home. The father did not have the slightest idea that his wife found his very presence obnoxious. It was only now that there were soon to be no children in the home that the strain of pretence would become quite intolerable for his wife. The rapist in question denied knowing that his terrified victim meant no when she said yes. He did not know how obnoxious he was to his victim.

In another case, the discovery of his use of soft drugs had reportedly caused a fourteen-year-old boy's adoptive parents to experience enormous disappointment in this, their hope-vested only child, on whom they had lavished thoroughly good parental care. Later, when he was nineteen, a discussion took place between institution staff and the family about the chance of his being released from Borstal, and it became clear that if he did not go home with them the boy would be in the position of seeming to be responsible for returning his parents to the hitherto-denied disappointment of their childlessness of so many years before. He had been to his parents the 'drug of adoption', intended to oust their unshared despair, but of course it was now looming again on the time-horizon of their late middle age.

In a case of stealing by a fifteen-year-old boy, the parents were invariably able to detect by their son's post-theft demeanour that he had been up to his old tricks again. Sure enough, on one such occasion his mother's jewellery was discovered in the window of a local pawnshop. 'I was right! I knew it!' she exclaimed. It transpired that the parents were in effect being given a crash course in intuition – the vital Good that they had lacked to a dangerous degree. In this instance the eventually acquired intuitive ability to know that something was wrong without it staring her in the face saved the mother's life. In spite of being 'perfectly well' she went to her GP, having suspected that the tingling in her left breast was 'evil'. The biopsy showed a malignant growth and the subsequent operation was therefore performed in time and was successful. The historical basis for the parents' initial lack of intuition was that both parents had been evacuated in their childhoods, to very well-organized institutions. Their own parents had visited them and had been told how things were with the children, but what had been lost was the ability of those parents (now grandparents) to know when things were not right without actually being told or having it spelled out. The grandparents had been forced to lose the knack of having a feeling, a hunch or intuition because of the war-time separation; so the parents, when themselves children, could not acquire or learn by unconscious example from their parents this faculty of intuitively keeping track.

Another common manifestation of delinquency is truancy. The repeated absence from school of a twelve-year-old boy reportedly entailed the collusion of his divorced mother. Stories were told about his mother giving him permission to be away from school, writing notes to excuse him and then claiming that she hadn't. Eventually it was realized that allowing a child's *absence* is as significant and important as insisting on that child's *presence*. The mother, who had legal custody, and who herself had been in institutions as a child, still guiltily thought of herself as fighting her ex-husband, using the child as a weapon – present with her and therefore absent from her ex-husband. The boy was being torn quite needlessly, because his mother simply did not realize that the power to allow him to be absent from her (not simply nor only to be present with her) went with her custodial authority. However, the themes of absence and presence took place in the once-removed setting of school.

So far the examples I have given each stress one single theme relating to loss of good authority. I have mentioned that the delinquent (I mean here *delinquent*, not delinquency) is an over-determined symptom – meaning simply that there are many roots to the symptom. In this case not one but three themes arise. (I should say here that theoretically there can be more themes than three, and that each theme can be exemplified in sub-themes.) (1) Violence towards helpless individuals; (2) Actions not words, including not only the form of a boy's offences, but the reciprocal need for physical restraint from his would-be helpers; (3) A machismo – or 'nothing-to-lose' – profile.

Three-themed Kevin was West Indian and came to Borstal via other junior penal institutions and swastika bedizened, would-be Nazi delinquent gangs. His offences involved brutal senseless attacks on helpless old people. At the trial of his brother who was up for assault, Kevin showed his caricaturing lack of Good regarding the use of verbal over physical communication. When his older brother was being sentenced after having pleaded guilty Kevin, present in court in the public gallery, required several policemen to restrain him when sentence was pronounced. He was heard to scream repeatedly that his brother was innocent – innocent – innocent. His brother's words, his admission of guilt, had made no impression on him. Later, when he approached his own custodial sentence, he constantly stated that he wanted a 'tough' Borstal, one from which he would not be able to abscond, where bars and locks rather than the rules and codes of an open institution would be the means of securing him. The social worker referred to Kevin's machismo, by which she meant a fantasied, masculine, nothing-to-lose attitude, which was exemplified by his continual tearaway demeanour, his repeated offences even while many cases had still not been dealt with in court, his dress (eagled and studded black leather, iron crosses and chains) and his severely self-mutilating tattoos.

Kevin, it seemed to me, was enacting his own father's hatred of the grandfather, who had deserted the grandmother thinking that he had got clean away with it, managing to ignore the fact of the huge loss that was being incurred by the children (including Kevin's father, who was six years old at the time). Kevin's father had no conscious antipathy towards his deserting father, but unconsciously he hated and wanted to kill him – not so much for leaving, as for imagining that he was 'getting away with it', because the deserted children seemed to make no fuss.

The old man whom Kevin had beaten almost to death

was reported to have said that Kevin yelled, 'You didn't think you'd get a fucking bar in your mouth at your age, did you, you old fart?' That was, I suggest, revenge against the old man who thought he was clever in imagining that nothing harmful could happen to him. because of his defence of old age and frailty; or that because he was old he could 'get away with it'. This is another example that goes some way towards suggesting the mode of thinking that is necessary in order to explain the fantastic and bizarre cruelty that is perpetrated by some criminals on the helpless – whether young, old or sick. Since hearing someone remark that the church had been sought out by German bombers, 'in spite of' its venerable age, I have called this the St Paul's Cathedral syndrome.

The 'actions over words' theme was exemplified in many ways (also infecting the professionals), and once it had been identified it was seen to be rife in the parents. I have mentioned, for instance, how at the trial Kevin did not appear to be able to take in and register his brother's plea of guilty. At therapy meetings he consistently said that the meetings were a waste of time – they were *just talk*. The social worker knew that there was also a probation officer involved in the case, but *he*, the social worker, had *forgotten* this fact. I, the psychoanalyst in the case, found myself *forgetting* the format of the therapeutic meeting – *a book of words*. The father had been full of talk about visiting Kevin, initially impressing the staff of the juvenile institution where Kevin had once stayed, but he never came again. The mother and father had sworn to stay together 'till death us do part', just as the paternal grandfather and grandmother had done; they were all divorced and separated from their children – scattered to the four winds. It had been just a matter of words, only words. Now when Kevin mugged to get money, he did not use threatening words, he went straight in; he caricatured the whole family's destroyed concept (or non-concept) of abstract structures such as marriage, care orders, probation orders, which to him – and them – were mere words. That is why he wanted good old concrete and bars, the 'tough' Borstal – '*Now* you're talking.'*

The theme of machismo or his 'nothing-to-lose attitude' was born of an unconscious need for punishment, that punishment being specifically the 'deserving of no help'. Kevin had inherited the theme unconsciously from his father who, at the age of six, had unconsciously 'wickedly' lost one of his primary helps in life, *his* own father, and had felt devastated at his desolation, at having nothing left to lose: his father gone, his world was gone, the wanted-one who had not even deemed it fitting to face the guilty loss anguish of his child. The inhuman aspect of Kevin is exemplified by the fact that he was being a composite of his devastated father's murderousness towards the coward grandfather. He *was* that relationship, he was not a person, but a taboo father-rejected-from-grandfather's-mind relationship. Hence Kevin – the father–grandfather murderous relationship's logical conclusion – and his self-hatred, self-damage and probable eventual suicide. Occasionally the hatred of his grandfather could be smashed against a symbolic vehicle – such as the mugged and beaten old man – leaving Kevin 'free' to be his father only, having temporarily eliminated his grandfather by vicious retaliation. All the above had to be understood as quickly as possible, before the last of Kevin's little brothers reached the fateful age of six, when, as it happened, Kevin was becoming old enough to leave home permanently.

* Never waste words on a mugger – just give him the money.

*

ATE The word 'resistance' has worthy connotations on the whole, but TPA seems to be saying here that the victim would be fortunate to be suddenly struck dumb, since words may be *meaningless* to a mugger. If he is determined to resist, then action is the only course – certainly not reasoning, banter or appeal.

Now, while stressing the inhuman nature of the caricature or portrayal that *is* the delinquent – like Kevin – I would like to mention again in this context my own leaning towards ecclesiastical rather than medical, psychiatric or sociological jargon. 'Falling from grace' is not a far cry from, 'there but for the grace of God go I', and the words 'scapegrace' and 'disgraceful' are or were both common everyday expressions in respect of wrongdoers and wrongdoings. A state of grace, with its connotations of serenity, is seldom or never in evidence in the possessed, or the delinquent, or the psychopath. Ecclesiastical jargon often comes up in ordinary conversation about cases. I remember a residential social worker referring to a boy as an avenging angel. On looking closely I found that the boy was unreasonably fair in relation to his peers, in that whatever they did to harm him either by design, accident or even forgetfulness he would repay them in malignant full. Eventually I met the boy's parents, whose personalities were the opposite of each other, and these personalities seemed to serve only to provide cause for eternal, mutual, reciprocal and equal denigration, probably each fitting some similar parental/grandparental configuration.

Because of my inclination towards an ecclesiastical viewpoint, I often tend to see what I call attempts at self-exorcism; the attempt to rid the self of projections or possession. These are numerous and varied. Exhibitionism, for instance, seems on occasions to represent a desperate attempt to get caught, so that the one who is finally caught can discuss 'the "projection" who did it'. The first usually appears to be shy, as if to emphasize how different he is from the uninhibited offender.

*

ATE TPA, unusually I think for an analyst, has some belief in God. It takes a faintly primaeval and basic form, consisting, in part, of making bargains with the Deity, but it makes his thought-processes more accessible to persons of a religious inclination. Dogmatic classic Freudianism is, to people of a different cast of mind, alien and impenetrable. It delights TPA to reflect that perhaps the word 'sin' comes from Sinai – a desert, a wasteland; he sees the delinquent as offering the chance of redemption for the sins of the grandparental generation, and he simultaneously sees delinquency as a form of demonic possession.

I had just accustomed myself to his Presbyterianism when he suddenly remarked reflectively that perhaps the Devil was only God in a bad mood.

*

TPA   The personification I keep referring to shows itself over-dramatically in crime. By over-dramatic, I mean from the point of view of someone who might be simply trying to understand what is going on. The effect of the drama usually generates anxiety or titillation and therefore *thought-destruction* around it in the perpetrator, the victim and the investigators.* For example, the boy who committed rape may have been dramatizing the type of relationship in which necessary rejection or saying 'no' to someone is difficult to accomplish or is side-stepped. However, the offence of rape usually engenders outrage, *not* an urge to understand the motives for the offence. Stealing clothes from washing lines may well have some deep, hidden meaning – perhaps representing disloyalty within a family. Such a theft, however, is much more liable to produce scandal or hilarity in neighbours or newspaper readers than the realization that the thief's father had a compulsion to gossip destructively about his own and his wife's private lives – washing the family's dirty linen in public.

Physical violence causes tremendous blocking of think-

---

* A classic everyday manifestation of thought-destruction comes to light when, three days after the event, we know *exactly* what we should have said to that swine – if only we'd been able to think of it!

ing, because of the universal feelings of fear, outrage and vicarious excitement it arouses. A vicious attack with a butcher's cleaver, which left a woman maimed and a jury horrified, was only understood by myself (a distanced authority) two years later: the attacker's parents were perpetually in conflict, the father wanting the mother to stay with him, the mother wanting to divorce and leave him. The patient, tragically loyal to the differing desires of both his parents, committed a series of crimes and misdemeanours that always included both a staying and a leaving theme. For example, the cleaver episode occurred at dusk in a London street; the patient, slightly drugged and needing money to get more drugs, grabbed a woman who was walking with her child near an underground station. No sooner had he done this than (as should have been expected outside a busy underground station) two passengers appeared from the station exit, and the woman now grabbed her assailant. In a flash he hit her with the cleaver. The understanding I came to was that he had grabbed the woman and then had wanted to relinquish his hold on her, all within the blink of an eye – almost as if he had both wishes at the same time. I wonder, is it significant that the word 'cleave' means both to split *and* to join together? Unfortunately it is difficult to imagine a court giving any credence to this kind of interpretation.

Cases of drug abuse usually create tremendous anxiety in people. This anxiety and the resulting thought-destruction are often denied for what they are and become metamorphosed in people's minds – almost institution-alized. Now any drug abuse, no matter what its origin, falls into a phoney acceptable category and comes to be seen as a particular kind of problem for which specific resources should be provided. This has the effect of superficially doing away with the anxiety, but it simul-taneously also does away with the need to understand the dynamics in depth, concentrating on the simplistic effort to stop the drug abuse *per se*.

In order to gain an impression of the seriousness and complexity of the underlying features that are liable to become lost by this approach, this naive, institutional collusion with anxiety-borne thought-destruction, I will describe some of the dynamics in two cases that at first were considered as fitting material for specialized help, since they were only seen as 'serious drug problems'.

*

ATE   Trying to abolish drug abuse seems to be proving as pointless as was Prohibition earlier this century. Even if all the outlets of supply are stopped the demand would remain, and even if it were possible to destroy every poppy and cannabis leaf in the world then many people would, deprived of drugs, turn to some other source for whatever it is they feel the need of: gratification? – whatever that may mean – oblivion, ecstasy, the transitory but pleasant sensation of omnipotence, of invulnerable well-being. It is frightening to consider what means they might choose, and this is the reason why it is necessary to understand roots and causes, not waste millions in effort, time and money lopping off branches as they appear, hydra-headed, from the hidden dream.

*

TPA   In the first case, a heroin mainliner appeared actually to be identifying with her embarrassingly symbiotic mother. The patient had been in several institutions and had let everyone down in spite of promises and safeguards. What I found she wanted was a referring agent who would speak for her, counter the reservations of the helping agency and keep trying to help over and over and over again, no matter what let-downs would inevitably ensue. The woman patient 'was' the heroin in the syringe, and her veins 'were' her own mother's womb; once she, the heroin, was inside, 'back inside her mother's womb', that womb – in spite of itself – would *have* to

tolerate this noxious baby. The patient's everyday difficulty in resisting the drug's temptation was proof that
the baby outside the mother could be 'walked away
from', rejected by mother, therefore the *resistance to that
temptation had to be smashed.* The mother-body would
now have to look after the horrible baby-heroin even if
that meant the death of the mother-body itself. For the
mother-body to resist the heroin temptation would mean
mother rejecting the baby. (This again, of course, is a
way of looking at things that is liable to be considered too
fanciful.)

In the second drug case, a wealthy family's pride
and joy, their sixteen-year-old daughter, was found to
be indulging in heavy valium abuse, one effect of
which was to shatter her logical trains of thought. It
transpired later that her sensible mother desperately
needed to realize that her own early life had been
an illogical series of disconnected events, moves and
muddles. It had been like a jigsaw, where the completion of the picture is often achieved in a haphazard way:
here a section there a section, sometimes with great gaps
between sections. The mother's obsessional make-up
now made it almost impossible for her to flit about
from one disconnected bit of herself to another since
this for her meant going mad. When she was four
years old she had been treated like a fourteen-year-old
by her Indian Army parents; subsequently, at the age
of six, she was treated like a four-year-old by the aunt
with whom she had to stay when separated from her
parents.

Other examples of offences that are thought-destroying, even if some are perhaps not very harmful in
themselves, are: exhibitionism, prostitution and sexual
offences of all kinds, especially those involving minors.
In these cases the mode of thought-destruction is by
titillation as well as anxiety. The unconscious thought-
destruction that is often present is reflected on a conscious level in commonly reported debates (on radio or

television, for example) concerning the inconsistency of punishment of offenders. In retrospect especially, very little conscious rhyme or reason betrays itself as to *why* certain crimes of violence are treated more leniently than other crimes, which have involved, say, deception and/or theft, or self-exposure – it is more likely that the reaction is mediated by primitive forces freed by thought-destruction.

When trying to get to the bottom of things, it is no help to be so anxious or excited by current events that one cannot think straight. The personification themes which I have laboured are best discovered in the relatively anxiety-free sidelines – ideally in the comparatively long-term therapeutic setting that will be described in the next chapter. These themes, once discovered, can be so accurately diagnosed and described that eventually the therapist and staff concerned can *guess* the offence for which a patient has captured the attention of the world at large. It is as though a vague image of the unconscious interpersonal relationships of family and professionals, present and past, can be gradually pieced together. Once this has been done, the very practised can distil the weak solution to the proof spirit of the offence. Put another way, all sorts of dealings – say between professionals, family members past and present – can be seen or deduced; themes often not very spectacular or important in themselves but none the less absolutely typical for that case. Once he has a firm grasp of the themes, it is possible for a really experienced person to work out the likely offence which the delinquent has committed, because that offence will exemplify exactly the same themes, though usually in a spectacular or important way. The offender, of course, since he epitomizes particular, ever-present themes, is liable to repeat his offences many times, thus assuming a habit-like aspect, meriting in turn the use of labels: thief, rapist, murderer, drunkard, addict, embezzler, confidence trickster and so on.

If adolescence, as I am sure it is, is a process of mourning – that is, accepting the increasing burden of having to face the loss of one's childhood and all that appertains to one's childhood, and grasping instead the ever-increasing impinging weights and reliefs of adulthood – it means that a child's belief in his omnipotence, omniscience and idealization of his parents have to be sadly shelved; he must put away childish things. Instead the sober tweeds of maturity – planning, remembering, maintaining, listening, connecting, practising and knowing – have to be tried on self-consciously, in front of a dusty mirror, and the reflection of this vaguely discernible new adult who is gazing back at the disappearing child is barely recognizable. And if adolescence is indeed a vital process of mourning what happens if a child's parents did not or could not 'adolesce' themselves? Say such parents had been forced to act as little 'grown ups' at eight years of age (premature ego development), and mentioning missing 'bad' divorced father was taboo because it would upset mother. Or, supposing the important events worthy of mourning took place prior to mourning/adolescence, for example the death of grandfather during today's child's father's babyhood? As long as the tweed suit of maturity, or even its left lapel or cuffs or leather buttons, are not needed, if the necessity to grow up can be circumvented, then mourning will be automatically unessential and, even when briefly donned, can be doffed as too itchy or too prickly. If, however, a parent has not mourned, that is, adolesced (and this he *must* do, in order to be an adult), his child provides him with a second chance; the parent's adolescent child can *be* the parent's adolescence.[2] The present child is possessed by the deprived child of the parent's past. The unconscious fantasy of the adolescence the parent lost or never had is projected into today's child. I am virtually certain that the body of today's adolescent retrieves the lost adolescence of his parent(s) and is possessed by it. He is now the theatre for its dramatically active exhibition. He is now a delinquent. A great deal has been written about projection and introjection, and/or possession. T. S. Eliot, in his play, *Family Reunion*, has his character Harry say, as he is trying to puzzle out what has happened to him (he had committed a murder), 'Perhaps my life has only been a dream dreamt through me by the minds of others.'[3] While having these projections inside him, the criminal often claims to have been unable to do anything about what he was actually doing – claiming he was in a trance; he was a spectator to his own performance; he was instructed by God; he felt different from usual; he felt as though he were somebody else; he did not know what he was doing; he cannot promise not to do it again; *and does it again* in spite of treatment, training, punishment and resolution.

A letter I received from a patient in prison said, in part:

My problem is I keep beating up the girl I want to marry. I've also got two children now, one boy 2 months old and a girl, seventeen months old, and I'm scared I might hurt them as well. Please believe me, Doc, I don't mean it, I just can't help myself, it's almost as if I've got somebody behind me controlling my arms. I know I'm doing it but I can't stop myself. I know it sounds like I'm exaggerating but please help me, I can't stand it anymore, I just want to live a happy life with my children or not live at all.

I think that what is often said about girl delinquents being worse than boys is probably true, and is due to the vital necessity the girl feels almost to shriek that she is possessed. There certainly used to be a noticeable tendency to think of girl delinquents as though they were 'basically normal'. What is left of the female patient's own personality must not allow any helper to be duped into making this mistake. She must not allow the helpers to imagine or hope that their own ideas of sweet femaleness will prove dominant and she is just going through a phase, but rather the would-be helper must be made to realize that the adolescent girl's personality is being invisibly paralysed and drowned by massively projected themes from the parent's unmourned past. The child must behave so badly that no one will be left in any doubt, no matter how much wishful thinking, that something is very wrong.

The real adolescent becomes tragically lost to himself and instead finds himself as the thankless, unrecognized bucket or container for all his parent's unconscious projections. His only escape from his unappreciated role is the rejection of himself, body and soul, by the very parent whose adolescence he, the real person in the adolescent, is going through. Either that, or committing suicide.

*

ATE I have always believed that if, just around the corner, there was a door marked 'death', then sooner or later most of us would find ourselves fiddling with the knob; yet few of us actually do commit suicide. We know, at some level, that the unbearable pain or anxiety will lessen as time passes, and we wait because, even suffering, we are in our right, our *own* minds. The person who is not a person, whose 'personality' has been invaded by alien themes, who has a blind and mindless knot of worms slithering around in his psyche, has nothing to lose – certainly not *himself* – for that has been displaced already. In seeming to destroy himself he is seeking to rid himself of the incubus that has taken possession of him; and perhaps the warily generous form of words, 'while of unsound mind', 'the balance of his mind was disturbed', is an unrealizing acknowledgement of this. We have all heard people, numb with shock, say, 'But he was perfectly all right when I saw him yesterday. He was talking about work and making plans.' Had the suicide victim been barking mad his friends and relations would have noticed. The prisoner who has decided on a means of escape is cunning, resigned and calm. The gnawing discomfort of foreign intrusion which can lead to displays of violence and destruction can be disregarded when the escape route has become clear.

CHAPTER EIGHT

Therapy

*An account and rationale of some
therapeutic techniques developed
over many years in many settings*

TPA Bowlby,[1] in his renowned paper, 'Research into the
Origins of Delinquent Behaviour', elaborates some of the
hypotheses that exist to this day in regard to the origin of
and susceptibility to delinquency (and therefore, one
would think, suggest therapeutic or preventative approaches). A current list would include such factors as:
broken homes, unemployment, bad housing, illness of
mother or child, poverty, war, heredity, large families,
head injuries, chromosomal abnormalities, bad family
atmosphere, peer-group pressure, subcultures, poor discipline, interparental conflict, brutality or unreasonable
severity by parents, ineffectual, absent or cold parents and
emotional overdependence. Bowlby particularly stresses
the primal importance of the good parent–child relationship – especially the good mother–child relationship – in the
early years, mentioning his own studies, which showed a
specific causal relationship between persistent stealing and
mother–child separation in the first five years of life.

Delinquents have a reputation for being untreatable –
they often refuse to accept treatment voluntarily and
compulsory treatment often draws criticism.

*

ATE The concept of compulsory treatment may be looked at askance because of the hypocrisy inherent in it. It is frequently a euphemism either for punitiveness or for a refusal on the part of society to be bothered with the offender; seldom a positive or curative measure (as the term 'treatment' might imply) for the benefit of the offender.

The vexed question of capital punishment rumbles on year after year as people sidle furtively round the basic issue. They debate endlessly on likelihoods and improbabilities – does hanging act as a deterrent? A preventative? What too many people are unnecessarily shy of admitting is that hanging somebody who has outraged human sensibilities can be a satisfying act of vengeance. TPA points out that the Bible only *seems* self-contradictory when on the one hand it advises the smitten to turn the other cheek and on the other speaks of an eye for an eye and a tooth for a tooth. Behind this lies the implication that while the private citizen cannot claim eyes in retribution, cannot take the law into his own hands, authority should do that for him. He should not be left unavenged, simmering and festering with resentment. While the Lord in the Old Testament said, 'Vengeance is mine,' Christ, upon whom we are supposed to model ourselves, was very firm with wrongdoers. Perhaps the state, the corporate body of all its citizens, should be permitted to exact vengeance where the individual may not – for that would be hubris. Perhaps the state in this one solitary sense is remotely God-like. Perhaps compulsory treatment is useless (apart from hanging which has, at least, the virtue of efficiency). The delinquent, who may be reproached for failing to respond pleasingly to this 'treatment', and blamed for ingratitude, can point out that he didn't ask for it.

*

TPA Freud, in his paper 'The Exceptions',[2] talks of the patient being asked 'to make a provisional renunciation of some pleasurable satisfaction: to make a sacrifice, to show readiness to accept some temporary suffering for the sake of a better end or merely to make up his mind to submit to a necessity which applies to everyone'. Freud goes on, however, to mention certain individuals who resist such an appeal on special grounds. They would assert 'that they have renounced enough and suffered enough already and have a claim to be spared any further demands; they will submit no longer to any disagreeable necessity'. Today we too find that the would-be healer's influence and arguments are powerless against such individuals, who are inhuman from time to time or constantly.

In the same paper Freud quotes the opening soliloquy in Shakespeare's *Richard III*, where the audience is enabled to share the impact of Richard's minute and bitter depicting of his deformity – compelling us to be sympathetic to his villainy.

> But I, that am not shaped for sportive tricks
> Nor made to court an amorous looking glass;
> I, that am rudely stamped, and want love's majesty
> To strut before a wanton ambling nymph;
> I, that am curtailed of this fair proportion,
> Cheated of feature by dissembling Nature,
> Deformed, unfinished, sent before my time
> Into this breathing world, scarce half made up,
> And that so lamely and unfashionable,
> That dogs bark at me as I halt by them . . .
> And therefore, since I cannot prove a lover
> To entertain these fair well-spoken days,
> I am determined to prove a villain,
> And hate the idle pleasures of these days.
>
> (*I.i.14–23, 28–31*)

Richard III may or may not have had a real hump, but he certainly had a metaphorical one. His father, Richard Plantagenet, Duke of York, died when Richard was eight years old.

Hitler, who also claimed to be an 'exception', is sometimes described as: having had a terrorizing father, finding the advent of his little brother just too much for him when he was five years old, having to leave the family home quite early, and perhaps even suffering from congenital syphilis. However, according to Dr Langer in his report to General 'Wild Bill' Donovan of the American Office of Strategic Services, the predecessor of the CIA, the Hitler family's old Jewish physician, Dr Bloch, had described Adolf's mother as being devoted and affectionate to her son, and Hitler's father, Alois, in terms that implied that he was fairly harmless – certainly not the brute he is often thought to have been.[3]

I have alluded to Richard's claim to be 'an exception'. Hitler's claim was given extra apparent authenticity by the dramatic parallels between his personal predicament and that of the humiliated desperation of Germany after the First World War. I have come to the conclusion, however, that the explanations and justification supplied to support the claim to being an exception, are not only unconsciously tailored to deceive and defeat the would-be helper (whether Freud, Bowlby or any other therapist), but are also required to convince the psychopathic so-called 'exception' himself as to the validity of his claim. In other words, the claim to be an exception is created by the individual in order to explain to himself (or itself) why he is unable to concur with the opinions about him, respond to the entreaties made to him, seize the offers of help, including therapy, react to the threats and punishments and identify with the reasoning raining on him from outside, and often from inside, himself. He stole because he 'needed money', raped because he had 'trouble with his wife', stole a car because he was 'miles from home', bombed for the 'cause'. (In the latter instance, belonging to a specific and well-publicized organization often gives extra power to a claim to be an exception. Any good authority government should either

stop publication of the names of illegal organizations or
legalize the organizations.)

*

ATE In time of war the soldier must, to some extent, be de-
personalized. He wears a uniform, is given a number that
lessens the significance of his name and is told to obey
orders without question or be shot. He is required in the
name of the country, the monarch, discipline, to do
things which in civilian life he would not do; and in order
to enable him to do these things he is freed from the
constraints and inhibitions that normally keep the individual in check. Reports from the battlefield do not
read: 'Joe Bloggs, Fred Smith, Old Uncle Tom Cobbley
etc., today killed a number of people.' They tell us that
such and such a division, army, regiment made a dawn
sally and inflicted what kind of casualties on the enemy.
So what? So this distancing confers rectitude and dignity
on men performing acts that in peace-time would be
frowned upon or lamented. On some level *everyone*
knows that this is the case and so it seems obtuse to
extend this amelioratory dignity to illegal organizations,
allowing them the courtesy of rank and military titles.
This is to admit that they are – as they themselves
believe – engaged in legitimate warfare.

*

TPA I have already tried to make it clear that even if
delinquents did not make their delinquency untreatable,
the primary task of therapy should not be merely the
attempt to change a delinquent into a non-delinquent. It
might in fact be more sensible to think in terms of how one
might drain a mosquito-infested marsh to curb the spread
of malaria – though to the ignorant marsh-draining would
seem quite irrelevant to the patient's fevered gibberish.
This parallel would hold good in terms of prevention, but
of course no amount of future marsh-draining would
help the individual currently suffering from malaria.

Treatment of delinquency necessitates the understanding of what I term the Lassie syndrome. Late one evening near Christmas, with snow deep on the ground, and with more coming down, Lassie arrives home apparently quite demented, refuses her supper and her place by the fire, preferring to pull at her owner's trouser leg, whining to get him to the front door. The dog, without doubt, is disturbed and disturbing, and certainly at first sight requires a beating or a sedative. Lassie's master, however (in spite of not having read this book!), allows himself to be virtually pulled outside the house and to the stable, where, with curiosity and trust, he saddles up his mare, and trots out after Lassie into a blizzard. After some miles' trek he is brought to two small children and their parents, who lie unconscious; obviously the family has been thrown from its cart. The 'therapy' involves understanding Lassie's disturbing behaviour and bringing warmth, milk and brandy to the lost family, where they are actually and very obviously needed. When these are provided, Lassie, the original designated delinquent, becomes serene and untroublesome. Whatever empirical treatment (a beating, education, an advertising campaign, banishment, kindness or sedation) might have been used on the presenting delinquent patient – the 'disturbed and disturbing Lassie' – and whether or not such treatment might have been successful, it is easy to see that the benighted family would have suffered an unfortunate fate. One can also see why psychopaths, delinquents, criminals and yobbos often hate their would-be helpers. Evil is not the opposite of Good – it is the destruction of Good, or that which turns Good into Bad. Empirical treatment in this case would be evil. Not only, therefore, are helpers unwittingly evil, but they are often professional – that is, they earn their living through evil.

*

ATE Lucifer, Son of the Morning, was the brightest angel in heaven. Being an angel – so the story goes – he was outraged when he learned that God proposed to send his son to earth in the form of a man, and that this man would take precedence over the angelic hosts. Worse, a mortal woman, the mother of this man, would become Queen of Heaven. As Adam disobeyed in the garden, so Lucifer disobeyed in heaven, and all his angelic goodness and beauty turned to evil and ugliness. He is not, contrary to romantic belief, a comely gentleman with cloven feet, but a monster of hideousness. And he is not the opposite or equal of God and goodness. The gates of hell shall never prevail. His principal adversary, the one charged with keeping him within bounds, is St Michael the Archangel.

*

TPA One of the most interesting and misleading aspects of the way in which difficult problems present themselves is that generally they appear as *impossible* problems, whether they are anxious-making, very anxious-making or excruciatingly anxious-making. It is worthwhile remembering that behind delinquency – an impossible problem (a disturbed Lassie) – are difficult problems (unknown persons liable to die from exposure). I have described the anxiety that delinquency commonly uses as a fanfare: the problem often is, however, that if the anxiety created is not very great, the onlooker fails to take it sufficiently seriously. Lassie's owner might simply think that the dog was fooling around. On the other hand, if Lassie made too much of a fuss (perhaps biting her owner's ankle in her attempt to prise him from his warm cottage), he might become so angry and upset as to lose his senses and simply regard the bitch as having gone mad, thinking, 'She should be put down – an animal who behaves like that!' Professional evil-doers – empirical helpers – often do treat impossible problems, thereby guaranteeing themselves jobs for life and further fuelling the sometimes conscious cynicism of the so-called client population.

In everyday practice, children occasionally playing truant from school or adolescents taking marijuana present examples of delinquency that are in danger of not being taken seriously, simply because they do not make the observer sufficiently anxious. The tragedy is that if this state of affairs persists the delinquency will have to escalate until, metaphorically, an ankle gets bitten. By this time there is usually no one left who *can* think. Therapy in delinquency certainly requires, firstly, stopping the biting of ankles, and, secondly, helping Lassie to realize (if she did not already know) that ankles are not to be bitten. Thirdly, trained minds are required, and time and space in which to use them. I have already said that the anxiety generated by delinquent acts tends to destroy the power to think. Therefore, in any therapeutic set-up (whether individual or team) it is essential to devise means whereby the trained good minds can be preserved as such, in order to maximize the power of thought and understanding. Of the several methods that have evolved, two come to mind easily. First, a multi-disciplinary team approach, whereby strong feelings such as anxiety can be shared in a mutually supportive system, and second, that certain professionals should be protected from the direct anxiety-provoking behaviour, with a view to their brain-functioning being preserved at all costs. These people might be psychoanalysts, or at any rate professionals, who have themselves undergone some kind of therapeutic process which enables them to be sufficiently aware of their own personalities to resist any tendency towards unhelpful non-professional intrusion. They must, for example, be able to see and confront their own need to protect a youngster from reality, or their own wish to understand or like a child quickly when the child is actually difficult to like and difficult to understand.

Both of these systems, of course, are inherently supported by the fact that such people are professionals and they earn their living thanks to anxious-making behaviour. This is in direct contrast to the non-professional helper such as the parent, whose own professional life and earning capacity may actually be damaged by a delinquent child causing anxiety at home. Delinquency is so commonplace that even if the futile, brainless 'therapies' of revenge, education, publicity, moralizing, consolation prizes, carrots and deprivations, *did* succeed, an economic disaster would ensue: there would be unemployment in the person industries: medical, sociological, custodial, insurance, electronics, administration and policing; rubber-truncheon and handcuff manufacturers and many others would go out of business. The real therapy or help is to understand and where necessary to share that understanding. The 'experts' are pushed by the pain of the sufferers – relatives, victims, society, the delinquent himself – who say 'do something' to him, for him or about him. To allow oneself to be pushed in this fashion is too easy. There is no virtue at all in addressing oneself at the outset to the delinquency *per se*. It is essential to maintain a sane dialogue from the start of one's involvement; never once to be merely the expert who will either succeed or fail to take the pain away. The expert has to know what he is doing at all times; at the very least he has to know that he doesn't know what he is doing – but he *must know that completely*.

I was once asked by a prison officer to see a drug pedlar. I did not allow myself to respond to the drug issue, but rather to the reason why the officer wanted me to see this particular inmate – after all, there were many other inmates he could have asked me to see. There was sufficient inter-professional respect between us to produce a thoughtful response from him. He said he didn't know *why* he wanted me to see the prisoner; he honestly didn't know, but he did want me to see him; *that* he *did* know. That was a start, a sure ground; I was going to see someone who someone else wanted me to see, for no reason that the latter knew of. Here we had undeniable facts; perhaps these facts had a bearing on the psyche of the inmate. When I asked the prisoner if he knew who and what I was, and whose idea it was that we should meet, he guessed correctly and then volunteered that he himself had thought now and again of asking to see me. 'So I'm here,' I responded questioningly, thinking of some new facts: he's saying he wants to see me too, and doesn't say that he's interested in the other fact, that is, that it was an officer who had wanted me to see him, and that he would not have seen me at all if it were not for the other's request.

At once he began a lengthy monologue about the conditions in the prison. I now remembered another fact – that a psychoanalyst is not an ombudsman – and I reminded him that he had told me that he'd wanted to see me: 'Surely it wasn't to complain about the institution?' 'No, you're quite right,' he said, and proceeded once again to complain about the conditions in the prison. I could see that the information I was trying to impart was not being received and/or retained, and that he seemed to be rejecting what I was saying immediately it came to his ears. Having recognized this impasse, I asked him what offence had brought him to prison, and what he felt about it. He explained that the flat he had been living in had been searched by the police, who had discovered a large amount of cannabis. When confronted with the evidence, he had been very surprised, wanting to pinch himself, since *although he knew that the cannabis was his, he felt it was not.* He wanted to tell the police that it wasn't his. Of course it was, only it didn't *feel* like that.

I perhaps began to see how the officer had got the feeling that he wanted me to see the prisoner. It was a case of intuition; the prisoner was not keeping his own feelings inside himself, but immediately projecting them into the mind of the prison officer, leaving the prisoner derelict, or, as he later said, 'out of his mind'. Discussion and exhortation with such a man (education about the danger of drug-taking – of how soft drugs lead on to hard drugs, the inevitable further involvement in fund-securing crimes, the dragging-down of innocents – together with other moralizings) had all been wasted in the past and would all be wasted in the future. The point that would have been by-passed, unrecognized, by these 'common sense' methods was that this patient wasn't able to hang on to his own feelings for half a minute before he unwittingly shot them off into other people: into other waiting psyches, who then would turn to the likes of me to look into the originator of their mind-possession, or *intuition*.

*

ATE The urge to know is an ancient human compulsion. People are reluctant to admit they don't know things – even if it's only the name of that bird sitting in the bramble bush. Experts are particularly loath to confess to not knowing, since they believe that such a confession would lower their status in the eyes of others. Certainly a senior wrangler admitting to a dearth of knowledge in his subject would look a trifle foolish, but those concerned with the welfare of human beings, whether bodily or mentally, have, as yet, an incomplete grasp of *their* subject and must be prepared to realize it in the interest of all concerned. Intuition, which can be defined by those who don't fully trust it as knowing something you don't know you know, has been out of favour in academic circles for some time, but is an essential tool for the psychotherapist, dealing not so much with facts as with misty, unacknowledged awareness struggling for release and expression. He cannot afford to be too clear-cut in his judgements, nor pontificate too easily. It is indeed essential that he should know when he doesn't know.

*

TPA I hope I have depicted clearly the importance I attach first to isolating very simple understandings, then to pursuing these (and their elaborations) while not allowing one's involvement to slip into non-understanding without at least noticing what is happening. In the case I have described, that understanding, which was of a slow, step-by-step nature, comes to a halt (for me at any rate) at the apparent phenomenon I know as 'projection', and which is sometimes described as 'being under a spell' or 'being possessed'. It is not possible to succeed in treating delinquency without maximizing all available understanding, whilst becoming more and more expert at recognizing projection. Although I don't really understand how projection happens, I am sure it is possible to at least become expert at detecting its occurrence. It is as though in certain people psychic deficits take up a particularly shaped metaphorical space or hole, which is then exploded out of the owner's psyche and smashes, invasion-like, into the psyche of another individual, more or less swamping the latter's ordinary mental functionings either constantly or intermittently. This means that the same body is now pervaded and run by a different spirit. The terrible truth about this phenomenon is that the projector has no *conscious* awareness of his psychic deficit, nor that he has sent salvo after salvo of these deficits even into his nearest and dearest, with devastating effects. Only the recipient experiences the phenomenon, helplessly watching himself behaving in an alien fashion, perhaps eventually and sadly accepting the growing commonplace quality of this alien which has caused his true personality to lapse.[4] Only then can others, including both third parties and the unconsciously hypocritical projector himself, appreciate the loss of sense, experience and morality in the recipient. Since the projections are no respecter of time, place or person, another refinement of the tools of therapy is the realization that the professionals who are dealing with a case are themselves not immune. They too will be invaded willy-nilly by the peculiar projections inherent in the case, they too will forget, get things wrong, become muddled, will not seem to learn by experience, will find time passing slowly, or time passing quickly, will confuse father figures with fathers and develop other uncharacteristic, even unprofessional qualities. The action needed is to capture the projections, realize where they are and deal with them. Once the professionals have started to do this, thereby stemming the unconscious, overwhelming tide that is invading them, then the non-professionals – the family – can follow the lead, identify with it and begin to stamp out the phenomenon in themselves.

*

ATE The helper who is prepared to 'suffer with', to experience temporarily the demonic effects of psychic projection that are destroying the delinquent, is displaying 'compassion' – which is not just another word for pity. It should not come *de haut en bas*, but be an empathy, a 'feeling with'. It is not a comfortable emotion experienced from the sidelines, but a willingness to share and participate in pain and discomfort.

The compassion that the delinquent and his family need in order to understand themselves is not a cosy source of comfort meted out by a kindly bystander but, rather, the hardest sort of labour, demanding self-awareness from all parties; the helper even fearfully needing to experience in himself the more or less unconscious tensions, imperatives and losses that bedevil the delinquent before he can begin to apprehend the roots of trouble. Self-awareness is seldom a source of comfort to human beings and real compassion offers no comfort to the 'enemy'. It is the only quality man can share with God and it was this that Christ came to teach us. Vengeance, justice, forgiveness, mercy, are Godly Old Testament matters which the sons of men are not qualified to handle with any degree of expertise or success. All societies make wild stabs at aping the Divinity but, perforce, seldom get it right. We are better suited to attempt the exercise of compassion, having been sent an example with the New Testament, the new dispensation. Christ has not yet come to judge the living and the dead and we have been given time in which to prepare for eternity. 'The sinner is at the heart of the Church'; were it not for sin we would not have known Christ. There are few truly evil men and those that there are are possessed by the Devil. Most sinners are possessed by smaller, sad human demons, and other human beings, if they are prepared to do so, can help to exorcize them, without recourse to bell, book and candle, by the use of their wits and a capacity to reject the pharisaical elements from their own personalities; to realize that we are all subject to subtle forms of possession, and powerless to defeat them without understanding.

*

TPA Some of the well-known methods of treating delinquency against this projection back-cloth – most punishments and attempts at education – I think are of absolutely no value, since the projections, *per se*, are not human and therefore do not respond in a human way. Even if the punishment *is* meted out, or the education *is* given at a time when the individual is not being a mass of projections, then the punishment or education is resented since the person is neither guilty nor uneducated – it is the projections themselves, which could be described as evil spirits, that are guilty and/or ignorant. The attempt to increase another person's sense of responsibility (Grow up! Act your age!) is equally useless for the same reason – that the projections are not human. So called do-gooding, whether by way of encouragement or attempts to make up for apparent deprivation in delinquents, is again bound to fail for the same reason. I think physical punishment may possibly succeed temporarily, since of course the real person and/or the projections exist inside the same physical body, with its capacity for pain. A beating might stop the misbehaviour, but the projections would then take other forms. Any or all of the above ways (punishment, encouragement and the rest) may *seem* to work if the delinquents are totally separated from the source of the projections – the source generally being the delinquents' families. However, this will be a false solution since over a period of time younger siblings will be seen to be in trouble in their turn as they become the new receptacles for these projections. If there are no siblings available, I have the strong clinical impression that the parent or parents soon become ill. It is as though they now become host to a disease, which can actually be the physical embodiment of the projections, the latter having previously been exploded into the children. Furthermore, as I have said previously, my impression is that cancer, especially leukaemia, is more common in these parents than one would expect in a random sample of the population.

I realize that this opinion may reflect unfavourably on certain institutions – especially residential – that concentrate only, or mainly, on the treatment of the individual delinquent, often using the modes I have mentioned: sticks, carrots, provision of stable relationships and many more. At best, and probably quite unwittingly, they simply change the direction of the unconscious forces. Physical confinement and separation are certainly expedient, insofar as anxiety is allayed about the possible damage that the criminal could wreak, but in time the projections will have their evil way by some other route. Theoretically it is possible that if a criminal can be incarcerated long enough, and the projections kept inside him, then when the projection sources die, the criminal will naturally lose the projections he is possessed of. It is likely, however, that by that time the true personality of such an individual would be wasted by disuse and long-term feelings of persecution. Capital punishment might rid us of the containers of very extensive masses of dangerous sub-human projections, but since my practical experience is non-existent in this area, I do not know if the projections would be buried with the criminal. If the executed criminal could be guaranteed to hold on to the projections once he was dead, *if they are buried with him*,* then for me at least, this would certainly go a long way towards justifying capital punishment.

The only worthwhile course of treatment, in my view, is to tackle the whole business of projection in a firsthand way. The case of the intuitive prison officer gave an indication of the fact that since the phenomenon of projection happens not only to patients and their families, but also affects those professionals who are dealing with the case, then if the professionals can: first, actually manage themselves to become infected by those same projections; second, realize the presence of them now within themselves; and third, manage to expel them from themselves and each other (always in the direct or indirect company of the patients or clients and their families), then it seems as though a template is given to the non-professionals so that they too may be able to do the same by means of identification.[5]

In Shakespeare's *Much Ado About Nothing* old Leonato, who thinks his daughter Hero is dishonoured and dead, rebukes his brother Antonio who is trying to calm and comfort him. Leonato says:

> I pray thee cease thy counsel,
> Which falls into mine ears as profitless
> As water in a sieve. Give not me counsel,
> Nor let no comforter delight mine ear
> But such a one whose wrongs do suit with mine.
> Bring me a father that so loved his child,
> Whose joy of her is overwhelmed like mine.

$$(V.i.3-9)$$

---

* Contrast Shakespeare:

> 'Friends, Romans, Countrymen, lend me your ears.
> I come to bury Caesar, not to praise him.
> The evil that men do lives after them;
> The good is oft interred with their bones.'

Julius Caesar (III.ii.72–5)

The professional must be, and be seen to be, like the patient, *possessing* – not just *observing* – the same pain or difficulty.

The overt pressing wish for therapy is headed almost always by key professionals and/or the family of the pressurizing delinquent who 'want him better'. Therapy is however the attempt to find, extract and then capitalize on this extraction of the lost (or absent) good authority. It may be compared to exorcism, and is designed to meet the latent but urgent need to avert a particular disaster, or a continuing series of disasters in the future.

It might be interesting for the reader to investigate for himself the family trees of some notorious 'delinquents' chronicled in history and literature. For example, a literary example can be found in Shakespeare's *Richard III*, where Queen Margaret addresses Queen Elizabeth:

> I had an Edward, till a Richard killed him;
> I had a Harry, till a Richard killed him:
> Thou hadst an Edward, till a Richard killed him;
> Thou hadst a Richard, till a Richard killed him. . .
> Thou hadst a Clarence too, and Richard killed him.
>
> (*IV.iv.40–6*)

The father of Richard III was born 1412, whose mother, Anne Mortimer, died in 1413, and whose father, Richard, Earl of Cambridge, died in 1415.

The historical equivalent is, of course, Henry VII, most probably the true murderer of the 'princes in the Tower'. As well as having a mother who married three times, Henry VII was born nearly two months after the death of his father. Although the fate of the two princes will never be known, it is a matter of record that, of the nine remaining heirs who might have posed some threat to Henry VII's extremely dubious claim to the throne (his mother was the heir to the son of an illegitimate (!)

heir of the third son of Edward III), one he married within five months of succeeding, three women he married off to good Lancastrians, one woman he sent to a convent and one woman he executed, together with the four remaining male heirs. An expression of Henry VII's so-called 'delinquency' can be seen in his attempts to pre-date his succession to the throne to the day *before* the Battle of Bosworth Field. This would have had the effect of making all Richard III's supporters into officially recognized traitors. However, Parliament would have none of it.

My third example is Adolf Hitler, a notorious delin-quent of our own century; it seems extremely likely that Hitler's father, Alois, did not even know who his own natural father was, and that Alois's mother died when Alois was five years old. Hitler's mother had been a foster child.

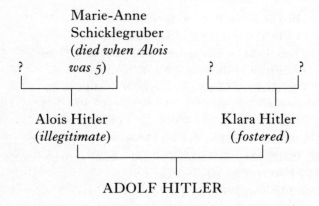

Marie-Anne
Schicklegruber
(*died when Alois was 5*)

?   ?   ?

Alois Hitler
(*illegitimate*)

Klara Hitler
(*fostered*)

ADOLF HITLER

Much store has been placed on the birth of Hitler's baby brother when Hitler was five years old. This event is usually given great prominence in attempts to explain Hitler's alleged sense of deprivation, which would in turn support his claim to be an exception. However, more importantly in my view, perhaps the age correlation between the two generations somehow triggered the reactivation in Hitler's psyche of Alois' loss of *his* mother.

The parents of the delinquent unconsciously identify with their missing good authority just as surely as they would have unconsciously identified with a present good authority had they been more fortunate. Those parents will therefore (totally unwittingly) provide the *absence of good authority* for their own offspring. In the first two generations the lack of the actual authority-holding parent is obvious (for example, the death of or desertion by the father, who has become the grandfather of today) but the *identification* with the lost authority is not noticed, since it is unconscious. If a child loses his father the missingness or absence of the father is visible – an emptiness, a gap – consciously apparent to the child, consciously apparent to anyone. On this conscious level, the child might feel bereft, or full of hate, may be pleased or philosophical. He will, however, quite *unconsciously* identify with his own hidden understanding of the meaning of the deserting father (see left-bastard syndrome, p. 119), but not the father as he was, prior to leaving. Instead the identification will be with the deserting father who now has myriads of new meanings for that child: the family having to move, not having a garden any more, a change of school, mother re-marrying, being worse off or better off, no more children being born, there being one fewer male in the family, and the irony of one's own wonderful father being away, whilst other less desirable people remain. These meanings are what the child unconsciously partly becomes, and in turn when he becomes somebody else's parent, he becomes, at least in part, unconsciously identical with all the meanings of the 'missingness' of his own parent.*

Perhaps a child might have gained a better life by

---

* It is very difficult even to keep track of the appropriate grammatical tenses when relating the mechanisms here.

losing his nasty father. Then, on becoming a father himself, he is likely to take care to be away from his own family a great deal since only then, unconsciously, can he be a good father. Whether or not he himself is able to be a good father, the Goodness will have become indelibly associated with awayness.

There are two main connected reasons, and one subsidiary reason, why identification with the missing parent's lost authority occurs unconsciously. First, good authority is not appreciated consciously, since it is not at all obvious when present, but is then taken for granted. Second, any strong feelings, say of loss, are owing towards this missing object, which might not even be represented by its visible human container, since that has gone. Therefore the feelings have nothing apparent or visible to hang on to and so are suppressed into the unconscious. How does a child manage to be satisfactorily, consciously, justifiably and directly angry with someone who is not there when he should be? The reason for the anger is the absence; and yet it is the completely unabashed, unapologetic, not-there-and-no-excuses-even absence that is so frustrating. What should one do? Flail about in the air, kick the cat or swallow hard?

One wonders whether the continuous swallowing of one's anger might produce cancer of the throat when the unconscious drama has been played out for twenty to fifty years, over and over and over, and when no cats (or children) representing solid thin air are any longer available to kick? Certainly cancer has been correctly predicted on a number of occasions in my own clinical work. In these cases either the last child was approaching eighteen years of age and/or I felt that since I could not hold on to the cases, because the family was moving, or the family's social worker was changing, the parents would need to cast about for another host for the themes which they must mourn.

The therapy has to identify the lost good authority at first hand, then capture it, look at it, see what would happen if it remained *in situ*, then kill it before it repeats its useless, obstructive or destructive schedule for the millionth time. It seems that the pressurizing delinquency tends to reach a crescendo as its accompaniment – the absence of good authority – is propelling a family, a parent, a sibling or the delinquent himself towards a precipice – or a chronically miserable slippery and uncomfortable slope on which to live. (The 'catastrophe' on the time-horizon.)

Bearing in mind that the eyes of all concerned (family and professionals) are overstrained and used up from observing the presenting delinquent, and that all brains are chewed up by a mixture of fear, worry, anxiety, anger, vengeance and vicarious excitement, it is essential to provide a therapeutic structure of such rigidity that, in spite of all the pushes and pulls towards concentrating on the overt delinquent, it is the absent good authority that is being prosecuted, persecuted, executed and turned the right way up again. People will also have blocked their ears, so that even if the therapeutic approach is stated ultra-clearly (as not being merely to cure the delinquent), and even if those present state that they *do* understand the approach, most families, if not all families, will have at first their own, mistaken idea of what *really* underlies the expert's obsessive intent. In other words, they still think he's trying to cure, make better, stop, change or turn the delinquent inside-out: 'You're the expert and we want you to do it *our* way.'

The delinquency specialist must hang on like grim death to the pursuit of his own objective, which must be to find and deal with the reason for the loss of the good authority. Some kind of logical starting point has to be agreed between all the parties, whether a single professional with a single client, or a large group of non-professionals, such as members of a family or institution with more than one professional helper (perhaps of several disciplines). This starting point I call the *focus*. I see to it that there is always a preliminary phase of deciding on, elaborating and staging the focus, and thereafter I make a very real effort to keep that focus alive (in my own mind at least), even if everybody else in the room or institution, whether one or one hundred people, seems to have forgotten the establishment of the focus and is hell-bent on discussing only the presenting delinquent.

Typical focuses are: to try to understand how it came about that Mr and Mrs Black felt the need to ask for professional help in respect of their son George. Or: to discuss a prison giving society a rest from a person. Or: for certain people to come together to express, share and discuss what they feel about a care order, a probation order, a supervision order, an institutionalization,[6] a hospitalization or even simply what the people concerned feel to be important and relevant. Or: the patient's general practitioner, house mother, prison officer or social worker wanting to know what the specialist understands about the patient. Or: the designated or presenting patient personally wanting and actually asking to see the specialist.*

The focus is to be borne in mind as part of the therapeutic structure. Other parts of the structure include, although there are many others, the venue, the time allowed, the order in which parts of the procedure take place, the knowledge of one's own status in the case and that of the other people, whether there have been previous encounters, the referral mechanism and the persons involved in the referral, whether there are likely to be future encounters. As a therapeutic encounter proceeds, certain themes emerge on several levels: intra-personal, historical, intra-professional, interprofessional, intra-familial, inter-generational and, in the therapeutic

---

* The latter focus is very often bizarrely characterized by my finding myself remembering that the patient himself had asked to see me, and yet the patient seeming to have completely forgotten. I have waited for fairly long periods before saying, 'Well?'

encounter itself, even affecting the recording or clerking and the keeping of notes. *These themes, though on several different levels, are eventually all recognized to be identical.* The specialist, particularly if he is a psychoanalyst, has an advantage in being experienced at locating and accurately capturing his own feelings and the feelings of others – conscious, semi-conscious and unconscious. From that point he is able to deduce what it is about a current situation, or about the presentations and sentiments of a personality or group of personalities, that has given rise to these feelings. The encounter itself can be captured in its conscious as well as its unconscious entirety. *The themes consistently recur* and will eventually be recognized; obviously, the more experienced the professional, the quicker this recognition will be. At one and the same time their presence will be validated by their evidence on the levels previously alluded to: present family, inter-generational history, individual delinquent, professional and therapeutic setting. The themes that come through in delinquency cases are all concerned with the loss of good authority. Some are fairly common, some less so, and very frequently the theme that emerges is completely new to the conscious previous experience of the participants. The latter is very exciting and is, to my mind, a valid substitute for the useless, destructive, sensational type of excitement which I feel is all too common in so-called professionals working in the field of delinquency. While the excitement of the chase after understanding has to be present in any individual or organization purporting to provide help, I have a deep, prejudiced loathing of the frequent dominance of that other vicarious type of excitement in some workers. It is to my mind just one more thought-destroying variety of delinquency's symptoms, like anxiety, fear and worry, which are planted by the delinquency itself in the mind of the watcher.

It is worth noting some very important characteristics of the emergence of themes at their various levels. A theme emerging in the self-observing mind of the therapist, or a theme emerging in the interaction at a therapeutic session, can be identified, captured and described very accurately, but it has to be borne in mind that the theme may be quite irrelevant to the case, and might be a result of the idiosyncrasy of that particular day, or the state of mind of the particular therapist, or any other coincidence (for instance a problematic current political climate in an institution or a personal difficulty facing a professional at the time). On the other hand, themes hiding in the presenting delinquency, or in the marriage of the delinquent's parents, in the cancer of a dead relative, in the relationships of parents to grandparents thirty years before, or in the difficulties existing between family members and/or their associated professionals, *feel* more relevant, but are not so easily available to immediate identification, and accurate description. That is to say, themes that one can most accurately identify tend to feel less relevant, whereas themes that tend to feel (and are) more relevant are usually more difficult to identify clearly.

A *theme* is established as valid by virtue of: (1) its constant recurrence; (2) its varying levels of presentation; (3) the increasing intuitive skill of the professionals; (4) the acknowledging of the almost *déjà vu* experience by the non-professionals: for example, 'That rings a bell!' 'That sounds familiar!'; (5) the exchange of knowing looks between the non-professionals.

It is possible, I think, that the phenomenon of *déjà vu*, familiar in everyday mental life, is the recognition and bringing to consciousness of one of these themes, which was previously perceived unconsciously at another level. The therapy requires the working-through of the theme on these lines: (1) a search for its origin; (2) how and whence it has developed; (3) the implications of its continuation; (4) how the destruction of its constant repetition compulsion may be brought about. As a result of the process of working-through, there is a strong chance that good authority, and therefore a more adaptable structure for living, may be achieved.

I know that as I have gained more experience, I have become less liable to make the mistake of seizing on a particular theme which is actually irrelevant, and more able to discern those that really matter. It is important that the therapist should be quite experienced before indulging over-much in making a fuss about where people choose to sit in a therapeutic session, their lateness, their dress, their Freudian slips of the tongue. Such wild analysis if irrelevant, or felt to be so, is at the very best extremely annoying and time-wasting. Corollaries must be drawn between the various thematic layers if the eagerness to understand is to be fired and fuelled where it is most needed – that is, in the family itself, in the tiny remaining self-observing part of the delinquent's psyche, which has more often than not been squashed to one side, and in the polite but often cynical key-professional, who may have known the family for years. Here are some examples of various themes and the levels at which they were detected. The first example, showing the same theme on five different levels, occurred in one therapeutic encounter with an individual patient.

Apparently I had already seen the nineteen-year-old prisoner alone once before. I scarcely remembered this when he asked, as I was walking through the main recreation hall of the institution, to see me 'again', and I agreed to his request with a feeling of ease; I recognized him, but could not remember anything of the details of our last session. I noted his name, the fact that he himself had asked to see me and the date in my work-diary. When I saw him some days later he asked me if I had found out what Dr Smith had had in mind when she referred him to me the last time. I needed to be reminded that I had agreed at the end of the barely remembered first session to seek out Dr Smith and ask her this (I assumed I had received from her a typical referral note), and I agreed apologetically that I would belatedly do what I had promised to do previously: contact Dr Smith to find out the reason for the referral.

The *theme*, which by this time I was aware of, amounted to the following. Here I was, engaged in something that I hoped might prove to be worthwhile for a patient, but realizing that the hoped-for result, if it did transpire, could never have transpired were it not for a beginning that I could not even remember in anything but the vaguest degree. That is, a hoped-for large benefit depended upon an almost-forgotten beginning. My natural wish to be seen as helpful, non-forgetful and non-rejecting had to be put to one side as irrelevant.

The above, it will be seen, contains the same theme twice. I couldn't remember the original referral from Dr Smith, which was presumably supposed to be helpful – inter-professional (1). Neither could I remember the first or original session, which had resulted in this hopefully profitable second session – the therapeutic encounter *per se* (2). I asked the prisoner about his parents and their relationship to *their* own parents. His maternal grandfather, a miner, had died in a pit accident when his daughter was a young girl. She had never got on with her father, though she had always tried to do so, but the fact was, he had wanted a boy. As a girl she was very envious of her brothers, who were always joining in and doing things with their father; the fact that she had been born 'penis-less' determined that she failed, unlike her brothers, to have a good relationship with her father. No matter how hard she tried, she was not a boy. She apparently didn't know the cause of her father's death, which I think is quite unusual. Once again, the details of the start or origin of a gigantic loss were not known, or had been forgotten. The thematic level here relates to the parental-grandparental inter-generational relationship (3).

I asked next about the offence for which he had been sent to prison. 'Shoplifting,' he said and went on to tell me of the enormous buzz experienced on the many occasions when he had helped himself to some article from a department store and had then wended his way through various perils – batteries of real and imagined short-circuit television cameras, trilbies and mackintoshes full of store detectives. His latest offence had been the stealing of a miniature bottle of rum, with which he had run the gauntlet of the system and this time had not beaten it. The tiny bottle of spirits had set in motion the television cameras, the store detectives, the police, the judiciary, the probation service, the prison service and, now, applied psychoanalysis. (The theme on this occasion is exemplified in the delinquent act itself (4): a little bottle of rum in relation to the huge penal system.) I asked about his brothers and sisters, and it turned out that he was the youngest. I have said that when the presenting delinquent is the youngest sibling, my theoretical view is that the theme still has to have a host in which to continue to survive, often having previously possessed all the children in the family one after the other. I believe that the key parent, who in this case was the mother, unconsciously needs to provide a host for the parasitic theme if the youngest and last child escapes or is protected from her projections – for instance, if he is in an institution or has left home for any reason. The host used is often the mother's own body, and of course the theme is a loss of authority theme *or* a loss-of-control disease. The woman's husband is commonly and unconsciously a fitting auxiliary ready to aid and abet the continuation of the theme until such time as the blighted generation is exterminated by it. (There is an implication here that delinquency is the overt and diseases like cancer are possibly covert natural righting mechanisms whereby psychic flaws can be eradicated in order to protect future generations. One often hears about the survival of the fittest in physical terms – not so much in psychological terms.)

*

ATE The concept of 'survival of the fittest' has no place in a Christian, or, indeed, in any spiritually evolved society.

It should be left behind up the tree with the shades of our apelike ancestors. The presence of deformed or inadequate members does not, in a prosperous community, imperil the survival of the species. While 'the right to happiness' is a mirage, the right of every human being to exist seems indisputable. On the other hand, the transmission of inadequacy from generation to generation is clearly less than desirable and presents another ethical problem for the Establishment to wrestle with. Most societies have a sneaking wish to bundle the malformed and the maladjusted out of sight, if not to massacre them.

A movement towards growth and wholeness is inherent in all organisms (but energy leads to entropy). 'Natural righting mechanisms' occur even within civilization and despite the 'unnatural' interference of medical science. If a psychological flaw can evade the notice of doctors and cause death then, presumably, this is one such righting mechanism, just beyond the bounds of ethical considera- tion and – at present – out of reach of interference by virtue of being insufficiently understood. The question of whether capital punishment might free society of a mass of unwelcome and unwholesome 'projections' is one I do not care to address myself to. Does expediency ever excuse injustice, or is 'justice' a mere unrealistic human construct? Perhaps the 'mark' is the answer. Let Cain pass by, for he belongs to God.

*

TPA Then I asked about his mother's health, and he said it was fine, though she had recently mentioned something about a small lump in her breast (5). Together we teased out the fact that she didn't like doctors, and that his father didn't like to interfere with his wife's independ- ence. Hearing about this small, possibly harmless lump jolted my thematically aware senses into memories of devastating system-invasive metastases, and hopeless open-and-close surgical operations.

The latter part of the interview with this shoplifter – our talking of his mother's relationship with her own father – is more difficult for me to remember in detail, but the muddled sense of it and the feeling conveyed were as follows. His mother, he said, just hadn't been born a boy, that's all there was to it. One couldn't expect a girl – even nowadays – to play football for England, no matter how strong or fast or skilled she was, even if she was marvellously well-educated at the best schools, even if she took to drinking with the lads on Saturday nights. We went on to talk in a very unselfconscious way about the terrifying, despised lump in his mother's breast – the breast that denoted her second-best, female status in the eyes of her father, the irony of it perhaps being a wished for penis substitute. We talked about his mother always hoping to be successful in her father's eyes by getting on with the right people and gaining encouragement and support from all quarters, only to find at the last that her father still preferred sons. It was sad to help the young prisoner see his mother's efforts mirrored in a sinister, deadly way by this penis-symbol lump that had been lurking in her so-female, not-male breast. From such a small start it was viciously able to take on all opposition from the hospitals, the doctors, the surgeons and radio-therapy. In fact it was monstrously achieving the patron-age of all her own body – welcomed to enjoy the sustenance of all its systems – its bones, its kidneys, its marrow. The welcome persisting till the sustenance itself begins to wither, the host's life-edifice crumbles, beaten to death by the tiny lump's huge expansion. This once three-quarter inch, manageable little lump, which had so terrified the husband that he wouldn't make his fright-ened wife go to the doctor, triumphs.

The thematic level of the above is the intra-personal somatic (that is, the bodily or physical, as opposed to the mental), in that the delinquent's key parent was being destructively unsupported by the particular kind of husband she had married. His *laissez-faire* policy towards her proved lethal.[7] (One might think of the somatic presentation of a theme – for example, in the form say of a cancer – as being an extreme *reification*, that is, forcing one to see the abstract as a material thing.)

Two days later I asked Dr Smith why she had referred the case to me. She *could not remember*, in spite of many memory-jogging attempts; looking through files and notes, asking associate staff if they had any recollection of the reason for the referral. This, of course, was again an interprofessional variation of the 'forgotten-origin' theme.

My second example shows three, or possibly four, levels of two linked themes. These were identified at the therapy sessions, which involved two teenaged brothers, their social worker, myself (the psychoanalyst) and the residential staff of an institution where the younger child was being cared for.

It was found that everyone present at the third session used up all the available discussion time slavishly repeating and hearing each other give the same information that they had already made known on the two previous occasions, instead of getting on and discussing the material. The words 'boring' and 'repetitive' were eventually used; I had actually predicted to myself what, yet again, one participant was going to say, before he had even opened his mouth. The first theme therefore was 'repetition', and was readily identified in the interaction of the session itself. We heard that outside the session, in real life, a sister of the boys had, for the second time in ten days, accepted a lift in a stolen car, having already been apprehended and officially cautioned for this kind of offence. Another unmarried sister had become pregnant a second time, while the older brother had lost not only his fiancée, but also his job. According to the social worker, who had visited both the ex-fiancée and the brother's ex-foreman, this brother had ignored his fiancée 'once too often', and had failed to see the warning signs of her unhappiness with him; and the foreman had made it clear that his absenteeism from work was getting 'beyond a joke', but again the young man had failed to grasp the implications.

We soon realized the significance of the fact that both the parents had died, first the father and, two years later, the mother. Both had suffered from mild warning (or pro-dromal) illnesses, and it transpired that the lives of the parents could have been saved if they and their children had been aware at an early stage that something was amiss. The two linked themes – consequences and repetition – were clearly shown in the lives of today's children and in those of the parents' generation. Nothing seems to have been known about the father's upbringing, but the mother had been brought up in an institution, so there had certainly been a loss of parental authority in that generation. The professionals who had been present at the sessions wondered whether institutionalization might indeed run counter to the development of the Good of an ability to change things for one's self, since inevitably it would entail one's becoming enmeshed in repetitive institutional routines, some beneficial, others possibly harmful to the young person concerned. The case illustrates one important difference from the first thematic example. In the first, the lack of good authority *was going to kill* the mother unless she were able to create it for herself, or have it created for her. In the second case, the mother *had already died* because of her loss of good authority, her own lack of recognition in her own body of the same beginnings as in her husband's fatal illness. I believe that after her death the children *had to deny themselves* any kind of early-warning system in whatever context or life situation, since to avail themselves of it would automatically present them with the knowledge of the means whereby they could have saved their mother's life. This knowledge would have brought enormous concomitant guilt. The themes of this particular case became known as the 'elephant's trunk'. In its working-through at a later session it was explained, perhaps a little patronizingly, to the youngest boy that, having been stepped on by an elephant once, you do not lie on the ground very long if you see an elephant's trunk coming around the corner – *unless* you want to be squashed. It was interesting to note subsequently that the middle brother, who had failed his multi-question examination for entrance to the army at his first try, had been able to learn by his mistake and, later, changed his technique on re-taking the exam. Instead of trying to complete *all* the questions, easy or difficult, in order, and in consequence failing to finish, he went through the whole paper first, completed all those questions he found easy and quick to solve, then returned to tackle the more difficult questions.

In a third example, a theme was established as valid on several levels at the very first family therapy session. The presenting theme was clearly seen as being concerned with the distortion of time and/or space. It was also noticed that everyone present gradually became infected with over-anxiety in their concern for the well-being of a nine-year-old boy. The meeting started late, because the case files were being unsuccessfully searched for in their usual filing cabinet whilst all the time they had been looked out earlier by another staff member (noted for her over-efficiency), who had taken them to the wrong room. When the boy's parents eventually arrived, they inadvertently became separated from one another; the father was found in the hallway outside the meeting room, waiting for his wife, while *she* was already in the meeting room, together with their son and the professionals. During the session, the social worker mentioned that the boy was unlikely to spend more than a short time at the residential institution – two years at the most! Halfway through the session the mother had to leave the room in order to deal with what she claimed was her first period for four years. The fact was discussed that in the past the son had never been where he should be, whether at home or at school. A member of the residential staff acted as clerk and recorded in longhand as much as she could of the conversations and events as they took place. To emphasize how pervasive the unconscious themes can be, I will quote what she had written; in this particular instance, the way in which a usually competent professional recorded a sequence of events was infected.

Dr Pitt-Aikens asked Mrs Jones [the mother] why they were late. Mrs Jones coyly [clerk's observation] said that it was embarrassing, but she would tell him. After four and a half years she had had her first period. She was a bit disappointed, as she was hoping for twins, she said with a smile.

Mother [Mrs Jones] walked into the room, the doorknob falling off in her hand. She was embarrassed, but sat down. Mr Jones then went on to apologise for being late, explaining that his wife had a painful leg.

Dr Pitt-Aikens added that periods take twenty-eight days, and that there might be a link between Eddie's [presenting delinquent's] idea of his stay at the institution lasting forever, and his mother's [Mrs Jones's] idea of being pregnant for four and a half years.

The mother also thought she had had cancer, a condition where cells multiply at a faster rate than usual, and where these cells are wont to be out of place. (Actually, her GP refuted her belief; she had had a simple cyst removed.) The prevailing over-anxiety amongst all of us, non-professional and professional alike, was based upon our heartfelt wish to do our best, and had originated from the mother's wish to look after her child as well as was humanly possible. This was in direct contrast to the attitude of her own mother, who had, amongst other things, thrown her out years before when at the age of sixteen she had become non-respectably pregnant. It was this chronic and widespread theme of anxiety to get things right and do one's very best that actually brought about the very opposite result – the chaotic disruption of time and space described on the various levels.

One problem about embarking upon and continuing with therapy is that often certain of the main characters who are in need of it do not wish for it. The therapist has no licence to inaugurate theme-chasing and working-through with parents who do not see themselves as having any difficulties at all, but instead point with anger at 'Lassie' as being the one who needs the treatment. This is the main reason for establishing the focus, that is, a relevant, understandable agenda that provides a licence for getting on to the actual themes. In my own work, after several years, a precise, naive-sounding definition of a procedure known as the therapeutic review meeting was evolved: *'A planned opportunity for professionals and/or non-professionals to meet, to express, share and discuss feelings about "X" (the focus), where attendance can be by invitation or insistence or compulsion.'*

If, for example, the focus is a child being admitted to a home, or coming under the legal control of a local authority through a care order, then there is an obligation to honour the agenda, so that even an interpretation concerned with unconscious phenomena *must relate to the focus*. For instance, whilst working through the case with the time-and-space theme earlier in this chapter, I said that perhaps the boy's wandering, which had brought him to court in the first place as being out of control, was like re-living the miserable period in his mother's life when, at the age of sixteen, her own mother had evicted her. The focus or actual item on the agenda was: 'The arrangement whereby the particular children's home was looking after and educating the boy on behalf of the London borough of —, which had legal responsibility for Eddie, represented by the social worker.' Somebody else wondered whether the reason things went wrong so often with the arrangement was because people anxiously tried too hard to get everything right. Weekends at home always seemed to result in people either missing trains or each other, or in misunderstandings that reaped compound interest. This last query had made it possible for

Eddie's mother to be asked if she was determined not to be rejecting, in the same way that she herself had been rejected by her own mother.

This approach, with its emphasis on trying to understand, using a focus as a starting point, meets with varying degrees of apparent acceptance and apparent non-acceptance, from both professionals and families. It is as well to observe a rule of thumb about this – that is, that no matter how compliant or resistant clients such as families may seem, there are unconscious meanings underneath the simplistic deductions one is tempted to make that 'so-and-so' is a cooperative client or just doesn't want help. For example, it might mean missing the whole point if parents who have chosen not to come to a therapeutic meeting are subsequently labelled as uncooperative. This labelling will not only hinder the working through of the intellectual *meaning* of absences – missing people, separations and so on – but will also spoil the opportunity of recreating within the session itself the emotional sensation of loss that is vital if the real meaning of such losses is to be understood and felt properly. The item on the agenda, or the focus, must be sufficiently all-embracing and unambiguous to take in all eventualities, and to thwart all so-called practical-sounding reasons for cancelling the session, such as 'the parents are not interested', or 'the parents feel too threatened'.

For example, if a social worker should conclude that the reason for the session is for family therapy then he might easily cancel a session if the family don't want to come. On the other hand, if the focus or item on the agenda is to discuss anything relevant to a child's being in hospital, then one might expect the social worker to want to be present at such a meeting, even if the parents have no wish to be. At one of a series of such meetings I was the sole participant, since the social worker, the parents, the children and members of the residential staff of the home where the children had previously stayed had all failed to turn up. However, I stuck like a limpet to the very rigid structure of the meeting and my bevy of empty chairs; I even told an intruder that a meeting was in progress. At the end of the hour I duly performed the one executive act required in such meetings, which was to arrange the date, time and place of the next meeting. At the subsequent meeting five weeks later, everyone assembled, which would not have been possible if the previous meeting, at which I was the only person present, had been cancelled – since no invitations would have been sent out.

The item on the agenda was once again '*Anything felt to be important and relevant to those present*'. The most important item that emerged, one which had consequent implications, was that mother's entire family had been lost in German concentration camps during the last war. We began to see how the lost good authority in this case was the loss of the ability to connect what were actually sequels of events across any period where continuity was tenuous. Such periods were real chasms of jeopardy for the family. When nobody turned up to the session, the temptation was to cancel it, since it felt so odd being at a meeting on one's own. The chasm of jeopardy was represented at that moment by the possibility of my succumbing to the temptation to cancel. If I had done so, the subsequent session – the sequel – would have been lost. The crucial 'therapy' was for me to exorcize my own natural inclination to cancel. The father had always thought the institution's care of his children was excellent but, paradoxically, had always condemned outright the court's care order – without which help from the institution could not have been enlisted in the first place. The residential staff, it appeared, had always noticed and commented on the exceptional non-communication between the two brothers. This strengthened our belief that the relationships in the family were a mass of gaps and consequent chaos. There had been a complete vacuum in the midst of both parents at times when links could only have been made by hanging on to orthodox tradition.

We wondered in the session whether the father's intervertebral-disc trouble had any symbolic meaning, in the sense that this disorder involves damage to the links of the spine. (It certainly got better.) He was quite incapable moreover of holding down a job with fixed hours, while monthly mortgage payments were to him an inconceivable notion.

It was felt that only the creation or the generating of ever-new linking crises associated with the children could enable this family to lurch its way through time. The marriage was held together simply by the children *being* children, and by the anxiety their conduct provided for *both* parents. The father's own parents had been divorced when he was six months old. Mother was maintaining a complete denial of the fact that her very early life had been split from her post-war, adult life by the Holocaust. Husband *and* wife were now coming nearer and nearer to feeling completely alone (though actually together), without any emotional knowledge of this chasm or of bridging. We all came to feel the relevance of the fact that the care orders had been instituted in the year when the mother had undergone her hysterectomy. When the children left home (if they *could* leave home), they would be leaving two parents who would now have a horrific gaping yawn of enormous boredom between them.

*

ATE If TPA's theory holds, then the effects of the Holocaust would be even more terrible than we know. Such deeds were done as perhaps cannot be mourned, because memory must reject them. When the unthinkable has happened – not in fantasy or nightmare, but in reality – then how can ordinary human beings come to terms with it? Perhaps it is asking too much and irremediable harm has been done to generation after generation.

*

TPA The working-through required in any particular case is unlikely to be distinguished by even the most skilled therapist hitting nails squarely on their heads, but will consist rather of discussions involving tentativeness, cynicism, sometimes excitement and often downright denial. These hurdles, which are to be expected, provide another reason why the understandable, relevant and agreed focus or agenda has to be adhered to and kept alive. There is no virtue in the therapist being on the right track if everyone else in the room thinks he is consistently mad and he gets no backing or support. The stated agenda or focus, whether involving two or several participants, or even one professional and/or non-professionals, is like a sheet-anchor; a kind of good authority in itself, allowing maximum freedom with maximum awareness. The freedom allows the possibility of discovering why one child rather than another in a family is *picked* as delinquent. On occasion family members themselves will become very animated at being able to see aspects of their own history being repeated through or in relation to their own children.

One mother, whose child, during his last week at the residential institution he attended, committed his first re-offence after a break of four years said, 'My father was killed on the last day of the war, V E Day.' This enabled us to see why she was unable to accept her child home long before; one loses one's authority at the *last minute*. She had been twelve years old when her father had died at the age of thirty-four; her husband was thirty-four when the care order had been made on her twelve-year-old son. These facts, with the understandings and their associated important feelings, therefore precipitated the possibility of a benign change, which duly came about against the background of a safe, trusted structure. For example the boy, when he found he did not like his first job, was able to change it for a better one with his parents' help, and not keep putting off the move.

Whilst working with and through a case, it is noticeable

that the delinquency itself holds fire – quite un-dramatically, no offences seem to occur and no huge anxieties take over. This gives rise to a subjective feeling amongst the professionals that they are working on the right lines. The hugest mistake, however, is to imagine that the case is completed just because there is no delinquency occurring. Unfortunately this error does happen, since the turnover of key professionals is rapid, and quite often a new key professional coming fresh to a case which is *not* giving rise to anxiety at the time will, quite properly on the face of it, elect to disband the therapy since 'Frank seems to have settled very well, and has kept out of trouble for a considerable period.' These are features that those with increased experience can be aware of, deal with when they arise, and even anticipate. This anticipation can extend to the development of such specialized intuition on the part of the regular therapists that they can anticipate the likelihood of a key worker leaving the case (perhaps by getting another job) be-fore the key worker himself has consciously considered doing so. (Magic!) These intuitions can become tricks of the trade, some seeming in retrospect to border on the bizarre.

A particular intuition-based stratagem, which I adopt occasionally, has an even less explicable quality. Its use becomes necessary when an important piece of under-standing has come to light, but then the relevance or im-portance of it is flatly denied by family members, who of course are the people most in need of that understand-ing. The feeling of the therapist in such a circumstance is generally one of disbelief that the client(s) cannot see what the therapist can see so clearly.

THERAPIST   So you smoke eighty cigarettes a day, do you?
You don't worry about cancer or bronchitis?
CLIENT   Oh no, it's not serious. It's only a habit.

When I first noticed these sorts of things I thought I had

missed something; now however I realize that this is Denial with a capital D, and calls for a certain technique or trick, which I call 'the least likely quarter'. This consists of looking around the room for what seems to be the least likely source of help. A father, who had complained about his burglar son 'taking nothing seriously', was asked about his own health. The man, a foreman dustman, said, 'I had a coronary ten years ago, and another one five years ago', and laughingly continued to say that he was due to have a third at any time. I, the therapist, was aware of my own exasperation, and asked whether he didn't think that the children worried about his and his wife's health. (The very overweight mother had recently returned from hospital after treatment for a serious kidney condition.) Father: 'Oh no, they don't know about hearts and things.' I turned to David, the eight-year-old son, and asked him what he knew or understood about heart trouble. David said, 'Oh yes, at University College Hospital they've got a ward full of taxi-drivers who've got bad hearts. All the veins in your heart get filled up with fat, and you just go pop!' At this point the father felt the hair-raising chill that we all did.

For some time in the particular type of therapy that I evolved for cases presenting as delinquency, I noticed how, over long periods, my ways of working remained static in their rate of return or value. Then, quite suddenly, periodic breakthroughs would occur, so that eventually the ground covered took only three sessions, whereas three years before it might have taken fifteen. There is therefore no empirical method of saying that such-and-such a case is finished because it has had the standard number of sessions. One should not be convinced that a case is finished simply because a child has left an institution, or a key worker has moved on, or, more deceptively, *that the delinquency has stopped*, or that no other siblings are being delinquent nor has any parent become ill. More and more themes and sub-themes could be uncovered, with more and more skeletons tumbling out of more and more cupboards. *Where* to stop? *When* is it technically appropriate to stop therapy in a case presenting as delinquency? Quite suddenly, as in all the stages of learning that had occurred to me and to those with whom I was working, the signal dawned. It became known as the Many Mansions syndrome. We realized that no one person or thing was ever going to signify that the case had been satisfactorily completed, but rather someone or something, by some sign, would announce that no one nor anything *would* ever announce that the case had been satisfactorily completed! This bears some relationship to the words of Jesus Christ: 'In my Father's house are many mansions: *If it were not so, I would have told you.*' [8]

I shall mention two examples. The first deals with a child who was on a care order; at the beginning of one 'maturer' session, when all delinquency had ceased and the professionals were no longer anxious, the social worker who represented the ex-delinquent's legal authority said it looked as though the mother was not going to be present this time, although she had said that she *wanted* to come to the session. When the hour-long session was three-quarters of the way through, the social worker again said that he was very disappointed in the mother, who had said she *would* come. The partial free-floating attention one develops in this work alighted on the discrepancy between the social worker's two statements. We understood the message: mother would have liked to have been with the people whom she had come to know over a period of many months, and who had helped her and her family, *but* although she would have dearly liked to have done so, life had to go on. It was rather like the situation when mourning has taken place following a death; the threads of everyday life have to be picked up again, and we have to do our best without the loved one. The case was not that the boy's mother *was* coming to the session, but that she *wanted* to come, which is quite a different thing.

In the second example there were three other professionals and only one member of the family we were concerned with at the meeting. Early in the session, as always, the chairman asked who else had been invited to attend, and heard that the mother and another sibling had been invited, but had chosen not to come. Ten minutes later, when we were each speaking our piece in turn, the son who was with us looked around the room and said: '*I* was invited.' This at first seemed a strange thing for him to say, but then we realized that we were being told something that should not have been necessary; in other words, the boy could not have been present unless he *had* been invited.

These Many Mansions examples are I am sure not contrived, but rather are unconsciously determined. As a confirmation that the Many Mansions syndrome was probably a valid tool, we noticed that discussions about cases at this stage produced a feeling in the professionals that these particular families had become 'ordinary' families, the type of family that does *not* have dealings with 'helping' professionals as a matter of routine – as do the families of delinquents. Somehow there is always a psychiatrist, a probation officer or a social worker being visited or visiting in such a household, and that way of life is taken as the norm. This is in contrast to that of 'ordinary' families (hopefully, most families), where visitations and concerns of that professional kind are rare or unknown. Furthermore, it seemed to us unnatural to expect such 'cured' families or individuals to continue coming to the hospital or any other institution for further therapeutic sessions. In fact, the whole professional/non-professional relationship felt distinctly unnatural at this stage, and it was arranged that any subsequent contact should take place in the homes of these now 'ordinary' families. In their wish to follow-up for purposes of research, the tables were turned – the professionals would now be helped by the non-professionals.

I have stated previously that the cessation of de-

linquency *per se* is no criterion when considering cessation of therapy. Certainly, however, the *inhuman* quality
stressed in Chapter Seven, which is present from time to
time or constantly, can be seen to quit the 'patient', so that
he becomes *dis*possessed either constantly or most of the
time. This quitting phenomenon is indeed an early
indication that it may be time to start thinking about
ending the therapy, provided the other signs are present.
The therapist must take care to ensure that projections
are not beginning to move out only in order to move in
elsewhere. The objective experience of dispossession,
which is very rewarding to see happening in a delinquent's – now an ex-delinquent's – face, is depicted by
Carlyle, when quoting the Prince de Ligne. The latter
was describing in 1783 the 'Great Majesty' that he had
only managed to see in portraits and hear about in
reports for ten years, which at last he now saw again as
the so-human Frederick:

> His eyes are too hard in the Portraits:
> by work in the Cabinet, and the hardships
> of War, they have become intense, and of
> piercing quality; but they softened finely
> in hearing, or telling, some trait of
> nobleness or sensibility.[8]

As I have stressed often, the parents of the delinquent
will be found to have lost, or never to have possessed,
their own good authority whilst they themselves were
children. One might ask, how then is it that the delinquent doesn't caricature *all* the hundreds of loss of good
authority themes from which his parents unwittingly
suffer? The answer, which only dawned on me very
gradually over the years and literally thousands of hours
of therapeutic sessions, is that *theoretically* it very well
could happen that the delinquent (once established as a
projectee) might potentially caricature all the hundreds
of possible themes. In other words, the delinquent is

probably the unconscious surviving evidence of the inter-generational natural history of the loss of authority in his family. The situation is somewhat reminiscent of the Ten Commandments given by God to Moses on Mount Sinai:

> For I the Lord thy God am a jealous
> God, visiting the iniquity of the
> fathers upon the children unto the
> third and fourth generation of them
> that hate me.

The iniquity in this case being the failure to provide good authority models for the next generation when it comes into its own age of authority.

With further reference to iniquity, it is well known that law-breakers *do* tend to specialize in certain crimes, and become known as 'rapists' or 'burglars' and so on, but sometimes they diversify their interests. I have come to understand why it is – if not how it is – that on a deeper level a delinquent presents, as a tight or compressed package, *relatively few* themes, where one might have imagined that, in theory, he could caricature hundreds. It seems that *only those themes that matter, in terms of an unconsciously scheduled catastrophe in the near future come to the surface.* It is as though the delinquent is immune from the projection of irrelevant loss-of-authority themes, or that they are not being projected towards him. I have not yet been able to discover more than half a dozen themes and sub-themes in a case, in spite of the fact that there may have been hundreds of lost-authority themes latent in the parents. It is, I am sure, not simply a lack of skill or a lack of time, but rather that the half-dozen themes were all that were presenting and all that it was necessary to detect and understand if the catastrophe on the time-horizon were to be prevented.

Michael and Enid Balint and their followers, meeting in seminars with general practitioners to discuss some of their cases, have capitalized what is probably the same phenomenon in a different guise.[10] These doctors (I used to be one of them in the mid 1960s) were encouraged to bring only the material which was in their heads, and not to worry about case notes or about details they had forgotten. The maxim that evolved and was found valid is that only the important and relevant facts 'gel' and come to the surface, in turn producing necessary under-standing, and therefore providing concrete help in respect of the case under discussion. In the same way, then, only the *relevant* themes of lost authority in a family with its delinquent member would gel and come to the surface in the delinquent.

Epilogue

TPA It has taken a long time to write this book – the temptation to wait until I understood more constantly competing with my wish to finish it. It seems reasonable to elaborate on one aspect, the importance of which has emerged late in this book's preparation. That is the predictability of delinquency and loss of structure.

I have stressed how the parent(s) of a delinquent will *always* be found to have lost his own parent's (or parents') authority during childhood. However, it also needs stressing that one cannot be certain that if, say, a child loses his father, such a child will necessarily parent a delinquent or even lose authority in any way over any of his/her own future children. That is, there is retrospective, but not prospective certainty. My inclination none the less is to believe that the phenomenon *will* be found to occur in this prospective sense; if this is true it is obviously a terribly serious state of affairs.

For instance, I have recently found in researching control subjects, that is, parents of non-delinquents, that although such parents may not have lost their authority over any of their own children in any sense, such parents occasionally will be found to have lost *their own* parent(s), for example, by death, when *they* were young. In these control cases I have discovered two phenomena which do not contradict the validity of a prospective possibility, but rather point to further areas that perhaps are worthy of investigation. First, in these cases I have often found that the grandparents lost *their* parental authority during *their* childhood, possibly implying that the need to mourn has been carried through to today's parental generation and been worked through to completion there, hence sparing the next generation. Second, the *siblings* of such parents are sometimes found to have lost their authority over *their* children, for example, the cousin or cousins of a non-delinquent (whose parents lost their own parental authority) might well be delinquent.

In a particular case, the father had not lost his authority over his child in any way, but his own father had deserted when he was ten. The present-day father's brother now had three children, all of whom were in care after constantly running away from home. It was found that the father's mother had been pregnant with his brother at the very time that the grandfather deserted the family. Probably therefore it was the brother who was most vulnerable in terms of being identified unconsciously with the business of the deserting grandfather.

It is fairly plain to me that the now prevalent rising tide of delinquency, cancer, obesity and alcoholism must be due in part at least to the insufficiently mourned 'awayness' or death of fathers during World War II. However, if I were wrong about this, then we could safely ignore the following:

Do we really want to make divorce for the parents of minors easier?
Should we not make parental suicide illegal?
Should we allow the immigration or emigration of minors without their parents, or for that matter should

we allow the immigration or emigration of parents without their children?

Should we allow single mothers to marry even the other parent before their respective children reach the age of majority?

Should we sterilize the children of divorcees, widows and widowers?

Should we allow minors to marry, or the grandsons of divorcees, widows or widowers to become president or prime minister or king?

I often feel that what I see as a kind of pseudo-democracy, comprising the premature trusting or over-respect for juveniles and lunatics, will reap a grimmer harvest of cancer and chaos in the future of two genera-tions hence, (The fifth) than a simple and easily envisaged totalitarian backlash.

I wonder whether failure to mourn is the supreme de-linquent.

*

ATE   Coming upon an idea from a new angle is as disconcerting and disorienting as finding that your house has been turned back to front when you weren't looking.

The outrageousness of the suggestions set out on pp. 189–90 caused me to protest: '*You can't say that!*' I had to follow the thread through several mazes to find that the house was still where it had always been and it was my perceptions that were at fault.

Putting aside the *idées reçues* of the present day, the niceties of the *bien pensant*, and peering again at the contentious propositions, they take on a familiar, if almost forgotten form – four-square and sturdy.

Do we really want to make divorce for the parents of minors easier? Take bad marriages. Undoubtedly they cause great unhappiness, but misery – even marital misery – is part of the human condition and all the lenient divorce laws in the world will not change that.

Everyone 'knows' that a happy marriage provides the best possible environment for bringing up children, but few are prepared to consider that an unhappy marriage provides a better environment than no marriage at all. The mistaken view that everyone (parents included) has a 'right to happiness' has led to increasing chaos as everyone flies off in all directions in pursuit of this mirage. The 'happiness' of individuals has never contributed much to society. Happiness is an accidental by-product and should not be seen as a goal.

Should we not make parental suicide illegal? Suicide was illegal until fairly recently. While the strictures of the law assuredly did not prevent people who felt so inclined from laying violent hands on themselves, the mere existence of this prohibition was a sign that society cared sufficiently about its members to *disapprove* of them doing so. The 'climate of opinion' is immensely powerful for better or for worse, and the concept of 'freedom' is frequently grossly misunderstood or misused. Does the knowledge that he will not be rebuked or punished for attempting suicide make the depressive feel much better? The apparently insane proposition that parental suicide should be banned, at least until the children come of age, is the simplest possible reminder that the death of a parent is deleterious to children, and that the deliberately chosen death must be more so.

Should we allow the immigration or emigration of minors without their parents, or for that matter should we allow the immigration of parents without their children? In the late fifties and early sixties, when West Indian immigrants were first encouraged to leave home and travel to Britain to work, nobody seems to have considered the possible ramifications. Anxiety has centred on the question of assimilation, with some afraid that it would not happen and some terrified that it would. What should have been exercising the minds of everybody concerned was the consequences of separating parents from children and children from parents – the loss of authority and the resulting inevitable delinquency in the grandchildren.

Should we allow single mothers to marry even the other parent before their respective children reach the age of majority? When a single parent decides to marry, the implication is that two parents are better than one – which is doubtless incontrovertible under proper circumstances. When, however, a single parent does marry, this can unconsciously devalue the child's previous experience. If he comes to believe that his mother cannot exist without 'help' he might grow to caricature what he sees as her dependency by being unable to help himself, by himself; he might be unable to hold down a job, give up drinking, etc. His early experiences and perceptions might be distorted by his translation into what is widely regarded as a 'better' state.

Should we sterilize the children of divorcees, widows and widowers? This startling suggestion is purposely designed to shock (I hope), so is in the same class as the question of parental suicide, that is, it is intended to bring home the nature of a problem in as immediate a fashion as possible.

Should we allow minors to marry, or the grandsons of divorcees, widows or widowers to become president or prime minister or king? Again this revolutionary sounding question is the merest common sense when you come to investigate it clearly. Calm stability is a most desirable quality in a leader and is likely to be lacking in a person who is unaware of precisely what it is that he lacks, or indeed that he lacks anything at all. Someone who has inherited a loss of authority is not suited to a position of high authority, no matter what his other qualifications. (TPA says it is horrifying to think of such an individual acquiring more and more 'outside' authority to try to replace that which is lacking 'inside'.) Primitive peoples were extremely fussy about who married whom and who should be permitted to take over the leaderships. Our more relaxed attitude to these matters which may, on the face of it, seem commendably democratic, is really rather dangerously careless.

*

I have been thinking about and discussing this book for what seems ages now – in fact in common with perhaps millions of others I have semi-consciously been aware of and puzzled by its message before I ever met TPA. I have been peering and prodding at the structure of the central theory and closely examining any bits that fell off in the process. It has, on the whole, stood up well, occasionally seeming to take on different lineaments as I approached it from different angles, but in the end retaining its basic form. For instance if the word 'authority' (which is presently unfashionable, being widely interpreted as blind domination, bossiness or nanny-like fussiness) is replaced by the word 'caring' then the whole concept appears in a different light. Unfortunately the word 'caring' currently has cant associations and means to many people nosiness, hypocrisy and nanny-like fussiness. One purpose of authority is to look after those in its charge, but as the word 'freedom' has such popular importance, 'authority' has assumed threatening connotations, and concepts of 'care' are more usually invoked (annoying different people according to their religious or political affiliations, or their views of semantics). The two terms, of course, should not be seen as mutually exclusive, but as complementary. The fact that both can now be used in a derogatory sense is confusing and irritating as one tries to hang on to their meaning.

Few people do feel particularly well cared for by the state, hence the cynicism with which the term is regarded. It is particularly muddling for the citizenry as one faction extols the virtues of self-help and another insists that we should rely on state benefits for the whole of our natural lives. Neither idea is particularly right or wrong, but they co-exist uneasily.

Once upon a time a great deal of invisible caring went on, which would not have necessarily been so perceived or described. Soldiers were housed and fed and clothed, and so were servants. The poorhouses and mental institutions or asylums were full, and while no one would claim that circumstances were ideal, people knew where they were – even if they didn't like it. While society and the state laid few claims to overt benevolence, then the populace, not having been led to believe that it would be carefully cared for from the cradle to the grave by outside agencies in a style to which advertising and the media – let alone the politicians – led it to believe it should be accustomed, was not infuriated and frustrated by impossible expectations; by the hypocrisy of empty promises incapable of fulfilment. The Victorians built prisons with cells designed for one inmate and, while the population was smaller, this does seem to indicate that they did not anticipate any enormous strain on penal resources such as we have today. The prisons now are crammed to overflowing with people who must, amongst other things, be cared for. These people, having got themselves into this position, are probably what could be described as inadequate – as is the authority or the 'missing' authority, which colluded in their plight. The inadequate authority might address the inadequate individual as follows: 'You cannot look after yourself properly. You need help. Right, we will help you not to look after yourself. You are not very good at looking after yourself, but we will be even better at not looking after you.' In a hellish sense *all* expectations are fulfilled in this way. More and more prisons are being built and will doubtless constitute a self-fulfilling prophecy. As people who were once contained in mental homes are 'returned to the community' to find a doubtful welcome, as more children leave home and fail to find work, so will the prisons get fuller – not necessarily because crime is increasing but because people must be contained somewhere, and somehow 'cared for'.

Every period of civilization has had its problems – frequently due more to the prevailing mores of the time than to acts of God or natural disaster – and they have all differed each from the other. The trouble is that what is known as the climate of opinion – which usually consists of a heavy fog – is so powerful that even the people who have formed it are quite unable to see clearly, and the rest of us are lost. It is difficult enough to stand back from present issues, and when they are further obscured by clouds of received wisdom it can seem impossible; while the clashing of ideologies adds to the overall confusion. If this book has appeared at times over-simple, it is because basic simplicities can disappear amidst increasingly sophisticated disciplines, and need to be restated, or even re-discovered. All sentient beings have always known at some level that structure – which can be defined as authority – is essential to communal living. The unscrupulous have always and doubtless will always capitalize on this knowledge and this is why it is necessary to isolate and reaffirm the proper, ordered sites of authority; to remember what service is owed to them, and what they owe to society. The rules are the same from the smallest to the largest unit, and the first rule is to be aware. And since life is inexorably subject to attrition, this awareness must first of all take into account the reality of loss, of missingness; of the need to acknowledge and understand what is lost, and if the loss cannot be made good, then of the need to appreciate and endure it without allowing chaos to slip in and fill the vacuum.

Appendix

Case Notes

Work with cases that both elucidate concepts discussed in the body of this book and highlight the artificiality of the classifying of delinquent types (to that end presented alphabetically)

Involuntary Absconding: 'I can't help it'

TPA This fourteen-year-old boy had been stealing cars and absconding from institutions on many occasions. He was well liked and well behaved in other respects but, when asked if he thought he could control himself, would reply that he *wanted to*, but *could not*. Over and over again he had been 'let off lightly'. One could see quite clearly that the time would come when judges, magistrates and authorities in general, despite having 'leaned over backwards' for a long time when dealing with him, would be bound to turn into the very authority figures that, it transpired, the parents feared and loathed. The boy's father was Lithuanian by birth, and the paternal grandmother was trapped behind the Iron Curtain. Since visits were forbidden, her son in England had not seen her for forty years. The family just seemed to accept the situation, and I was puzzled for a long time by their emotional blankness about this sad state of affairs.

I also discovered that the maternal grandfather had been killed on D-Day. Certainly the family's hatred of authority came through loud and clear. It was easy to see the way they attributed their hatred to the oppression they had experienced at the hands of the Soviet authorities in the father's case and at the hands of the British army authorities in the mother's case. (She blamed the army for the death of her father.) It was only when the usually very competent social worker seemed to imagine (quite incorrectly) that a probation order was more powerful in authority terms than a care order that we began to realize the vested interest this family had in pretending to themselves that *authority if it is to be effective is always authoritarian – even punitive.*

It emerged that the father at the tender age of fourteen had volunteered during the war to join the German army. (This is perhaps one of the reasons why the Soviet authorities still would not allow visits for the father or the grandmother.) He had volunteered quite on his own – his father was already dead and his mother had had to be away from home at the time. We began to understand that the father would become intolerably guilty if he were to face up to the fact that he had volunteered whilst his mother was absent. He preferred to believe that even if she *had* been at home, she could have done nothing to reverse his recruitment. In fact, in 1943 all that his mother needed to have done was to present herself at the recruiting centre and produce her son's identity card, which would show his date of birth. This would have been sufficient to force even the mighty *Wehrmacht* to give up its fourteen-year-old recruit. As it happened, when she *did* return home the boy had already left for the Russian front. Now, nearly forty years later, we could understand how the father unconsciously compelled himself to see that 'ordinary' authority (like that of his mother over her teenage son) would have been no match for 'authoritarian' authority such as that of the *Wehrmacht*. The fourteen-year-old grandson's inability to stop absconding caricatured a 'force mightier than his own', and his taking and driving away vehicles underlined the fact that all that was necessary would be the mild authority of the car owner, supposing the latter were to be sitting in the driving seat. This would be quite sufficient to withstand the marauding, more anxious-making authority of the thief himself. (He also, of course, accepted father's repressed guilt.)[1]

All Sorts of Offences

I saw this boy because staff wanted to understand why he was apparently so determined to get into any trouble that presented itself. I found that the patient was periodically enacting his father's unconscious wish to 'mess about', exercise his 'puer' as against his 'senex' and 'just be a bit irresponsible for a change'.[2] The patient's offences had become intolerable to others at school when he was fifteen years old. I discovered that the father had lost his own mother and stepfather when he was fifteen, never having known his natural father. Therefore, adulthood for father had begun somewhat early, suddenly and harshly.

Arson (1)

I had been asked to see this boy, but no reason for the referral had been given. It seemed to take ages to get going once we had met. I gave him some extra time, but in spite of this I still didn't really succeed in getting him going during the whole of the session. I thought the arson that had led to his conviction might epitomize a problem concerning 'minimal smouldering with the possible prospect of getting going or blowing up'. I gathered that he thought his mother had an ulcer, which of course can sometimes be dormant and then flare up into something more serious, such as a perforation.

Arson (2)

In a meeting with this patient it became clear that he would prefer to call his arson 'an accident'. Unfortunately for him, I felt that this was a rationalization. In fact, very likely he 'meant it' at the time, but just could not remember doing it. We went through the actual mechanics, as far as was possible, of how the fire had started in a car he had stolen and abandoned when its tyre burst. He said he had then seen it burst into flames while he was walking away. We realized that an expression he used while talking to me – 'out of his mind' – meant that he was probably identifying with his drunkard father, who had frequently been 'out of *his* mind'. We went on to discover that the father had committed suicide when he was losing his wife to another man. The important irony was that he hadn't thought that he was worthy of his wife (and this was fair enough as far as it went), but what he could not have known – what was 'out of his mind' – was that within six months of his death she would marry another drunkard, one who was a con-man to boot. His death therefore had made no difference whatsoever to the standard of life to be experienced by his widow.

Arson (3)

Barry – 'on his own' – had caused a fire in which a warehouse and its contents valued at half a million pounds had been 'burned to the ground'.

It was the 'on his own' and the 'burned to the ground' that caught my free-floating attention while discussing the case with Barry's social worker. His mother, it transpired, was a huge, unhealthy woman who suffered angina and for whom the surgeon had been waiting several months to perform a vital operation – waiting till she had lost sufficient of her sixteen stones. Barry and his mother fell out frequently. The latest episode involved his unwittingly locking his mother out of their home. She had become wildly angry and had broken down the door to get back into the house and physically attack her son.

It turned out that mother had been deserted by both her parents soon after her birth and I felt this had left its unconscious mark in at least two fatal ways, each corresponding to the themes of 'burned to the ground' and 'on his own' that I had picked up. In the first instance her bulk was a way of unconsciously stressing her existence in contrast to its denial by her deserting parents (a half-million-pound warehouse which did exist and then didn't is not forgotten lightly either); in the second instance it was realized that slimming is essentially something one has to do for oneself – only rarely are others able or willing to help actively in incarcerating the would-be slimmer and wiring up her jaws. Doing things on one's own – whether slimming or making one's way alone to a hospital appointment – was, it seemed, inconceivable to the mother. The aloneness was akin to the repressed feeling of having her existence denied and being left on her own as a baby. She actually complained that her husband didn't help her to slim. Moreover, it wasn't difficult to see why she was so furious with her son who had not realized that his gigantic mum was not 'not there' but was, larger than life, locked out in the back garden.

Sadly the mother died before she could be helped in her own right. Her son, though, was helped through a subsequent depression and was able to understand why he had committed arson. Until then, he had been very disturbed and baffled by his behaviour.

Sexual Assault on a Juvenile, and Breaking and Entering Premises Without Stealing

I was asked to see this boy so that I might try to understand the meaning of his offences, which were apparently disconnected. The themes represented were as follows:

Assaulting juveniles. This produces a dramatic response to the corruption or intrusion on 'innocents', including a determination on the part of all types of professionals to go to great and unusual lengths to eradicate the likelihood of a recurrence. *Entering premises without stealing*. This produces nil or very little effect, as against an actual burglary, which is much more likely to be noticed and may spark off a chain reaction in its wake.

On a deeper level, these themes had been thrown up because about four and a half years previously, at the time when the patient first began to get into trouble, his mother had pleurisy *or*, as the boy said in a throw-away, seemingly unconcerned fashion: 'She had something to do with cancer of the breast.' In discussing the case further with the patient, I came to the conclusion that the mother might well be suffering from a recurrence of her illness. She was a very shy, 'innocent' type of woman, who had no children of her own, the patient being an adopted child. As the discussion went on, I suggested a meeting between myself, the patient and his mother. His whole mood changed and he became quite upset at the very idea of his mother being asked to 'come near this place'. Consciously he could not tolerate the assault on his shy, juvenile mother, but like her he would prefer to think of her as healthy. In the same way, a person who inspects the premises after a break-in and who does not notice that anything is wrong unless something is missing, does not for one minute think that a thief has 'cased the joint' and will be bringing a pantechnicon the following night in order to clean the place out. I had to go to very great lengths to get the mother to go to her own but new doctor. Her husband at first seemed much more worried that his wife might be asked to undress for a physical examination than that she might die.

Accident-Proneness

This little twelve-year-old suffered from bed-wetting and soiling as well as being a chronic truant and thief.

The dominant theme, which I termed 'once something
has started it goes on', caught my free-floating attention
when I heard that although he had sniffed glue and had
brought glue into the institution where he was staying,
he still did not regard himself as a glue-sniffer – 'I would
not like to sniff again.' He apparently admitted that he
tended to go along with what other boys were doing but
he was *quite adamant* that even if he were offered a sniff
of some glue by his friends he would refuse it. I
wondered why he had to make such a fuss about that.

I heard that his truancy constituted a 'continuing
pattern of absences', many of which were 'supported' by
letters from his mother. Reasons for absence ranged
from 'tummy upset' and 'cold on the lungs', to 'transport
strikes', 'bronchitis', 'anxiety about his reading', plus
some other occasions which mother could not explain.

It was in a meeting comprising professional staff,
mother and child that the theme of 'it's one thing leading
on to another' really made itself felt. One of the procedures in the format of such meetings is that a brief account
of what happened at the previous meeting is read out at
the beginning of the new meeting. This is particularly
useful for people who had not been able to be present on
a former occasion. This time, after the minutes had been
read, the mother, when it came to her turn to speak, said
that she was fed up with hearing about a certain boy who
had been bullying her son. He had been brought up last
time and the time before and she didn't want him
brought up again this time. When it came to my turn to
speak I pointed out that since the mother had mentioned
the boy who had been brought up in the reading of the
minutes, several people had referred to this boy; that is,
the very thing which the mother said she did not want
had in fact happened. I wondered if it were possible that
this was the same as having lots of accidents (the boy was
sitting there with his arm in plaster) insofar as it seems
that previous accidents, in some almost magical way,
cause further accidents. Certainly one would imagine

that, having had one accident, one might be more careful and be liable to have fewer. Paradoxically the converse occurs in the situation known as 'accident-proneness'. (I must add that her son had been in hospital on several occasions with fractures, head injuries, etc. over a period of about three years.) Likewise the mother, by saying that she did not want the other boy discussed, had actually initiated the discussion, which would in turn be minuted, read out next time and possibly be discussed yet again, mentioned again, *ad infinitum*.

In response, the mother said that she found it extremely difficult not to say something about the other boy. She angrily protested that if she did not say anything she would just have to button up her mouth and stew. On further discussion we learned that the mother, prior to her divorce, had indulged in constant bickering with her former husband. Rows simply could not be allowed to rest. Mother since her divorce had achieved what she called 'peace and quiet', which none the less she agreed she found extremely lonely. It was not difficult to believe the social worker's later description of the eight-foot-high privet hedge round the mother's garden and the fact that she had voiced some vague fears of becoming a recluse. In other words, the boy's accident-proneness actually depicted the mother's inability to stop herself becoming involved in bickering situations, that is, perpetually dragging up former difficulties in her relationships. Alternatively – as her *only* alternative – it seemed she had to cut herself off completely.

Burglary (1)

A patient whom I, as well as many others through the years, had found very difficult to get through to required what could be termed an *extra* effort if one was to communicate with him or understand him. I felt intuitively that for a considerable period he had, by being like this, been the 'mysterious part' of his mother. I thought that on reaching sixteen perhaps he had unconsciously tried to expose the meaning as well as to withdraw from his role of 'mystery man', by making the role unacceptable and public, that is, by committing many serious burglaries out of the blue. Soon after he had embarked on this new role – which amazed all who thought they knew him – his mother was suddenly diagnosed as having cancer of the breast, which of course is another malignant mystery.

His incarceration, I thought, meant that he had unconsciously, guiltily absconded from having failed to continue in his unconscious role of carrying his mother's 'mysterious part'.

Burglary (2): *Bound to be Caught*

I was asked to see the patient, since it was felt he was acting in a 'paranoid' fashion. It seemed that the boy *did* feel he was being talked about, but I came to the conclusion that this was an introjection of part of his father,* that is, of his father's common sense, of which the father was not aware, and therefore couldn't use.

We deduced that the father ought to have been talking to himself about *him*self, since he had bad kidneys, rheumatism, a bad heart, a recent hernia repair and yet had not slowed down at work one bit, and would no doubt kill himself. We also realized that if the boy had reflected for one minute before attempting burglary, his common sense would have told him that he was bound to be caught.

Burglary × 3 and Theft × 10

This eleven-year-old boy had committed at least thirteen offences within the space of six months. It emerged that he

---

* That is, one receives projections; once received, from the recipient's point of view, these are called introjections.

had a tremendous wish to have that which he could not have.

It became clear that there was a strong desire on the part of all the family members involved to reconstitute original families. It was realized, however, that such a reconstitution would be impossible, since both of the boy's parents had now remarried, and both had new children from their new marriages. The new partners themselves had previously been married with children before the eleven-year-old was even born. The fact or theme of never managing to have that which was wanted (that is, the reconstruction of the original family) needed to be faced, since there were now several 'original' families. Somebody, inevitably, would have to lose out.

Mr A. and first wife
raised family *No. 1*

Mrs B. and first
husband raised
family *No. 2*

Mr A. marries the
former Mrs B.
They raised family
No. 3 (including
boy delinquent)

Mr A. and third
wife raised family
No. 4

The former Mrs B.
and third husband
raised family *No. 5*

The six adults had now produced five families of children.

Child Abuse (*1*)

On average I take part in psycho-therapeutic meetings concerning families 250 times per year; I have done so for say sixteen years. That is a total of approximately 4,000 meetings. These meetings are extremely structured and the first part of any meeting involves the election of a chairman and a clerk or secretary. The elections take on average one and a quarter minutes, but are seldom recorded; the clerk does not write, 'It took one and a quarter minutes to elect myself and the chairman.' Over a period of sixteen years, therefore, there is an unrecorded but actual loss of 5,000 minutes of discussion time.

About three times a year a great fuss is made at the election of the chairman and clerk – particularly in respect of the clerk. Quite serious arguments have developed, usually of what might be seen as a petty nature, with professionals putting forward reasons why they should not be clerk on this occasion: pressure of work, wishing to contribute more to the meeting without having to be concerned about 'writing things down', etc. On average these 'great fuss' elections take seven minutes, though on one famous occasion the argument went on for twenty-two minutes. It has been found that when the election takes as long as seven minutes it is duly recorded as having occurred, namely, 'It took seven minutes to elect myself as clerk and Mr X as chairman.'

It would seem therefore that in sixteen years the very apparent, that is, recorded loss of discussion time would take 336 minutes. So the recorded time lost in sixteen years is actually many times less *than* unrecorded *discussion time lost over the same period.*

It has been found that in nearly all cases where there is a longer than average – therefore recorded – election, there is some question of incest being a possible feature within the family under discussion. One only hears about the incest that one hears about; one does not hear about the incest that one does not hear about. Could it be that the incest that one does not hear about is many times more prevalent than the incest that one does hear about?

Child Abuse (2)

A fourteen-year-old girl accused her stepfather of having sexually abused her. It had already been noticed at a previous meeting that it had taken longer than usual to elect the clerk. On another occasion the meeting ran out of its strictly allotted hour of time without the next meeting having been arranged. A future meeting was however arranged outside the hour, but it was realized that this next meeting could not strictly be regarded as of the same series as the earlier ones – it was the first of a new series. It was seen that the meetings had 'committed suicide' and that they would have to be reconstituted, that is, they would have to be started on a new life. This model was seen to be exactly the same as was being used within the family. The stepfather was under suspicion of having abused his teenage daughter, but did not seem to connect a possible court case, with its attendant publicity *vis-à-vis* his past alleged offences (that was one life), with his future plans to stand for public office (his next life), which would without doubt be destroyed by any hint of bad publicity. The mother had married or cohabited on several occasions and in fact had sported five surnames, to my knowledge during her lifetime. The child herself had 'attempted suicide' many times and had surprised professionals by the new lease of life that she invariably took on on returning from hospital.

On interviewing people who have been apprehended and imprisoned for sexual offences against children within the family, they have very often confided to me how subtly the sexual activity both started and grew, to become apparently normal within the family, not assuming its usual sense of abnormality to the prisoner until discovery and publicity ensued.

Drug Abuse (1): Heavy Drug Involvement, Including Several Overdoses

I was asked to see this boy in the cells after he had been more extroverted than might be expected in the particular institution he was living in. The patient epitomized the position in which his father was placed at that time. The latter was endeavouring to start life again with another woman, having left his second wife. It seemed very probable that the father was going to find himself in the same ultra-boring situation in which he had found himself during his two previous marriages, and would be likely to feel suicidally trapped.

The boy's dyed yellow hair and 'buzzing' lifestyle were designed, I concluded, to achieve an 'anti-boring surprise effect'. I felt very despondent about the prospects of this boy and his twin brother, since I could not hold out much chance of anyone enabling his father to take back his own suicidal feelings of being *bored to death*, but being too old to change wives yet again.

Drug Abuse (2)

At first I found this boy rather dim and rather ordinary, but he gave small signs that made me realize that he was actually extremely bright. I also noticed that he talked a lot, in an idealizing way, about his drug-taking. Another theme that I picked up was his ability to make members of staff and his family nag him about his tendency to take drugs. I felt that he was 'being', in part, his mother. She also seemed, from social-inquiry reports, a very ordinary person but, I felt sure, was like her son, extremely bright yet in danger of being compelled to continue living a boring, depressing, 'skivvy-like', sometimes suicidal existence. His drug abuse, I sensed, was an attempt to nag the 'mother' inside himself and enlighten her to 'her' true potential; his ability to make other people nag him was an echo of the same aim. I felt I ought to meet him with his mother. Sadly, I didn't overcome the boy's objection to this notion and later heard that she had been admitted to hospital, having taken an overdose. Nowadays I would write to such a mother, offering to see her whether the son objected or not.

Drug Abuse (3)

I noticed that the patient who had been addicted to heroin was an adopted son; I had almost missed this important point. I was inclined to think that the two reasons that had led his parents to adopt him were: (1) overt: to have children; (2) covert: to avoid the pain of *not having children of their own* (this being akin to a pain-relieving drug – such as heroin). The boy and his sister were both eighteen years old, that is, they were their own legal authorities. The parents therefore were being returned, much older, to their former childless status, with no chance of further 'treatment' for the condition alluded to in (2) above. I suspected that the reportedly quiet and ulcer-prone father and the mother who suffered with her 'nerves' were in fact disguising a great deal of fear on their own and each other's behalf about the return of the pain that had threatened them eighteen years before. It seemed to me that the patient caricatured the above drama.

Drug Abuse (4)

This boy was referred to me by the staff in an institution where he had been found to be an extremely annoying patient. I felt that he was an expert, quite unknowingly, at doing things to people's minds, disturbing their concentration, distracting them from the job in hand and so on.

For this metaphorical crime the boy was punishing himself in like manner: he was 'smashing himself out of his mind' by taking drugs, thereby assuaging the unconscious guilt. However, since this was an unconscious process, I felt that it would be liable to repeat itself over and over. One could predict that unless the cycle were to be understood, and unless it was discovered with what he was identifying in his parents the only way he could break such a cycle would be to die.

Unfortunately, I never met the parents, they did not answer letters from me or the staff, and sadly, their son did indeed die soon after his release from the institution.

Drug Abuse (5)

I noticed that at first I had thought the patient was an ignorant, perhaps stupid, person; later, however, this was disproved. It became clear that the first impressions of him which were gained by people around him were invariably incorrect, as mine had been. Therefore, he must have often failed to know where he stood. Strangely, he had tended to boast that realism was a major part of his character. (Fancy thinking you know where you stand in relation to the world when everyone in the world has got the wrong idea about you.)

His drug-taking, which was usually in company, seemed to give him and his fellow drug-takers the experience of feeling (justified or not) of being 'on the same wave-length', that is, they all felt that their feet were on the *same* metaphorical *ground*, whether real or imagined. It was difficult to be certain what the origin of this dynamic was, since I had no opportunity to follow up the case by meeting his parents in the flesh. I suspect however that it may have had something to do with the fact that the mother and father came from families whose class origins were very, very different, and that only later, perhaps too late (since they were now divorced), did they realize just how *different* they were from each other on account of the dissimilarity of their *groundings* or 'wave-lengths'.

Drug Abuse (6)

The prisoner had himself asked to see me, and at first I found it very hard to understand why. Eventually I realized that his request was actually to do with something quite simple. He wanted me to put in a good word for him in connection with his possible release date. I therefore made an initial 'overall diagnosis' of a person who tended to complicate things unnecessarily. On further discussion it became clear that both he and the staff had feared that it would be extremely difficult for him to come off pills on admission to the institution.[3] However, to his and the staff's surprise this turned out *not* to be the case.

It transpired that he was identifying with his father, who was still working in spite of having had two heart-attacks. The father had countless complicated reasons as to why he could not and should not retire. I met the prisoner's mother and father, and it was interesting to note that the father indeed had no concept of cutting his losses. He was prepared to wait until retirement at sixty-five rather than at sixty.

My Father was a Drunk – I Don't Drink

This case underlines the distinction that needs to be made, but which is often not understood, between conscious identification and unconscious identification.

It was true, the father *was* an alcoholic, and the son, now imprisoned, did *not* drink to excess – or to anything approaching excess. However, when I passed through the unit often the young man (whom, I noticed, I could not like) would greet me loudly, would slap me on the back and rant on at me in an over-effusive, embarrassing *bon-ami* manner: 'How's that old Jag of yours?' 'Cheer up, you're not dead yet,' and so on. I realized that the only thing missing from this banter was *the offer of a drink*. It became clear that quite unconsciously the boy *was* after all identifying perfectly with his father's only method of socializing. It was solely the father's readiness to offer a drink that made him acceptable in the bar of a public house, and it was the same catalyst that had dulled the appreciation by the father of his own pathos and was ruining his health.

A Prospective Gaolbird

I was asked to see this boy because he had spent so much of his life in institutions, and it was felt likely that he would continue to do so.

I found that the boy caricatured his father's denied terror of crisis and of change. His father had left home at the tender age of fourteen, and had been fortunate enough to find a good, steady, living-in job very quickly. He could have become a waif or stray if he had not taken the chance of committing himself, or he could have been sufficiently unlucky to have been picked up by a Fagin, and to have gained 'unfortunate stability'. It transpired that the father had maintained this 'stability' to an extremely destructive degree: he had kept the same lowly job for years; he had not taken a larger house for his wife and six children, even when the local council had offered it; it was reported that the births of his six children had been far too much for his 'never-very-well' wife.

I felt it was worth noticing that the last child in the family had been born about the time when: the patient's sister was approaching the age that would entitle her to leave home. This would mean destabilizing the father's situation. At the same time the patient and his brother were making their first significant contact with the police. The father at this stage, then, was moving into a new and *insecure* position, and he needed help in facing this. Not only was there the loss of his children as they grew up and left home, but also the realization that his sick wife could not possibly continue to produce more and more new children in order to prolong the almost-institutionalized status quo in his family.

Our prospective gaolbird was the embodiment of this denial on the part of his father: he portrayed the evidence of how hard it can be to settle without a great deal of maturity, help and luck, as well as the error of denying the fact of growth (he was himself physically extremely small).

*

ATE TPA tells me there should be more in this chapter under G because some case histories have proved inaccessible – not to say lost. They were about a gambler and a glue-sniffer; he told me about them and I will attempt my own version of what I remember of the telling of their themes and problems. By chance I was reading W. Somerset Maugham's short story, *Portrait of a Gentleman*, which is about a gambler, when I started to think about the gambling boy. I have always thought of gambling not as a mortal sin, but as a peccadillo in the same sort of class as brewing illicit gin – an offence more against respectability and accepted mores of society than against actual virtue – and beyond that I have seldom given it a thought.

The gambling boy, whose chosen mode was playing fruit-machines, was strongly disapproved of. Everyone was thoroughly cross with him. Then, with a little digging, it became apparent that his father was the type of person who *could not* take a chance, and refused to consider taking a new job in case it did not work out. He would not even buy a new car in case that turned out not to be worth the money. His wife, thoroughly fed up with the constraints this placed on their lives, was planning to leave him.

Here is Somerset Maugham on 'John Blackbridge', who may be a real person or may not. He had

personal dignity, rectitude, humour and common sense. 'The amusements of mankind,' he says, 'have not as yet received proper recognition at the hands of the makers of the civil law, and of the unwritten social law,' and he has no patience with the persons who condemn the most agreeable pastime that has been invented. Namely gambling, because risk is attached to it. Every transaction in life is a risk, he truly observes, and involves the question of loss and gain. 'To retire to rest at night is a practice that is fortified by countless precedents, and it is generally regarded as prudent and necessary. Yet it is surrounded by risks of every kind.'

The father of the gambling boy had caused his son to inherit a mirror image of his own no doubt inherited loathing of gambling, and his hatred and disapproval were projected out into all those who had to deal with the boy. I think.

The glue-sniffing boy was the child of travelling people. They whizzed around the country working with zoos, circuses and safari parks, and everywhere they went they got themselves into messes. Then they moved on, never returned to sort things out and had a horror of 'going back'. Every time the problem boy was mentioned, words like 'going back' or 'lapsing' were used: 'Is he going back to glue-sniffing?' His mode of illustrating his family problem of not going back to sort out realities was unusually live and dangerous, but it did cause everyone furiously to think – which is the purpose of delinquency.

I think I've got it right, but it is a difficult notion – floating away as it does from one's mental grasp. The child unconsciously 'inherits' an already 'inherited' hatred or fear of gambling, or hatred or fear of 'going back' from his parent or parents, then this is projected into the outside world which then takes a conscious dim view of his gambling or consciously fears his reverting to glue-sniffing.

*

TPA *Indecent Assault on a Woman: Using an Offensive Weapon*

This fourteen-year-old boy could clearly remember events before and after the attack on a twenty-two-year-old woman, but could not remember the incident itself. It emerged that before the attack he had been discussing sexual matters with other boys at school – 'dirty' talk at school is of course common enough. He also mentioned how the other boys had teased him in a sexual way. The lack of memory of the incident itself portrayed the shared difficulty of the boy's parents in facing facts: they tended to fantasize instead. The mother was very confused about the difference between firmness and punitiveness. When it was pointed out that she had a family of seven children, which must have been difficult to cope with, she imagined this was an attack, rather than a statement of fact. Her husband was a man who, rather than face the difficulties of this world, tended instead to shrug his shoulders philosophically. Both parents thought that their son, in spite of total academic disinclination, could be a fighter pilot – the examinations along the way 'did not exist'.

The blotting out of the actual offence by the boy caricatured the area between fantasy and reality; in the secular world everyone is allowed to fantasize in a sexual way, *but* exercising those fantasies in reality is taboo. It was plain to see that the chaos in the family – resulting in the electricity and gas supplies being cut off at their home, and all the children having to be adopted or placed in care or fostered throughout a wide area of London – was due to the total non-appreciation of the difficulties and necessity of facing reality on the part of both parents.

Non-Accidental Injury to a Child

On discussion with a twenty-year-old father, I found that the background of non-accidental injury to his child possibly involved the wife, himself and the babysitter. Facts emerging included the information that the baby-sitter was being paid 17 pence per hour (the going rate being 50 pence per hour). On interviewing the patient I noticed an unwitting tendency to by-pass any complicated or difficult questions. It was simpler for him to say, 'I don't know,' than to try to make sense of something and then put his thoughts into words. For instance, when I asked him whose idea it was for him to see me, he said, 'I don't know.' However, on looking at the referral form I saw that it was he himself who had asked to see me. On further discussion I felt it probable that during a period of unemployment both the patient and his wife had become very depressed; when they became employed again their depressions 'lifted', but were projected into their baby. Babies, I think, when depressed are liable to damage, since their musculature becomes very lax and therefore does not protect their vital organs or their bones. (Contrast this with the archetypal happy 'bouncing' baby.) My opinion was that neither the patient nor his wife was capable of thrashing out complicated details inherent in any relationship, but were by-passing these by the 'I don't know' technique. Therefore more and more unresolved issues were piling up in a most depressing way.

I didn't think that the child had been actively damaged by anyone, but the results were every bit as serious as if this *had* been the case. If the child was being looked after by someone who was herself being treated badly (that is, the babysitter), he might not be lifted up as gently as was needed, taking into account his limp and therefore non-protective musculature. I was interested to realize that this child-abuse case, by its very nature, incurred a 'no stone left unturned' approach by the professionals involved, as distinct from the patient's 'don't know' lazy technique of by-passing difficult problems. The patient told me that his mother had been institutionalized as a child; that his father had been beaten when a child by the grandfather; and that the grandfather in turn, when a child, was said to have been beaten by the great-grandfather.

Out of Control Truancy

A fourteen-year-old boy had been the 'man of the house' periodically, and had been very supportive to his forlorn divorcee mother. She had had six children and several miscarriages. It was very obvious how careful people felt they had to be about not provoking the boy into one of his huge explosions of destructive temper. The staff also found themselves worrying about what name they should call the mother by: 'Mrs X' or 'Miss Y'. Eventually it became clear that this atmosphere of touchiness was preventing anyone from talking about what were felt to be sensitive matters. It was a great relief to those present when at length the mother said: that she didn't mind whether she was called 'Mrs X' *or* 'Miss Y'; that of course she wanted more children, in spite of already having had six, and not having a man living with her at present; how difficult it was having an attractive fourteen-year-old son who would be able to give her a child.

We had not thought it would be possible to bring these important matters into the open, without the mother either exploding with anger or withdrawing herself from the meeting. The staff involved wondered whether, because of the need to keep these feelings hidden, the mother might have reproduced in an asexual way, that is, by producing a tumour. In subsequent discussion with this intelligent woman, the 'outlandish' notion was greeted by her not with scorn, incredulity or plain acceptance, but with a demeanour that indicated that we were confirming her intuition. She said, 'Yes, *and* I smoke like a chimney, *and* I had a phantom pregnancy when there was a man in the house.' At the subsequent meeting we also heard how, following the above discussion, she had sought the advice of her GP regarding a lump in her breast – and that this had been removed surgically.

*

ATE 'Breast lumps' are used by TPA as a form of shorthand for a larger query. When he is worried that the projections may be seeking another host in maybe another guise he will often ask whether the parent of the delinquent has noticed any such thing. Breast lumps are comparatively easily discernible and less threatening than some forms of cancer, being often susceptible to early discovery, treatment and cure. They are also quite common. Besides, the breast is the seat of nurture.

When witch-hunting was all the rage, a woman suspected of witchcraft would be stripped by the witchfinder and searched for any extra bodily excrescences. Any lump – probably a wart or a tumour – was regarded as rock-solid evidence of black magic. It was considered to be an extra nipple at which the witch suckled her demon, her hellish associate, and once uncovered, the witch stood no chance.

En passant, there are very few pure black cats in this country because they were all thought to be witches' familiars and also put to the stake, stoned or drowned. What I'm saying is – in view of the fact that by the clock of eternity all this was happening just a fraction of a second ago, we should not be over-confident about the validity of our present ways of dealing with those who appear to present a threat to society. Rationality offers no safeguard against idiocy. The witch-hunters, having defined the problem to their own satisfaction, were behaving perfectly rationally when they burned the offenders; and our present legal system, when its practitioners stick doggedly to the letter of the law, can have egregiously peculiar results.

*

TPA *Habitual Petty Crime*

Members of staff had commented that this fourteen-year-old patient seemed positively unable either to understand or to take advice. Things seemed to go in one ear and out the other; he appeared incapable of foreseeing what would be likely to happen if he were to behave in certain ways. For instance, he seemed oblivious of the near-certainty that he would be caught as a consequence of his many 'stupid' misdemeanours. When I met the boy's parents, I noticed that the father smoked five cigarettes during the session. On my asking him whether or not he feared for his health, he said that he *didn't smoke*: 'It was just a habit!' The bizarre dynamics (or unconscious facts) that unfolded were that he completely denied the first two years of his life, when he had been brought up by his natural parents. He declared that his adoptive parents *were* his real parents. It became clear that this father was a person who utterly denied 'starts', and that this attitude stemmed from his denial of his first two years of life. Therefore it seemed, quite literally, that he denied his cigarette-smoking because 'he had never started'. The presenting delinquent was identifying with his 'start-denying father', who seemed at the time to be heading straight for a serious respiratory condition. I discovered two weeks after this interview that the father had lung cancer.

Rape (*1*)

(Town, outdoors – where typically the victim screams – or should scream)

This patient's rape offence took place in the city. Therefore there was a fair chance of his being caught, or of his victim being rescued. I felt he had a need to get things straight – his victim had yelled and screamed from the onset of the attack. It was interesting to discover that he described his mother as being 'as twisted as a corkscrew'. On the other hand his father, who had died after breaking his back ten years previously, epitomized 'straightness', being lost and as yet unmourned. I felt that his rape offence could be equated with a wish-fulfilment. In other words, I suspected that unconsciously (and accurately) he had picked a woman in a situation where she was liable to 'put him [his mother] straight' in so crushingly forthright a fashion as to be almost refreshing.

Rape (*2*)

It was impossible to ascertain who the referring agent was, or the reason behind the referral. I simply received an unsigned note from a staff member, asking me if I would 'kindly see Mr X'. On meeting the patient he and I agreed that it might be profitable to understand something about the rape for which he had been imprisoned. His tremendous difficulty in managing to concentrate long enough even to remember what exactly had happened during the offence became very clear to both of us. He put forward tentative suggestions that maybe he had 'done this', or maybe he had 'done that'. The quality of vagueness that he felt in relation to the incident was almost tangible to me as the observer, and frustrating to the patient. We decided that he had become a caricature of his mother who, it transpired, was vague to an absolutely maddening degree – so much so that quite severe hardship had resulted in the family, especially to the younger siblings. Mutually, we began to feel that perhaps the aggressive element in the rape was a product of intense retaliatory feelings towards the *vague* (reminiscent of his mother) erotic feelings, which he himself remembered having had towards the woman before the attack. He wanted to kill his (mother's) vague feelings and to come (get his mother to come) clean.

Rape (3)

(Country or indoors – where typically the victim is silent – or should be silent)

In discussing this man's case with members of the prison staff, it became clear that he simply did not realize how glad people were to see the back of him – he got on their nerves. Although they felt that they actually had been violated in this way, they were incapable of saying so until after he had gone from their presence. I felt sure that the patient did not realize the effect he was having, and I also felt that there might well be some connection between this fact and his actual rape offence. Later, in discussing the man's relationship with his wife, we noticed that he had asked her quite casually, to bring to the prison on the next visiting day various materials, books, radio batteries and so on, to the value of about £8. He had fondly imagined that the total cost would have been about £2. We felt, in discussion, that it would be worth meeting the wife on her next visit in order to ask her about the possibility of a mutual collusion in this unwitting financial 'rape'. We could see quite clearly that if he were treating his wife like this, in many contexts (notwithstanding his actual rape), then his relationship with her, though good on the surface, might very possibly have flaws that would eventually cause the family, with its three children, to crack open.

Sexual Offence (*1*) : Sexual Offence on a Nine-Year-Old Boy

I was asked to see the patient because staff were concerned about his offence and his shyness. Having discovered that he was an illegitimate child, we gradually perceived that: (1) his natural mother had been too timid or too shy to keep him against the inevitable scandal and her parents' opposition, and (2) on the other hand, his 'unnatural' or adoptive parents had braved possible ridicule about their own infertility when adopting him. The shyness resulted from his identification with his natural mother, whereas his unnatural act with the nine-year-old boy was an identification with his 'unnatural' or adoptive parents.

Sexual Offence (*2*)

In discussing various things with this patient, it became clear to me that it was the mind-sticking indelibility of his sullied reputation following sex offences with children that was the principal feature or theme.

On asking about his family, my free-floating attention caught a nuance of history, this time in connection with many of his relatives, close as well as distant, who had had TB. On closer inquiry it transpired that his doctor-hating mother had a severe cough of some duration. I envisaged in this patient the personification of the old wives' tale of tuberculous sufferers being sexually over-active as well as the bringing-together in him of the old stigma of having TB, all topically depicted by his becoming grotesquely marked by the current stigma of being a child-molester.

Sexual Offence (3): Bizarre Sexual Offences[4]

This sixteen-year-old boy was known to be in the habit of stealing women's underclothes from washing-lines, and even of entering private homes and institutions for the same purpose. On a few occasions he had indecently exposed himself. It became clear that he was the same age as his father had been when the latter's elder brother had committed suicide. The delinquent's own older brother was liable to go blind quite shortly if certain surgical procedures were not successful. It gradually emerged that the father, at the age of sixteen, had felt totally unable to talk to his suicidal older brother and to take him under his wing. My colleagues and I were actually becoming involved in an unconscious wish to turn the clock back; to give the father a second chance (living through his younger son) of saving his dead older brother by proxy. It would have been essential for the father to have been his older brother's confidant, because it was said that the grandmother was a weak woman who had never been 'any good' since the death of her husband (the grandfather of the delinquent) six years before the suicide. I should mention that when these understandings began to unfold, it became possible for the present-day older brother to behave more sensibly. He had been warned by the surgeon about the danger of losing his sight. He was not to gad about going to discotheques every night, but was to take things very easily if his corneal grafts were to be given a chance to heal. There was little doubt in my mind that we might well have witnessed history repeating itself in the form of the suicide of the present-day older brother if the first corneal graft had failed and left him virtually blind.

Shoplifting

An addiction to shoplifting on the part of an eleven-year-old boy was found to epitomize his mother's inability to stop farming-out some of her children to friends, relatives and local authorities. She did this, it transpired, in order that she could take proper care of the two or three children who remained with her. This exhibited exactly the same dynamic as the shopkeeper who, unable to do two things at once, couldn't keep a sufficiently sharp eye on potential thieves at the same time he was serving customers. This case is important in that such a mother would commonly be thought of as bad, or rejecting, *but* she was actually unconsciously, compulsively and repeatedly reproducing, then consciously finding reasons for moving a child out of her orbit because only then, in her unconscious view, could she possibly be a good mother to those remaining. The mother's siblings had been separated during the war years: the grandmother had felt able to look after her two babies, but the older children had had to be evacuated.

Silly Offences

This illegitimate young patient identified with his natural parents who 'did not think'. Sadly, I felt that this was the only thing the boy *had* inherited from them. He had never known them, but his unconscious notion was that they had not thought that a pregnancy would result from their intercourse. On working through all that had come to light, we eventually agreed that he would be well advised to relinquish, if somewhat sorrowfully, this one and only legacy from his natural parents. After all, if they had been 'thinking' people, the boy himself wouldn't have existed.

*

ATE   I was curious to know what the 'silly offences' were –
'wasting police time and walking old ladies' dogs without
their owners' consent or knowledge.' No malice intended
– just thoughtlessness.

*

TPA   *Someone to be Frightened of*

A boy who had been on the fringe of involvement with
extremely violent individuals in the past asked to see me
because of his fears of getting more deeply involved
unless something were done about him. His mother had
given birth to him when she was fourteen. She had been
abandoned at birth by her own parents, as had two older
sisters previously. I sensed that he was harbouring
maternal projections of tremendous hatred against *very*
bad parental figures, by which I mean neglectful or
rejecting figures who not only reject but imagine that
they have got away with their neglect. The boy's mother
had since met these parents who had abandoned her, and
on the face of it got on very well with them. The kind of
crime that I felt the boy would become involved in,
would be acts which involved cold, business-like violence;
he himself would not be directly involved, but was more
likely to direct those associated with him towards violence.
He would be able to distance himself as the grandparents
had distanced themselves from the fact of their actual
though denied violence in rejecting their own three
newborn daughters. It appeared to me essential that he
should at least make a sincere effort to convene a meeting
between his mother, himself and me in order to give her
the opportunity of taking back these projections. By
return of post she replied she was 'leaving the country'
but, as often happens when a parent has at last been
offered such an opportunity, her son's anxieties subsided,
and since his release he has avoided further trouble.

Stabbing

This army man's wife had left him. Some days after her desertion he was attending a drinks party, at which two girls began to tease him about what they suggested was his sexual ineffectiveness in respect of his runaway wife. On his getting angry with the girls, his mates threw him out of the party. He went home, but got into more and more of a rage, eventually grabbing a knife, going back to the party and stabbing both girls. My understanding of this offence was that this man portrayed a difficulty in allowing himself to be aware of provocation, and as a consequence had been unable to take necessary avoiding action at an early stage, before the provokers got too carried away with the excitement of their provocation and, therefore, before he eventually reacted violently. Painfully it emerged that the patient, at the age of thirteen, had lost his father through lung cancer and bronchitis, caused, according to the patient, by his father smoking at least sixty self-rolled cigarettes a day, combined with his job of spot-welding in a fumey atmosphere. I felt that this man had been denying the even more painful psychic truth that if his father had not continually provoked his lungs in this way, *he need not have died*. The denial of this 'if only' type of truth has to apply across the board. That is to say, it had to apply in every similar context otherwise the particular issue of father's death would break through to his son's consciousness in a devastating fashion: he would be thrown back into realizing the painful fact that *father need not have died*. As it happened, he was having exactly those 'if only' feelings in respect of his own offence, and was bemoaning the fact of the loss of his job, of his wife and of his reputation – all because of a lack of resistance or ability to realize and deal with the presence of provocation. (I might mention the game that children love to play if they get the chance – poking a wasps' nest. No doubt they gain the satisfying learning experience of what constitutes too little or too much provocation and what can be done to avoid the results of the latter. It might even be seen as sadistically comical to watch children who come unstuck when they get stung because the provocation went too far, plus the fact that the wasps could fly faster than they could run.)

Handling of Stolen Goods

I noticed that this patient had an ability to make me know and care about him, but that he didn't seem either to want to know or to care about himself. His self-mutilation and very heavy drinking underlined my notions that he didn't seem to mind damaging himself, and that he had a tendency to forget himself. In discussing his background it transpired that his parents had abandoned him when he was very young: they didn't want to know about him, nor did they care about him. He identified with his parents by not seeming to want to know himself, nor to care about himself.

His offences involved the handling of stolen goods, which highlighted his apparent non-awareness that others might get to know that he had been involved in the transfer of these stolen goods. It was as though the idea of anybody being capable of deduction – knowing where the goods had come from, whose hands they had passed through and where they might be going to – was foreign to him.

Streaking

The young man had run naked across a playing-field whilst a game was in progress. This was found to depict in caricature or joke forms[5] his mother's need to know when it was appropriate for her 'to run for her life' (figuratively or literally) from her awfully violent but awfully wealthy husband. It is seemly, for instance, to run out of a burning building with no clothes on (newspapers often mention such fugitives – 'naked' or 'only in her nightdress') but it would be excruciatingly embarrassing to find one's self outside one's house, naked, and to realize at the same time that the fear of fire had been groundless.

Taking and Driving Away (1)

The patient epitomized the need to transform the mundane or ordinary into the 'special'. His indulging in the offence I saw as getting into *a* car which is *the* car of its owner. He was identifying with his father who, on returning from military service in Malaya, found his fiancée, Elizabeth (*the* Elizabeth), married to someone else, although they had kept up a correspondence whilst he was overseas. On the rebound, the father got the patient's mother pregnant, and like a 'good Catholic' he married Elizabeth number two (*an* Elizabeth). The patient, if he had not been conceived, could have allowed his father to get over being jilted by his 'special' Elizabeth, number one, and eventually to marry another 'special' woman (say Susan), *but* of course the patient would not then have existed.

Taking and Driving Away (2)

I was asked to try to understand the meaning of this young man's many offences of TDA. It transpired that the patient's four grandparents had very poor marriages, but that these had survived for considerable periods. According to the boy, 'there were no objections'. His own parents had a similar marriage, which was again characterized by mutual 'no objections'. The patient was possibly another man's child, but his mother's husband at the time of the boy's birth was said to have raised 'no objections'. The earlier reporting of the patient's indecent assault on a twelve-year-old girl, when he himself was fourteen years old, occurred as a result of her father's having gone to the police. He did this, according to the patient, in spite of the little girl having had 'no objection'; she and the young man were in fact still friends at the time of my interviewing him.

It seemed apparent therefore that to him 'no objections' was a theme charged with many hidden implications. He needed to define clearly when and where an objection would be made and who was going to make it. His experience had taught him that people who made 'no objections' were not to be trusted; that transmission of the 'no objections' theme could provide chronic unreal situations, as in the two marriages of the grandparents already mentioned, and could lead eventually to very dramatic reversals and let-downs which might now affect both his own and his parents' marriages and families, where there were still young children. All this now helped to enable some understanding of his many TDAs – often he had let it be known that he always became excited at the idea that he could drive off in any car he chose – Bentleys, Porsches, anything – and nobody would raise a finger.

Taking and Driving Away (*3*)

This little Gambian boy had been driving cars away since the age of ten. The fact that he absolutely lived for cars was paralleled by the fact that they were the mode by which he fell into trouble, that is, they were good *and* bad. It was important to learn that both his mother's parents had been killed on her first birthday. It would seem that from this point onward she had unconsciously denied the juxtaposition of good and bad: the death of her parents was a bad thing; the day being her birthday was a good thing. Unconsciously she had solved this conflict by avoiding debating in her mind whether something was good or bad in reality, and choosing instead the easiest rather than the best option.

It is not difficult to see how such a method of reality-testing – perhaps *just* doing what you fancy, rather than choosing what is best in the circumstances – is bound to bring dire results sooner or later. The boy in question said that he often took cars all on his own, and when asked how he had learned to drive, said proudly, 'I don't know. I *just* can, and I have never crashed one. I *just* like driving; I *just* nick a car, drive it around for a while, park it and hope it will still be there next day to pick up. If it isn't, I *just* nick another one.' I thought it sad that, when asked what his hobbies were, he said, 'Football, bikes and driving cars.'

Violence (*1*)

A twenty-year-old man had been transferred from another institution because of his extreme explosive violence towards an inmate, the latter having to go to hospital after being kicked unconscious by the patient, who had had to be restrained by other prisoners. I saw him because of his own worry regarding his 'usual non-anger' with associated 'loss-of-control tempers' after a long interval of such 'non-anger'. I found that he was identifying with and portraying his father, an industrial roofer ('the best in the business'), to an incredible, psychic degree. Such remarks as 'my father has an instinct for it. He's too fast for his labourers to keep up with; he can feel sky-lights under three inches of snow,' were being applied to a father who was almost blind.

The patient later said that his father '*had to go to work*' even if he had flu and there was snow on the ground, he 'had to', and 'not for the money'. I thought the father was satisfying his creative/aggressive instinct by sublimating it into work – and nothing but work.

The patient also said that '*if my father goes completely blind he will not be able to work*'. I realized, and suddenly so did the patient, that it was not *if*, but *when*, the father would become blind. The tragedy was that the father's 'instincts' were becoming better and better with the gradual loss of his sight, so that when he *did* lose his sight completely, his 'instincts' would be at their maximum, but would only have one other outlet, suicide.

Violence (2)

Staff were worried about this very strong man who had a history of extreme violence. I noticed his tattoos and that many had been taken off by surgery. In discussing the tattoos, he surprised me somewhat by talking of having some more put on. He reminded me a bit of Humpty Dumpty: how easy it is for an egg to fall off a wall, *but* 'All the king's horses and all the kings's men, Couldn't put Humpty together again.' Certainly, this man's violence had been of an explosive variety, and apparently all this conduct had resulted in tremendous remorse on his part. I felt that he caricatured a non-realization of how difficult repair might be following an action or inaction, such as destruction or non-contraception. The latter particularly referred to the fact that he had fathered a baby, to whose conception he had not given a great deal of attention and who was now being cared for by his ex-girlfriend on her own. On looking into his background it turned out that his mother had certain medical symptoms that she was tending to ignore, that is, she was unwittingly being extremely self-destructive.

*

ATE Body ornamenting has a long history. The ancient Britons wore woad – I believe to alarm the enemy. The men of some tribes spend their days painting each other, I can't remember why, although I read a work of anthropology attempting to explain this phenomenon. Maori and Australian aboriginal men and women are variously tattooed and cicatriced for ritual, religious purposes. Sailors used often to be tattooed, perhaps for a reason similar to the practice of wearing differently patterned knitted sweaters according to the place they came from – so that their drowned bodies would be recognized. Now many murderers are found to be tattooed. Perhaps this is a reverting to the primitive, aggressive urge to terrify an adversary or victim, although that doesn't explain why so many men have the name of a loved one indelibly marked on their bodies, thus giving themselves trouble when the loved one is superseded by another. Perhaps that is a symptom of a more amiable, though no less foolish, human urge – to proclaim an unchanging fidelity. In the heat of passion the lover has no real concept of the future.

*

TPA *Violence* (3)

The patient had asked to see me because of his mood swings. These periodic changes in mood always resulted in a fear of being violent and seemed to follow through, on occasions, to actual violence. When I mentioned that the session was drawing to a close he claimed to be having at that moment just such a change of mood and a feeling of rage. We realized that he was 'being', that is, internalizing, the adults who were important in his life, who passed him around like a parcel and had done so since he was three years old, apparently as the mood took them. 'Mum-to-Gran-to-Nan-to-Father-to-Mum-to Nan.' The violence belonged to his real self as a reaction to the 'moods' of his internalized fickle relatives.

Violence (4)

In discussing this man's previous violent behaviour it became clear that he felt no guilt at all about it. Apparently he felt 'good' about his violence, in that it was all out in the open. It was difficult to understand what this paradox represented, but on looking further into the family situation it turned out that the father was someone who did not interfere; he appeared to think that interfering was always a bad thing to do. On talking further to the patient about present goings-on in the family it transpired that the mother had cancer of the colon and would in all probability die although she had, in the patient's view, very probably discussed her early symptoms with her husband. The latter had 'not interfered'; he had not insisted that she should go to the doctor. The violence of omission was 'bad', clandestine, as opposed to the 'good, up-front' violence of his 'all in the open' son.

What Happens 'Normally'

Spitting
A very common delinquency which provides the idea for an experiment.

Take a tumbler and half fill it with water. Spend ninety seconds producing as much saliva in the mouth as possible without swallowing. Then swallow the saliva and take a large draught of the water from the tumbler. How acceptable to the experimenter was this procedure? Give marks on a scale of one to ten.

Half fill a clean tumbler with water, then collect as much saliva as possible in the mouth for one and a half minutes. At the end of the period spit into the glass of water. Then, using a teaspoon, mix the saliva with the water and leave for one minute. Finally, drink a large mouthful of the mixture and rate the acceptability of this second procedure on a scale of one to ten.

The spat as against the unspat saliva represents in physical form the fate of projections that have been put on to 'A. N. Other'.

Littering

A crime that is ascribed to things called litter louts. Is there anyone who has not strewn litter, who has in some magical way coined a distinction between their littering and the littering of the litter lout?

Wish to kill

There is no shortage of interest in situations where the husband or wife have killed or attempted to kill their spouse and/or the lover of the spouse. What are the driving forces which bring about the wish which without the balance of other forces of reality-testing might go on to action? When human beings have relationships, for instance get married, it is likely that they *do not* want to marry as well as *do* wish to marry; or that they wish to have relationships, simultaneously with the wish not to have relationships. If parents exist who have had to suppress this ambivalence, that is, only consciously own up to the wish to relate, or the wish to marry, and suppress the wish not to relate or not to marry, then where does the wish not to marry go? I suggest the child of this union might unconsciously inherit the dilemma. This cannot be a particularly rare phenomenon. Perhaps later on such a child in its own adult relationships can project the rejecting half of the inherited ambivalence on to his own collusive partner. The consequence is potentially disastrous, since the partner may now feel completely negative towards *him* and will often simultaneously experience consciously a huge freed positive quality and direct that for safekeeping towards a handy other. The first partner is now affected not only by the rejection *per se*, but by its making no conscious sense – until of course he or she reacts with anything from pathetic blackmailing collapse to violent upsurge, thereby falsely seeming to legitimize the rejection in the eyes of all – even perhaps himself. Most developing, that is, potentially close relationships, will to some degree go through this phase. Without society's traditional taboos and standards or without the catalyst of children, one must deduce that very many relationships will *appear* to have failed and to all intents and purposes this will, sadly, be the case.

Silent phone calls

Not many people I know have never received a silent phone call. Not many people I know feel the same way about them, nor do they seem to agree on a common strategy as to how to deal with them. There is no shortage of responses: fear, amusement, sympathy, annoyance, etc. Nor is there any shortage of suggestions as to how to deal with the phenomenon: take the phone off the hook, obtain an ex-directory phone number, shout at the silent voice at the other end, say nothing etc. The themes that readily come to mind about these phone calls are that they are untraceable; that there is, none the less, a danger that the unknown person may learn something about the recipient of the phone call, for example, the person might answer with his name and other members of the household might answer with their names, thereby unwittingly allowing the silent caller to build up a picture in his or her mind about the entire configuration of a household. One might try to ascribe motives to such a person, knowing full well at some level of consciousness that there is no way of validating such theories. One might actually argue with another member of the family as to how to deal with the phenomenon and end up in conflict based on someone and something that should mean nothing: a red herring jerking a family into opposition and conflict over something that should not exist. The very few patients I have come across who have confessed to making these kinds of calls have indeed come from families where at least one parent should not have existed and whose life situation meant very little in terms that I or the patient could understand (as though such a parent was indeed an irrelevance, a red herring). One can almost imagine a policeman looking for clues, looking for motives and putting aside explanations as being so illogical as to be dubbed red herrings. What if the perpetrator is the personification of such a fish?

*

ATE We had a spate of anonymous phone calls. One of the sons, suspecting that he knew this persons identity, eventually addressed the caller by what he imagined to be his name, thereby posing me with an interesting dilemma. Since the name was that of a friend of mine, should I apologize to him for my son's rudeness in supposing him to be mad enough to make anonymous phone calls? I imagine an anonymous phone caller would be outraged at being identified – for various reasons, not least the insulting supposition that he was who he was.

*

TPA ***On being unable to get through and/or being unreachable***
Surely one of the commonest and most painful predicaments facing couples is the business of non-communication, where each partner, possibly inheriting an

unconscious difficulty from their parents,* strives but fails to achieve the mutuality they most crave. The physically stronger partner is likely to feel or even act violently 'to get through'. The weaker of the pair is liable to withdraw, even finding him/herself deserting in order to make a communicative impact. Paradoxically, these attempts to get through simply make the other feel more estranged, more violent or more liable to withdraw or desert. How awful if one's armoury of communication only includes complete withdrawal. The above situation may metamorphose into a projected one. Child abuse may in fact be a caricature of the difficulty in getting through. A very small child who is developmentally unable to respond to threats, entreaties, cajoling, teasing, reasoning, spoiling, etc., becomes a licence to one parent or both parents in collusion so that they can vent their anger at their failure to communicate on the child. This preserves a tragic equilibrium in the couple, the equilibrium is the direct result of the baby sacrifice thrown into the non-communication maelstrom.

On not getting up in the morning

It is not uncommon to wake early in the morning, to lie momentarily, hoping to get back to sleep, when suddenly a worrying shimmer of thought intervenes, heralding a tossing and a turning for several hours. Often, when it is too late (because one has to go to work), the most delicious temptation to sleep at last sweeps over one. I suspect that the arrival of this somnolence is dependent upon the very fact that it is now time to rise. It seems to me that if one did not have to go to work the enticement to sleep would similarly not present itself. Where do all

---

*The mother of one such man had denied the fact of her pregnancy – it was not allowed to 'get through' to her. She said, 'I was so innocent in those days. I thought if I bound my tummy up tight it would go away – this went on for some months.'

those forbidden sleeps settle, up and down the country and no doubt throughout the world? Do they not reside in loafers – those we dub as being too lazy to go to work? Are the loafers not the custodians of our projected, hidden desires for one of those blissful slumbers, which our collective superegos might deny us for all time? Presumably the lazy stay-a-bed is liable to be the recipient of projections from his family of origin, whereby he can enact the impossible wish, which is perhaps in some instances exactly what his family of origin desperately needed to be granted but was simply not to be.

Goodbye – be good

A child who has learned that its extended absence rather than its presence means that it is good in the mind(s) of its parent(s) is in a tight and hopeless spot – and so is the next generation. It will receive no loving parental reward for being 'away-good', since loving parental rewards mostly involve contact or proximity. Since, however, contact and proximity destroy 'good-awayness', the child would immediately no longer be good. It is now bad and must 'quite justifiably' forfeit its loving parental reward.

How much tact then is needed to send a child to bed?

When an 'innocent' people is disinherited, do its future generations produce some no-need-to-hope (fanatical) individuals who may then 'enjoy' the results of having projected the assault, degradation, even murder of hope on to innocent airplane passengers (no hope if something goes wrong) or on to hostages (hope may be cruelly kept alive and might be found worthless after a searing, considerable lapse of time)?

The child who constantly appears in the night asking for a drink of water may not be as dangerous as the terrorist planting his bomb, but the intrusive, demanding, disruptive purpose is the same – 'remember me'.

*

ATE 'Criminality' in the domestic environment can appear in many guises, not merely the more obvious ones such as child- or wife-beating or neglect.

Once upon a time there was a midwife somewhere in the Balkans who worked out a nice little sideline selling poison to the village women. Many an inconvenient husband or unwanted grandparent was dispatched by this means and nobody suspected anything until the deaths mounted up to a really unusual extent, whereupon a few autopsies and exhumations took place and all was discovered. Nothing too odd about that; since women traditionally do the cooking, it is certain that before forensic science reached its present level of refinement many a disgruntled housewife will have had recourse to various substances – injurious to one extent or another. The really bizarre fact to emerge was that a woman had used the poison to murder her son because he had reached his twenties and it made her look old. Not a bad mother, she had sat at his bedside and sung hymns until he expired. That was a crime but then, on the other hand, it was positively criminal of the lad to grow up and indicate in the most graphic manner that his mother must be getting nearer to the grave than she cared to accept.

Then 'driving people mad' could certainly be construed as a crime and perhaps all members of families are guilty of this to some extent – leaving doors open or lights on, making the same remark at the same time every day that God sends, playing the record-player too loudly, going to wash the car the minute dinner is put on the table, sucking their teeth, smoking Havana cigars in bed – the list is endless and all these things cause people to react in ways, and say things, that they will regret. They lose their tempers and are forced to see themselves behaving in a manner that surprises them. Whatever happened to the kindly, tolerant creatures they considered themselves to be?

*

The Yorkshire Ripper – A crime of common interest

TPA The search for the Yorkshire Ripper presented me with a very special opportunity, to test the three-generational theory of delinquency and my knowledge of themes and how they present in professional contexts and to try to elaborate a family-tree for the Yorkshire Ripper. At that time there really seemed no prospect of his being caught, in spite of the enormous interest, cost and labour being expended. In this case, there would be no clues offered up by the delinquent *per se*, no mother nor father, no current family, no grandparents – nothing save the themes that one might find scattered amongst the newsprint and beamed over the radio and television.

The primary theme was obvious and soon sprouted sub-themes in my mind. The primary theme was quite simply, that 'he couldn't be caught'. Imagine a policeman trying to catch a criminal and giving any credence to this kind of clue. In what sort of family can one be sure which child is stealing the jam? Most assuredly, a family with a single child must be the answer. Where even if the jam stealing is never actually seen to happen, given that the jam is disappearing and that there is only one child, who could be stealing it? It must be that child. By reverse token, a family where a child is stealing the jam and in which it would be difficult, if not impossible, to find out which child it was, must be a family with more than one child. I figured that one of the Ripper's parents (probably his mother) was one of at least three siblings. (I thought that in a family of two children it might be relatively simple to deduce which one of a pair was committing this domestic crime.) Sub-theme (a) 'Somebody must know' – at least one of the three children of the Ripper's grandparents probably knew who was perpetually stealing the proverbial jam but said nothing. (b) 'Non-disclosure of *modus operandi*' – it would be silly for the Ripper's grandmother to come down to breakfast and announce that not only had jam been stolen but she wanted to know who had done it. This would at one and the same time confirm the ease with which such a crime could be perpetrated, and if it was already being done by one child, then if another sibling had a mind he too could indulge himself with impunity. No doubt, the police's reasons for non-disclosure of *modus operandi* in West Yorkshire went along those lines. They could not have wanted any murderously discontented West Yorkshire husband to be issued with a pre-packaged fall-guy. At the same time, should there be any further killings, they wanted to see telltale signs which could only be those of the Ripper himself and not some sign that they had fatuously planted on themselves by publicizing it.

(c) The third sub-theme comprised innocence and guilt – no doubt in a family of covert jam-stealer(s) the guilty and the innocent children will be merged since there is no possibility of discerning between the two. It was noticeable how the press described the victims as being from the red-light district on the one hand and being innocent students on the other, as though, somehow, it made a great deal of difference. It was stated over and over again, a covert judgement was made as to the upstandingness or low-down-ness of the victims.

(d) The fourth sub-theme was depicted in the two kinds of interest taken in the case: one kind, epitomized by the slow, patient, almost plodding, determined work of the police; their thankless, undramatic, unrewarding yet relentless efforts bizarrely matched by their opposite in the press with its extreme spikes of interest, particularly at around the time of the latest murder. I thought it likely that in quantity the police effort was unsung, massive and consistent, though a murder had not occurred for months. A derivative of this theme was that the press looked as if at any moment they might cast aspersions on the police; that is to say, that the interest of the press might come into conflict with the determined, patient, thankless interest of the police. I began to imagine grandmother slogging away with her jam-stealing family, patiently doing her best in spite of the great difficulties she would encounter at the hands of her unruly brood. She, this hypothetical grandmother, reminded me of the old woman who lived in a shoe, she had so many children she just didn't know what to do. The press I saw as being interested when there was something dramatic to be interested in, or when they felt it was time to show interest. I developed a picture in my mind of a tired, poor old woman looking after at least three children, being greeted by her husband who would have been away from the family, off for months, or nights, or years, in prison, in the pub, with the fishing fleet or on his lorry but creeping back dutifully, looking for an opportunity to ingratiate himself with his slogging spouse – 'What's the matter, dear?'

'It's nothing,' she replies.

'Don't tell me that there's nothing wrong, I can tell it from your face.'

She, knowing from former experience that to confide in her husband would simply give him the opportunity of showing to himself, if no one else, that he had a part to play in this household, which he rarely encountered, would continue to hold her peace until eventually, through tiredness, or plain inverse bloody-mindedness, she would confide that the children had been stealing the jam. She had now committed the awful error of disclosing the *modus operandi* and licensed her husband to exercise his promiscuous, spiky interest in his family for his own, if no one else's, gratification. Off he goes to the bedroom at three in the morning to wake his (at least) three children with the terrifying, crazy-sounding shout of 'Which of you has been stealing the jam?' No doubt on some occasions a child might look shifty, or guilty – the prostitute child, who would be leathered for her demeanour. On another occasion, a child might at three in the morning look puzzled, wide-eyed and innocent, wondering what on earth was going on.

'Don't you look so bloody innocent,' he would yell as the innocent was leathered as well, or as badly as the 'guilty' child had been on a former occasion.

The grandfather might leave the bedroom with the traditional sergeant-major threat to his company that if there were any more of this sort of trouble he'd have that man's guts for garters. It's the crafty old soldier who realizes that this terrifying oath is only an oath. Misdemeanours can go on unhindered if the perpetrator keeps cool and is not intimidated (I wondered whether this military threat had any resonance with the actual crimes perpetrated on the unfortunate women). As a result of the grandfather's intervention, all the children now know that jam-stealing is there for the taking and apprehension for such a crime is virtually impossible. No doubt grandmother hid the jam, no doubt the children found the jam, no doubt grandmother sometimes wondered whether the jam, which was now not where she had put it, may have been moved by one of the children or perhaps she herself had hidden it – where she knew not. I thought of grandmother becoming more and more depressed, more and more tired, and far from being helped by her husband; actually being in an even worse state as a result. Might she have committed suicide? Did the Ripper's mother know what was going on and could she have told the Ripper's grandmother? Somebody must have known who was stealing the jam. I came to see the Ripper's mother knowing and doing nothing about it, watching her own mother deteriorate into confusion, mental hospital and/or suicide. I wondered about the police and whether they might find themselves in an analogous state on the professional front, coping not only with the difficulty of the case itself but with the extra burden of the media's promiscuous interest.

So now I had a picture of a constant, hard-working, hard-driven grandmother looking after at least three very difficult children, with no support worthy of the name but periodic local interference with what she was trying to do and brutal treatment of her children by her mostly absent, but when present violent, husband. I imagined that the Ripper's parents, probably the mother, was one of these awkward children – the one who knew. She it would be who would need to recreate the self-same situation in her own family; she would require a 'not-getting-caught child', a child who would get away with it, who would never be apprehended, who would drive her mad. She also would have more than two children putting her through the same kind of hell.

Here I took a leap. I guessed that the Ripper was no longer under eighteen, that is, a minor, but that some-how, since he had stopped being his mother's persecutor, mother had had to produce her own. I wondered for a long time what kind of disease mother might have engaged in her body which would fit all the themes alluded to. Dr Martin Scurr of London said that dissemin-ated lupus erythematosus fitted very well. Everything fitted, even the name lupus, with its werewolf con-notations, its tendency to come and go, seeming to leave the patient for months and returning ferociously, putting the fear of death into patient and loved ones alike, its predilection for women, its tendency towards exacerba-tions in ultraviolet light, even the butterfly rash across the cheeks reminiscent of outstretched hands raised in horror across the face, reminding me of Freud's Wolf Man – that grandfather with his threats to cut open the stomachs of his grandchildren, the butterfly fantasy that Freud attributed to the behind of the maid, which I now felt more likely to be related to outstretched protective fingers, the inter-digital spaces depicting a swallowtail butterfly. Angina is a common enough and serious centrepiece in disseminated lupus, the death might result from failure of the many systems that are involved in the sinister disease. I calculated the minimum age of mother, based upon the Ripper's age being a minimum of twenty-three (eighteen plus the number of years that had elapsed since the start of the murders). If she had her first of at least three children at twenty-two, she would now be a minimum of twenty-six, plus eighteen, plus five (again, the length of time that the murders had been proceeding); that is, she was at least forty-nine years old. She would have at least three children (none less than twenty-three years old), and was herself one of at least three siblings. I thought it quite likely that the Ripper himself might be married, but he would not have any children since children stole jam and drove mothers mad. However, since it had been the traditional job of the Ripper to provide 'comforting' punishment for his mother to expiate her guilt *vis-à-vis* the grandmother, then the Ripper would have to become the disease, and the students and prostitutes would have to be the ones to be killed, and the West Yorkshire women the ones to be driven mad with fear. I did meet Mr Oldfield, the senior police officer in charge of the case, at Dewsbury police station and corresponded with Professor Kind, then director at Aldermaston Forensic Science Laboratory. Perhaps it is not difficult to imagine my trepidation when facing these two experts with the proposition that the most likely route to catching the Ripper was first to appreciate that by definition he could not purposefully be caught. Like the were-eel that he was, even if he were held in the hands he would slip through the fingers. My suggestion was that the eel would need to be caught in company with a large volume of water, that is to say, it was conceivable that the family-tree might be identifiable. The family-tree I submitted along with the notion of the Ripper's mother dying of a disease like lupus or having succumbed since the most recent murder was kept fairly simple. I suppose I could have increased the volume of water by indicating that the hypothetical grandparents, as depicted in the family-tree, might well be matched numerically and characterologically by the family – parents and siblings – of the Ripper's wife, if indeed he had a wife.

*

ATE I am now so caught up in this theoretical caper after the identity of the Ripper that I cannot tell whether it makes sense to me or not. Anyway, I am struck by the irrelevant thought that in this day and age no child would bestir himself to steal jam and no one would care if he did. He would steal the vodka or the cans of lager and that would be really annoying.

I think that the police might be annoyed when offered psychiatric theories. Mr Oldfield once remarked to TPA with a mixture of acerbity and weariness that at least 'all you chaps agree on one thing. He hates women.' If I had been in his shoes I should myself have been cross to hear this from those highly trained persons, but I suspect he was over-simplifying. Nevertheless the application of psychiatry to problems of delinquency does irritate a lot of people, not only those with the old-fashioned approach to thief-taking. There is a feeling that those who have put themselves by their actions beyond the pale of civilized society don't deserve thought, understanding or compassion – and I dare say some of them don't. Still, it can only be useful to try and discover why they do what they do, even if there is then nothing much that can be done about it. It is even more depressing to dwell on the nature of the Ripper than to contemplate his crimes, and so of course the newspapers, who do not wish to bore their readers, concentrate on the more spectacular aspects.

After Sutcliffe's capture we went to see three crime reporters on a national newspaper, hoping that they could tell us something about his grandparents. Because they knew nothing sensational they said they knew nothing, then proceeded in a rather apologetic fashion to furnish details which bore out the theory to a degree which was gratifying and also rather frightening.

Bibliographical Notes

Chapter One

1 (*p. 8*) William Buchan, MD, FRCP, *Domestic Medicine, or, A Treatise on the Prevention and Cure of Diseases by Regimen and Simple Medicines, with an Appendix, Containing a Dispensatory for the Use of Private Practitioners*, 10th ed., p. 353 (Edinburgh, 1783)
2 (*p. 10*) Max Gallo, *Night of the Long Knives: June 29th–30th, 1934 – Hitler's Purge of the SA*, Lily Emmet, trans. Souvenir Press (London, 1973)
3 (*p. 13*) *Care Orders (1970): Part 1 of the Children and Young Persons Act 1969 – a guide for courts and practitioners*, HMSO (London, 1970)
4 (*p. 16*) Regional Plans for Community Homes (1969), Children and Young Persons Act 1969, Section 36–50, HSMO (London, n.d.)

Chapter Two

1 (*p. 19*) T. Pitt-Aikens and M. Bowman, 'The Borstal Matron', *Prison Services Journal*, No. 30, New Series, April 1978, p. 11

2 (*p. 20*) *Powers of the Criminal Courts Act, Section 2, 1973*, and *The Sentence of the Court, A Handbook for the Treatment of Offenders*, Para. 55

3 (*p. 27*) T. Pitt-Aikens and J. Russell, 'Delinquency in Delinquents' Social Workers' (in preparation)

4 (*p. 30*) George Orwell, *Down and Out in Paris and London*, Penguin (Harmondsworth, 1975)

Chapter Three

1 (*p. 34*) Colin Murray Parkes, *Bereavement: Studies in Grief in Adult Life*, Tavistock Publications (London, 1972)

2 (*p. 36*) Howard Parad, ed., *Crisis Intervention*, Family Services Association of America (NY, 1968)

3 (*p. 40*) T. S. Eliot, *Four Quartets*, 'Burnt Norton', Faber and Faber (London, 1942)

4 (*p. 49*), Robert Jay Lefter, 'Suspicion of Counterfeit Nurturance', *International Review of Psychoanalysis*, Part 4, Vol. 3, p. 76

5 (*p. 51*) Emil Zola, *L'Assommoir*, Leonard Tannock, trans. Penguin Books (Harmondsworth, 1970)

Chapter Four

1 (*p. 66*) 'Crime, a Challenge to Us All', a report of the Labour Party's study group, June 1964

2 (*p. 66*) The Child, the Family and the Young Offender, Home Office, Command 2742, HMSO (London, 1965)

3 (*p. 66*) *Children in Trouble*, Home Office, Command 3601. HMSO (London, 1968)

4 (*p. 67*) *Home Office Commission on Local Authority and Allied Personal Social Services*, Home Office, Command 3703, Chairman, Frederick Seebohm (London, 1968)

5 (*p. 67*) *Royal Commission on Local Government in England Report, 1969* 3 Vol., Command 4040, Chairman, Right Honourable Lord Redcliffe-Maud (London, 1969)

6 (*p. 69*) 'Perversion as a Regulator of Self-Esteem', in I. Rosen, ed., *Sexual Deviation*, Chapter 3, pp. 73–8, Oxford Medical Publications (Oxford, 1979)

7 (*p. 69*) Ibid.

8 (*p. 69*) Walter C. Langer, MD, *The Mind of Adolf Hitler: The Secret Wartime Report*, Secker and Warburg (London, 1973)

9 (*p. 78*) Dr Benjamin Spock, *Common Sense Book of Baby and Child Care*, Duel, Sloan, Pearce (New York, 1946)

Chapter Five

1 (*p. 84*) John Bowlby, 'Research into the Origins of Delinquent Behaviour', *British Medical Journal*, Vol. I, 11 March 1950, pp. 570–80

2 (*p. 85*) J. Laplanche and J. B. Pontalis, *The Language of Psychoanalysis*, The Hogarth Press and the Institute of Psychoanalysis (London, 1973)

3 (*p. 86*) Tom Pitt-Aikens, with Rachel Rosser and Paul Kind, 'A Three-Generational Study of Loss of Authority and its Relation to Delinquency' (in preparation)

4 (*p. 87*)

OFFICE-BOY ACTOR
FILM CHANCE WHEN
LICKING STAMPS

Until yesterday Arthur George ▆▆▆▆ was just an office boy for Fox Films in London, and despite what his colleagues might say, he could lick stamps with the best of them.

Mr Albert Parker, the United States director

of the company, is making a talking picture called 'After Dark' for Fox Films at the Walton Studios, Surrey, and in it there is a boy who is a 'card'.

Mr Parker could find no 'cards' among the self-conscious children available to British film studios. He went to Fox Films in London to say so, but on his way he passed Arthur George ███████ as he sat at his desk.

It was a fateful moment. Arthur was licking a stamp!

Mr Parker's dejected progress changed to a gallop of triumph. He rushed into his production supervisor's office as if he had won the St Leger. 'I've got him,' he cried. 'He is here right under your nose!'

Arthur himself is pleased, but not impressed. He said in his matter-of-fact way, 'I suppose they know what they're doing. Anyway, I like to make people laugh.'

5 (*p. 88*) Lily Pincus, *Death and the Family: The Importance of Mourning*, Faber and Faber (London, 1974)

6 (*p. 93*) 'Apoptosis: physiological controlled death of cells – equal in importance and therefore requiring balancing with mitosis.' E. Duvall and A. H. Wyllie, 'Recent Progress in the Study of Cell Death', *Hospital Update*, 19 March 1983, pp. 297–314

Chapter Six

1 (*p. 107*) Sir David Henderson and R. D. Gillespie, *A Textbook of Psychiatry for Students and Practitioners*, Chapter 12, p. 384, Oxford University Press (Oxford, 1956)

2 (*p. 108*) 'New Approaches to the Treatment of Young Offenders', UN: European social development programme report, May 1977, SOA/ESDP/1977/3

Chapter Seven

1 (*p. 122*) Joost A. M. Meerloo, MD, 'Father Time', *Psychiatric Quarterly*, Vol. 24, October 1950
2 (*p. 139*) Donald W. Winnicott, 'Mothers' Madness Appearing in the Clinical Material as an Ego-Alien Factor', in Peter L. Giovacchini, MD, ed., *Tactics and Techniques in Psychoanalytic Therapy*, Part 6, Chapter 20, Science House (1971)
3 (*p. 140*) T. S. Eliot, *The Family Reunion*, Part II, Scene II, *Collected Plays*, Faber and Faber (London)

Chapter Eight

1 (*p. 143*) Op. cit., see Chapter 5, note 1
2 (*p. 144*) Sigmund Freud, 'The Exceptions', in *The Standard Edition of the Complete Psychological Works of Sigmund Freud*, Vol. 14, The Hogarth Press (London, 1966–74)
3 (*p. 146*) Walter Langer, op. cit., see Chapter 4, note 8
4 (*p. 154*) Masud R. Khan, 'Exorcism of the Intrusive Ego-Alien Factors in the Analytic Situation and Process', in Peter L. Giovacchini, MD, ed., *Tactics and Techniques in Psychoanalytic Therapy*, Part 6, Chapter 19, Science House (1971)
5 (*p. 158*) Ibid.
6 (*p. 164*) Peter Bruggen, John Byng-Hall and Tom Pitt-Aikens, 'The Reason for Admission as a Focus of Work in an Adolescent Unit', *British Journal of Psychiatry*, Vol. 122, No. 568, March 1973, pp. 319–29

7 (*p. 172*) J. M. Elwood and W. P. Moorehead, 'Delay in Diagnosis and Long-Term Survival in Breast Cancer', *British Medical Journal*, Vol. 280, 31 May 1980, p. 1291

8 (*p. 183*) John 14:2

9 (*p. 185*) Thomas Carlyle, *Frederick the Great*, Vol. 10, Chapter 8

10 (*p. 187*) Michael Balint, M D, *The Doctor, His Patient and the Illness*, Introductory, Pitman Medical Publishing (London, 1956)

Case Notes

1 (*p. 201*) Sigmund Freud, 'Criminals from a Sense of Guilt', in *The Standard Edition of the Complete Psychological Works of Sigmund Freud*, Vol. 14, The Hogarth Press (London, 1966–74)

2 (*p. 201*) Douglas M. Daher, 'The Senex-Dominated Youth: Issues and Problems of the Adolescent Grown Too Old, Too Good, Too Soon', *Journal of Adolescence*, No. 4, 1981, pp. 295–306

3 (*p. 214*) J. Richard Eiser and Michael R. Gossop, '"Hooked" or "Sick" Addicts' Perceptions of their Addiction', in *Addictive Behaviours*, Vol. 4, pp. 185–91, Pergamon Press (Oxford, 1979)

4 (*p. 226*) Alice Thomas Ellis and Tom Pitt-Aikens, *Secrets of Strangers*, Duckworth (London, 1986)

5 (*p. 230*) Sigmund Freud, 'Jokes and Their Relation to the Unconscious', in *The Standard Edition of the Complete Psychological Works of Sigmund Freud*, Vol. 8, The Hogarth Press (London, 1966–74)

Index